FRAGMENTS OF TENDER HEARTS

FRAGMENTS OF TENDER HEARTS

An Anthology of
Fantasy Love Stories

Cat Devlin, Nastasia Bishop-McHugh,
Kristen Bales, Becca Ryden, Starr Z. Davies,
Anthony B.T, Louise Heywood, Rae Windsor,
Hypatia Rhodes, Sam Trathen, Onika Howdyn.

Astronaut Publishing

ASTRONAUT PUBLISHING
www.astronaut-publishing.com

First published in Great Britain in 2025

With thanks to the following team at Stardust Book Services:
Cover design, chapter art, and formatting by Fakel Barros
Editing by Nastasia Bishop-McHugh
www.STARDUSTBOOKSERVICES.com

ISBN: 978-1-0683265-3-0

Printed and bound by CPI Group (UK) Ltd,
Croydon, CR0 4YY

FIRST EDITION 2025

Content Warnings

It's important to take care of yourself when reading. This publication contains multiple stories, each with their own set of content warnings. To read a complete and comprehensive list of warnings for each story, please visit our website here: www.astronaut-publishing.com/fragments-content

General content warnings include:

Violence
Physical torture
Suicidal intention
Murder
Death
Sexual servitude
Domestic violence
War
Pregnancy
Blood
Grief
Animal death
Religious trauma

Spice Ratings

Our spice rating is as follows:

* Sweet embraces, gentle kisses, or no intimate physical contact
** Loose descriptions of intimacy or fade to black
*** On-page nudity and graphic descriptions of sex
**** Like 3 stars, but wetter, wilder, and more graphic
***** Filth. Only the wicked are safe here

CONTENTS

PLAYLIST

THE DRAGON AND THE SONGBIRD
"Elendil's Oath" by Gealdýr

THE STEALER OF NAMES PROVES HIMSELF TO BE A TERRIBLE DEMIGOD
"Never Love an Anchor" by The Crane Wives

DEATH WEARS A FEATHERED CLOAK
"Would That I" by Hozier

A FIRE REKINDLED
"End of Silence" by Entropy (feat. Alexa Ray)

SOULBOUND
"War of Hearts" by Ruelle

ECHOES OF THE LOST
"I Can't Hear It Now" by Freya Riding

BOUND BY FLESH
"Lullaby of Woe" by Ashley Serena

SONG OF BRINE AND BONE
"Siren Song" by Grace Power

EVEN THE WEEDS SAY LET HER GO
"Harpy Hare" by Yaelokre

THE JERSEY DEVIL
"Burn Your Village" by Kiki Rockwell

THE ARE OF SUMMER
"Little Dusty Dreams" by Keep Shelly in Athens

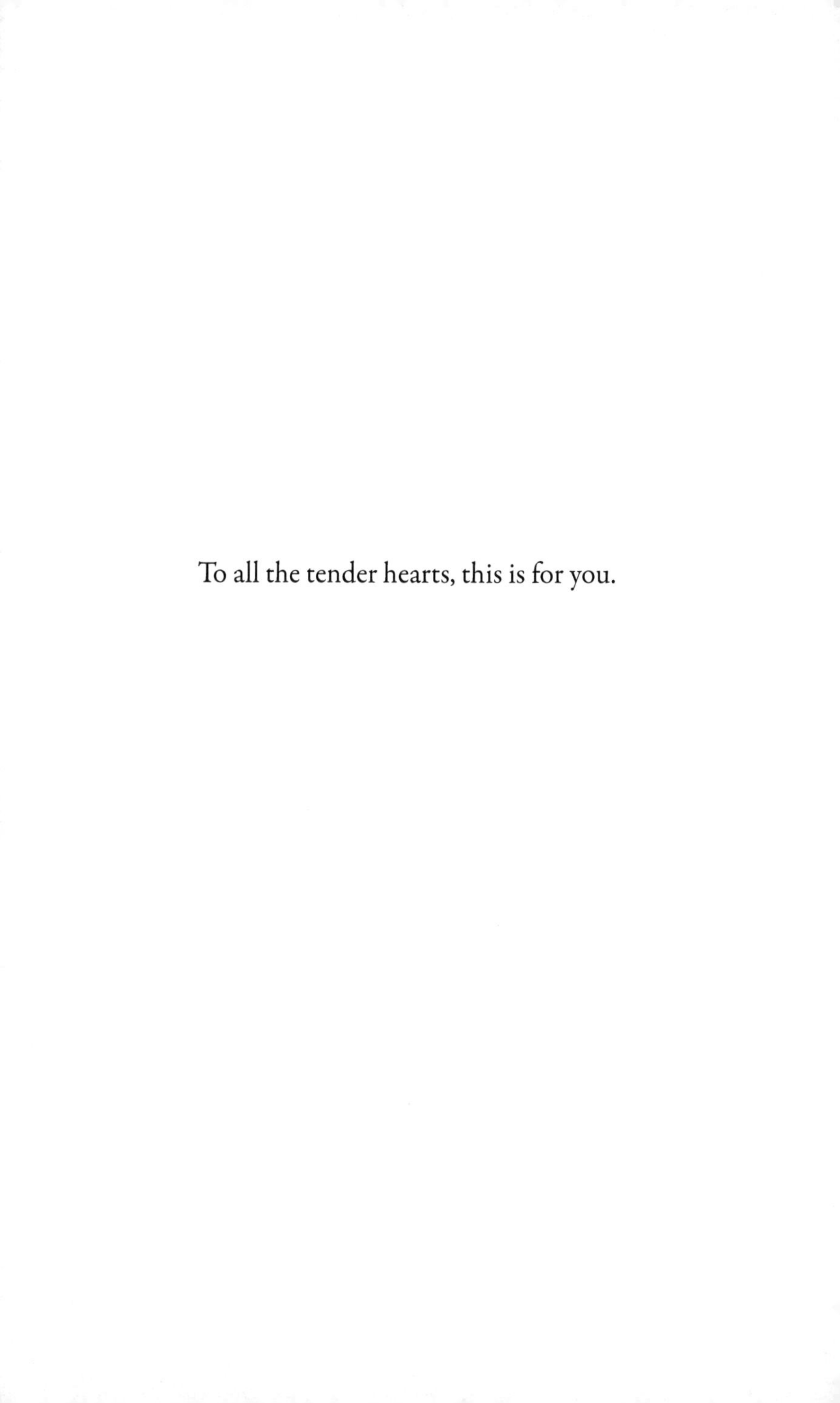

To all the tender hearts, this is for you.

FRAGMENTS OF TENDER HEARTS

THE DRAGON AND THE SONGBIRD

CAT DEVLIN

1

THE WITCH MADE ONLY ONE PROMISE when she caged me in this lonely castle: that I would never leave. Not by rescue – she killed anyone brave enough to come for me and left them where they died, like macabre trophies whose flesh slipped from their bones and rotted the air. And not by escape – my tower was a prison whose steps had crumbled away centuries before. Thrust high above the sea like a spear aimed at the sky, only Ceritha knew the spell to reach me.

Still, even dead, men tried.

The slain reanimated when night fell. They desired living flesh, and I was their only opportunity to get it – perched just out of reach. So they came, scratching, scrabbling at the stone, and tried to scale my tower. I shivered in the dark, damp cold of my chamber and counted the seconds between each scrape of bone and the inevitable *thunk* of a body when its grip failed.

They rose again, climbed again. The pains of flesh and bone were no longer a deterrent to what they wanted. Their voices husked back and forth, trying to lure me to throw down a rope. Promising to rescue me if I did. *Lies.* I huddled in the dark, hugging my shoulders, ignoring their call. How long would it take for them to reach my window? To climb through and feast on my flesh?

My only comfort was the dragon's roar. Each night, the Witch's dragon thundered in the caves below the castle, fighting his own madness. The sound shook the battlements and rattled the stone, but it also drowned out the dead.

Morrdryn.

The last living dragon. Even as far away as my father's kingdom, we knew that fae serpent's name. Some claimed the Witch had fed him the souls of evil men until he was mad with a craving for death, and some said she'd trapped him with a collar of iron that poisoned his heart. However she'd done it, he was an enforcer of swift and violent wrath against anyone who opposed her. He was the reason men called this cursed water the Nightmare Sea, and he was the reason they feared *her*.

Ceritha came to my tower room each night by a set of stairs she summoned with her magic, and she sat on my bed and brushed my hair until it shone like spun gold in the firelight. She combed through my tresses, as gentle as any mother, and I sat still for her while she told stories of the others who'd come before me – women she'd taken with gifts like mine, and women who'd died in dragon fire.

"Some dragons hoard treasures of gold," she said, smoothing my hair back. Her eerie, milk-glass eyes gleamed as they settled on me. "This one hoards *bones*, sweet Liora. So many lovely bones. And if you try to escape, he will have yours too."

"I would never try," I lied, offering a sweet and vacant smile. "You've been so good to me, Ceritha. Why would I ever leave?"

I could not tell if she believed me, but she did not threaten me further.

"Sing," she ordered, and I sang as the harp sings for its master, but in the old fae tongue my grandmother had taught me. There were few left who knew those ancient songs, but when I sang, the dragon went quiet, as if this one thing was enough to pull him from madness and make him listen. Was the sound such a strange and foreign thing? I had begun to think that he was trapped, like I was trapped, as alone as I was, and some part of me hoped my voice helped him keep whatever scrap of humanity he had left. I had to know he wasn't so lost to fury he didn't recognise himself anymore, because I didn't want to lose myself too.

I didn't want to go mad here, alone forever.

After my songs were done, she clipped locks of my hair and crafted her spells in a little pot she kept in my hearth. Perhaps she did not know who my grandmother was, or perhaps she thought I had no witchcraft of my own. But I tracked her every move – how long she stirred, and what trinkets she added. Night after agonising night, song after song, I watched and learned the Witch's spells.

Then I made my own.

A chill crept over me as I leaned out my window into the rising wind. The Witch had come and left already today; she did not like storms, and across the sea, the first squall of winter charged down on us. It was growing dark, and when night fell, the dead would come as they always did.

All that stood between me and freedom was the dragon.

My gaze swept down the dizzying drop to the waves below. That was *his* domain. Even now, I felt the weight of his otherworldly gaze watching me. *Waiting*, as if he knew I would come. Fae creatures were tricky, my grandmother used to say. They had magic of their own, and no bargain with them could ever be trusted, but there was no one else. There was no other way off the island.

I could not escape, the Witch had told me. Not from this tower, not from the dead outside, and not from the dragon who lived beneath us, waiting to devour me whole. But in between the taut snap of wind-worn pennants, beneath the fear churning in my gut, desperate rage surged through me. I had vowed, with every dead hand that reached for my tower, not to end up like all the others. I had prepared my spells as best I could; if I didn't go now, I might not get the chance again.

I would escape, I had to – and that meant I needed the dragon.

I pulled the stopper on a potion bottle. Beneath the smoky glass, the golden strands I'd used from my hair gleamed with light. I poured the liquid out onto the rough brick lintel of my window and waited. As the liquid trickled over the edge and down the wall, the stones began to shift and grind together. One by one, they slid out of place until a stair formed and wrapped around the outside of my salt-pitted tower. It wound all the way down until it dropped over the bluff and cut a trail straight down the cliff face to the sea below. Then, before I could rethink my choice, I crept onto the first step and ran down the stairs towards freedom.

2

HALFWAY DOWN THE STAIR, A GREAT, rending screech of claws cut across the rock.

The sound cleaved the air behind me, beside me, all around me. It screamed through my ears, made the bones ache deep in my body, squeezed tears from my eyes. My knees buckled, and I grabbed the wall for balance. A cascade of stones rained down on my head, but I did not look up. I did not dare look, no matter how my gut twisted.

I knew what was there. I could hear him breathing behind me.

Monster.

Dragon.

I ran. I pushed myself forwards down the treacherous cliff path on steps carved out of the stone by my magic. I made it another fifty feet before I skidded to a stop, chest heaving. The jagged edge of the cliff rose towards my tower on the left, and to my right, the stairs were open to empty air – and blocking the entire path was a group of men. Or rather, what *used to be* men. Pirates maybe, shipwrecked and washed up on these shores, where the dead never stayed that way. Lightning flashed overhead and illuminated twelve of them, clutching swords and shields while the rain ran in rivulets down their armour.

The dead man in front sucked his teeth as he grinned. "Where you going, princess?"

I swallowed. The dragon was coming, the dead were in my path, and both of them wanted me.

"Move." I tried to make my voice sound fierce. The hairs on the back of my neck prickled as the stone groaned behind me. "Now."

His men pushed forwards instead, bones and steel rattling as they jostled for a better look.

"The Witch said we keep what we catch, Cap'n."

"Been too long since we had a feast this fine."

Behind me, the rock groaned beneath a sudden enormous weight.

"Aye." The captain dragged his lifeless eyes over me. Half his face had rotted away, and the loose edges of his decomposing cheek jiggled as he spoke. "How about we tie you to the rocks, my girl, then eat you down to the bone?" His sinister smile was full of missing teeth. "Maybe we'll leave a little for the crabs, eh, boys?" His grin widened as his hungry men jostled forwards. "Maybe not."

Claws scraped over stone. My teeth chattered as goosebumps ran up my arms, but I wouldn't look behind me.

"Please... move," I pleaded, but there were twelve of them and only one of me, and the dead only cared about one thing.

Behind me, a low rumble began at the back of a dark, violent throat.

The captain grasped at my sleeve. "Come here, sweetling."

I jerked my arm away and scrambled backwards, but that growl pushed at my back. A scream trembled on my lips, but all that came out was a hoarse whisper. "*Run.*"

My legs did not obey.

Too late. The stone shuddered behind me as the beast moved. I threw myself flat against the cliff face just as a slab of rock cracked away and punched through the space where I had been only moments before, taking half the stone steps with it. Bodies *thunked* and crashed below; those remaining cursed as they, too, leapt back.

There was nowhere to go.

My pride evaporated. Reason fled. I cowered against the cliff as the dead came for me again, and I did the only thing I could think of: I tried to reason with the monster.

"Please, Morrdryn... help me."

A gust of hot air, of *breath*, hit my back. I squeezed my eyes shut and prayed as I had never done before. Whatever plan I'd had evaporated. The way I'd imagined meeting him – this wasn't it.

I hid my face away and begged for my life.

A *weight* settled behind me, heavy and dense, but when I risked a glance, there was nothing there. Only blackness, where stone and steps should be – a dark void, deeper than night had ever been. For a moment, that's all I saw. No cliff, no path. Nothing but a deep, impenetrable dark.

Then it *moved.* The bulk behind me *breathed.* A creature formed out of that shapeless mass, and I realised I was staring at gleaming black scales stretched across an expansive chest. I followed them up, up, *up* to a massive head that reared high above me, crowned with horned spikes and dripping with rows of sharp teeth as long as I was tall. The heat rolling off his body engulfed me, and the monster's gaze locked onto mine. Those bright and burning eyes blinked, slow and deliberate. A coal of dark flame kindled to life in the back of his throat, and I screamed as his head snapped forwards.

3

I FELL TO MY KNEES ON THE STEPS AND curled into my body. The heat of the flame engulfed me, singeing my unbound hair and burnishing the rain right off my skin, but it did not burn me. It burned *them*. They screamed as rotted flesh vaporised into char inside the shell of their armour. Some leapt from the stairs into open air and fell, steel and bones clattering all the way down to the bottom of the cliff as they went.

Then there was only silence. I became aware of the rain on my face, of the wild waves crashing against the base of the cliff. Of my body, shivering and cold, but still alive.

And not alone.

That monstrous face watched me. The great beast clung to the side of the cliff, talons gouged in deep to hold his weight – a gargantuan, sinister creature of shadow and smoke. It was dizzying to tilt my head at that angle, but the dragon's eyes burned into me, and I could not look away.

My breath froze. His head snaked down, sniffing me, and I squeezed my eyes shut as I pressed flat against the stone. I did not dare move as he growled, low and menacing. But then the beast's form *shifted*. The great webbed wings flexed and contracted until they disappeared into his shoulders. The horns shrank, and those molten eyes collapsed in on themselves, swallowed by darkness. The edges of his bulk softened, and his shining scales melted from hard diamond into flesh and cloth.

A man stood on the edge of the broken stairs above me, framed by the cliff face on my right and the fall to the bottom on the left. He was tall, with wild dark hair that crowned his head. His gaze held me transfixed, with eyes that gleamed as cold and distant as the shimmer of stars in the night sky. When his eyes met mine, it was as if we stood apart from the world, like *he* had pulled me outside of it, and as I stared up at him it seemed he looked *deeper,* saw *farther*, than anyone ever had before. That implacable gaze raked over me. "Have you come for your death, little Songbird?"

I shook. All over, uncontrollably, with the cliff behind me to remind me how small I was before this creature. How fragile. There was nothing warm, or friendly, or *human* about him, but there was no one else to turn to.

"Not death, faery. A bargain." I tried to force the fear down, to make my voice sound bigger. I lifted my chin and squared my shoulders – I would not be afraid. I would not look away, no matter how my knees trembled.

He laughed. "Do you know what a deal with my kind costs?"

"I know the Old Ways."

"Do you?" He stepped forwards, and I stepped back. His mouth curved into a dangerous smile. "Then, you know you're already in trouble."

Another step. He was driving me back, towards the bottom of the stair, but I hesitated, held by that unrelenting gaze as his heat travelled straight down into my belly. I knew I should run, put distance between us, but he moved first, trapping my body between him and the wall at my back.

"I..." My breath let out slowly. "I need your help, Morrdryn."

"*No*, my pretty Songbird." His breath washed across my cheek, and the scent of him, like sea and smoke, filled my senses. His voice was a spell, full of a dark promise as he said, "I'm not the bargaining kind of faery." He caught my chin in his fingers, forcing my gaze to his. "I'm the kind who *devours* you."

Those words chased fire down my spine. Every hair on my arms stood on end, and my pulse raced as those sharp eyes mapped my face. For so long, I'd been alone. I'd pushed down hope of anything more than shadow and death, but now, looking into that quicksilver gaze, dangerous longing fluttered in my chest. The rain sheeted down, and the wind tore all around, but somehow, in some magical way, it didn't touch us.

Maybe I shouldn't tempt the monster, but I couldn't help myself.

"Then... why haven't you?"

The corner of his lips pulled into a faint, amused smile.

I drew a sharp breath as his hand caught my hip and his body pressed flush with mine. There was no space between us now, no hiding how we fit together, and I did not miss how his lips hovered just a breath away. As if he, too, felt this pull between us.

"Is that what you want?"

Oh yes.

It was a trap, I knew it, and still I shuddered as Morrdryn brushed his thumb across my cheek. Just that whisper of a touch burned like a fever over my skin. He was toying with me, he had to be, but what if he wasn't? So many lonely nights converged into a single, new idea: what if he'd watched for me at my window like I'd looked for him so often at the base of the cliff?

I couldn't help myself as I closed my eyes and leaned into his hand. We stood amid fire-blackened stone, and he caressed my skin like he had not been a monster moments before, like whole men had not just been reduced to ash in his fire, and all I could think of was that I wanted *more*. That maybe he needed me as much as I needed him.

"She's put us both in a cage," I whispered. My heart raced, and I wanted nothing more than to lift my chin and kiss him, but I pushed against his chest, trying to get space; I could not allow myself to be seduced by this spell. Not before we got free. "Help me, and we can both escape."

His brow furrowed, and something uncertain flickered in his gaze – a flash of curiosity before darkness drowned it again. "I've wrecked ships, destroyed armies." A dangerous edge laced his tone. "Do you know how many I've killed? Why would I help you escape?"

"So why listen to me sing?" My chest felt suddenly tight; the gravel in his voice stung. "Why didn't you kill *me*?"

"Do I need a reason?" he snarled. "I said *no*."

"I'm not your enemy and you're not mine," I shot back, jabbing a finger in his chest. "*Help me.*"

Something snapped; his eyes went flat, and the beautiful lines of his face shifted into hard steel. He stepped back, and as he did, the real world collapsed on top of me again. The frigid wind and rain rushed back in as the thunder of waves crashed against the cliff below. I hugged my shoulders against the sudden absence of him as he looked down at me and scowled.

"One way or the other, you'll end up dead." His eyes flashed cold. All dangerous flirtation was gone, replaced by a vicious snarl. "Go back to your tower, Songbird, before the Witch makes me drag you back."

"That's not true." I shook my head. "Wait. Don't go—"

But Morrdryn's sleeve slipped through my grasp as I reached for him. He shook me off and left me standing there as he descended towards the frothing sea at the base of the cliff.

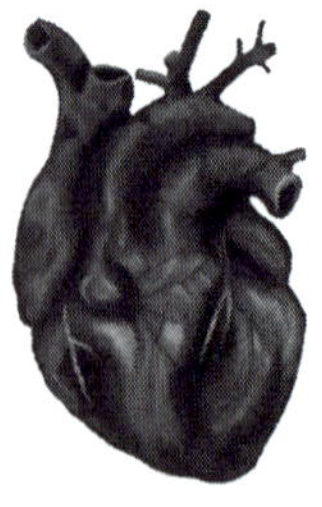

4

I WAS A FOOL, BUT I CHARGED RIGHT AFTER him. I needed the dragon to escape, but I hadn't expected to be drawn to him like this. His scent lingered, and I hadn't known I could feel so bereft for someone I hardly knew. There was more in him than the savage monstrosity the Witch made him out to be, more than just a distant, tormented spirit living in darkness beneath my feet. He was an inky well of chaos, implacable and terrifying, and for some strange reason, I wanted to dip my hands into his soul and cleave it to mine. Whatever this feeling was, it was enough to make me ignore his warning. I had to get him back.

"Morrdryn! Stop!"

The waves broke hard and fast against the rocks, whipped to fury by the wind. One caught me and knocked me against the cliff. I yelped as my shoulder hit, and then I slipped on seaweed and fell against the sharp, uneven rocks.

The waves crashed over me, the water so cold it made my lungs seize.

"Help," I gasped as the water broke away. My voice was barely a whisper, hardly loud enough to be heard over the thundering waves, but I tried again. Louder, working against the cold. The sea sucked at my dress, trying to pull me down with it, and I coughed and spluttered as I scrabbled for a hand hold on the stone.

"I told you to go back," Morrdryn growled as he caught a fistful of cloth at the small of my back. He cut me a hard glance as he hauled me up beside him. I clung to him, to the solid safety of his warm body. I could go back and try to escape another way, but the dead would tell the Witch what I had done.

I didn't want to think about what she would do.

I shook my head. "I can't, and I won't."

He caught my chin and pulled my gaze up to his. I shivered at his touch, my defences destroyed under that searing glare, my arguments erased. If he said no again, I was lost. Doomed. But before he could say anything, another wave hit us and tore him away from me. The sea flung him against the cliff with a heavy thud as if he were not a dragon, as breakable in human form as any other man. Then another wave came, and another, raking us against barnacle and stone, pummelling us both as we clung to any handhold we could find. My hands and arms streamed blood from a thousand cuts.

Morrdryn found me and pulled me up again. I followed his gaze as he pointed towards a gloomy cave at the base of the cliff. High above, a flash of lightning lit up my tower. It stood high like a looming spectre of judgement; it had been a cage perhaps, but it was also *safe*, and if we didn't get off these rocks, the sea would macerate us until there was nothing left. This was my last chance to go back, that dark spear seemed to say – and if I stayed with the dragon, *she would know*.

I wasn't going back.

I nodded to Morrdryn without question; we were both soaked to the bone, and blood streamed from a cut above his eye. He slid an arm around my waist and half-carried, half-dragged me off the rocks and into the shallow lagoon at the mouth of the cave. Darkness fell over us as we splashed through the frigid ankle-deep water and then collapsed on a sandy bank inside.

"Steady now, Liora."

I coughed and sputtered, trying to get the water out of my lungs. "You know... my name?"

"And?" He rolled his eyes and pulled me close, tucking me against the warmth that burned inside of him. I panted, grateful for the heat against my body.

I cut him a dry look. "Do you learn the names of all your victims?"

In that liminal space at the mouth of the cave, where dark and light collided with waves, he brushed the hair out of my eyes. "Just the ones who vex me."

"Here I was, thinking we might become friends."

I smiled as my head fell against his shoulder. He felt so good, so *warm*, and even though I was still a little wary, my fingers curled against his back, and I closed my eyes, letting myself bask in that fiery embrace.

"I was... curious," he said, after a moment. "I haven't heard that language in a long time, and it seemed... brave to sing to someone like *me*. I wanted to know who you were."

"Oh." *Brave.* "No one has ever called me that."

I met his silver eyes; heat flushed my cheeks under the intensity of his gaze. We were so close I could feel his heart beating hard in his chest, as if each pulse were trying to leap up to meet mine. "You just seemed... so alone. And so was I."

He frowned and ran a strand of my wet golden hair between his fingers. As if he were seeing it for the first time, as if it were a marvel to him. "I'm a monster, Liora. That's what she made me." They were harsh words, ground out and pulverised into the truth. His glance flicked back to mine. "Why do you care if I'm alone or not?"

"Because when I was afraid, you were there. You endured, so I endured too. I just wanted you to know... I heard you too."

I glanced towards the storm outside. It raged still, as if Ceritha had sent it on purpose to crush us. But in here, strangely, I felt *safe*, held in his embrace and soaking up his warmth. "Even the storm fears to cross your threshold," I said, turning a curious glance up to him. "You have so much power, Morrdryn, why do you follow the Witch?"

Silence met my question. But a muscle in his jaw ticked as the thought dug under his skin, worked its way inside – until finally, he sighed and pulled me up with him. His hands held my shoulders and pointed me towards the interior of the cave. "Look. *See* all of it."

A narrow cleft opened in the cliff above, slanting faint light through the cavern's gloom. The ancient chamber vaulted above us, its walls written with a story of violence. Morrdryn's fire had burned so hot it melted the stone in scorching arcs across that broad ceiling; obsidian gleamed where the molten rock had cooled too quickly. He'd raked deep gouges into the stone and slammed himself against the walls so hard the rock was cracked and dented with an impression of his body.

"A long time ago, she put a collar around my neck." He scowled as he traced the base of his throat, as if he wore it even now. "I tried to leave – at first." His jaw clenched, and he shook his head. "But this is what I am, Liora. What she's made me."

I saw the bones.

In ancient stories, dragons always hoarded gold, but there was none of that bright metal here, only bones, strewn across the cavern floor and piled against the base of its walls. This was a treasure hoard of the dead. A trophy case of skulls, spines, femurs, and rib cages – and all of it gleamed within the melancholy dark, bleached white by salt and sea.

At the centre of it, arrayed in a circle around a large, flat thrust of rock, four white dragon skulls looked back at us.

"Falemor, Líodd, Caile, and Dáguinn," he said against my ear. "My kin. The last of us." His tone was flat. "Between the iron and her magic..." He gritted his teeth. "When she's in control, I'm not, Liora. She made me kill them, and... I won't be able to stop it happening to you, either."

Finally, I understood what he wanted me to see, and something cracked open inside. There were so many things we'd both endured. Isolation. Loneliness. Fear. It was impossible to imagine how it hurt him to kill his family, to be as massive as he was, with no ability to control his own body. To be unable to stop a frail, hateful woman. The Witch had bent him to her will until he'd destroyed all he loved, until all anyone would recognise was a monster.

"You've been trying to tear it down," I whispered. It made sense now why he raged. I'd thought this was a lair, but it was a prison, *her* prison for the dark and twisted creature she wanted him to be. He couldn't fight, and he couldn't leave, so he'd resisted in the only other way possible – he'd been trying to pull it all down on top of him. "You—"

His hand slipped to my throat. I swallowed, acutely aware of how his fingers wrapped around my windpipe, but I did not fight. Call it madness, or desire, but the feel of his rough grip made something wild rise in me too. He'd had the chance to kill me if he wanted. He could've let me drown in the sea. That wasn't what he'd wanted at all – it wasn't the choice *he* would make.

Now his warm lips pressed against my ear, equal parts dangerous and tempting, as he whispered, "So you need to go back, before I have to do something I don't want to do."

I closed my eyes as every part of my body shivered under his voice. "No."

The icy wind thrashed through the cave, and I had to bite my lip to keep my teeth from chattering, but I turned in his arms and met his gaze. Thick red blood stained his temple where he'd hit his head on the rocks outside. It smeared across his face and neck, dripping down underneath the collar of his leather vest.

"I came looking for a dragon because I wanted to escape." My eyes softened as I swept his black hair away from his brow. "I can't leave without you."

Morrdryn caught my wrist. Our wills locked together as I pushed against his grip and he held firm, but still I did not relent. Then my fingers slipped through his, and he let go. I traced around his wound, dragging my fingers through the blood and then down the sharp blade of his cheek.

"You don't know what you're saying."

"How do we get the collar off?" I whispered.

Something vulnerable flickered across his expression as I looked up at him. A shadow swirled there, as if the dragon inside him coiled just behind those silver depths, sharp and wary of a trap.

"Liora..." he warned.

I dragged my fingers over his lips and silenced him, boldly smearing his own blood across his mouth. Then I traced down around the base of his neck. He stood still as stone, his whole body rigid, wound tight and ready to spring. The heat that rolled off him sent up curls of steam into the chill air. His magic *hummed* in the space between us, drawn like a taut string, threatening to tip this tenuous balance between us.

I wound my arm around his neck and lifted on my toes, pressing my lips to his skin. To that place where a collar might rest, if it had been a physical thing. He sucked in a harsh breath, but I kissed his skin anyway. He tasted like crisp, clean water, smelled like fire and ash.

Thunder cracked above. "I'm not leaving without you."

Morrdryn's dark eyes searched mine. Silver swirled around the black, pupils dilating, and a low, possessive growl rumbled in his throat. When his hand slid up and cupped my cheek, I held my breath.

Then, like a stone toppled, his head tilted forwards and his mouth claimed mine. His breath crashed into my own as his hands tangled in my hair. Fire, that's what he tasted like – raw and dangerous. His tongue was like molten silk as it pushed against my mouth – insistent, offering no quarter. I moaned as I opened for him, and he swept in like the tide, commanding me. Devouring me.

The wild sea slammed against the rocks as another wave surged over the top and flooded into the cave. I was lost. Fallen. I tilted my head as he pulled away and kissed down my neck, and my entire body shuddered under his mouth. Morrdryn's flame was under my skin now, singing back to me – and I welcomed it.

He lifted me around the waist and carried me into an alcove of pitted stone, where skulls and bones were set upon the ledges like grisly trophies of a bygone era. It should have frightened me, but I couldn't think with his mouth on mine, with his strong hands caressing my body. Bone crunched underfoot, but I didn't care. There was an aching need in the centre of my body, a warmth that flooded through me as he set me on a narrow ledge and pushed my knees apart.

He slid my dress up to my waist, hands skimming across bare thighs. I groaned as I squirmed for him, already slick with desire. He smiled, running his nose along my neck, breathing in my scent.

"Shh," he whispered, like a devil commanding me to sin. Those sharp eyes fixed on me, and something dark and hungry swam in them. He'd barely touched me, but he knew what he was doing to me. Those lips curved into a lazy, dangerous smile as he dragged the pad of his thumb over my mouth. He growled. "This is mine."

"Yes," I panted. Outside, the storm raged, but in here, among old bones in this dark corner of his lair, something forbidden kindled between us. I could just make out the line of his pale jaw, the shining silver of his eyes, the confident gleam of his smile as his fingers traced everywhere. Across my jaw. Down my neck. Over my shoulder, pushing my sleeves down to bare my skin. I shuddered as he pressed a kiss there, grazing his teeth across the curve.

"I'm going to claim you in every way that matters."

"Even my heart?" I meant the words playfully, but when his head shot up, I bit my lip, suddenly shy. This didn't feel like a game anymore.

Morrdryn took my face in his hands. "*Everything,*" he breathed, and kissed me tenderly.

My head fell back in ecstasy as his hand slid under my skirts and against my damp core, the rough pad of his thumb pressing against my clit. A needy groan slipped from my throat as I let my knees fall wider. A sudden, wild thrill raced through me. This was a language I had never spoken, but it was one I knew all the same – one of want, of longing, of aching need – all converging under the point of his thumb.

"Good girl," he said, eyes shining with approval.

One by one, he pulled the laces that bound the front of my dress, loosening the bodice until it fell open. Underneath was just my kirtle, and as I balanced on the ledge, I pulled the wet woollen dress over my head and tossed it aside.

Those silver eyes gleamed as he took me in, savouring every inch of my bare body. He brushed strands of my drying hair back so no part of me was hidden from his view. "So beautiful, my Songbird," he said in rough wonder.

Fire flushed across my skin, and I moaned as fresh warmth made my thighs slick. He felt it; the corner of his mouth curved up as his eyes flicked back up to me. "And so ready for me."

His finger traced a line down the centre of my chest, and I held my breath as he skimmed right between my breasts. I whimpered as that finger circled around one breast and then the other, as my nipples hardened under his touch. He didn't even touch them, but just the hint of it, the *tease* of it, was enough to send a fresh rush of heat between my legs.

"Morrdryn." His name was a plea as I clenched my hands and leaned back, trying to draw him with me. I wasn't sure which part of me wanted him more. "Teasing me isn't fair."

Morrdryn only shook his head and grinned. "I'm fae, Songbird. *Fair* isn't part of the deal."

The gall of the man. I reached for him, but he laughed and sank to his knees before me, pulling one of my legs over his shoulder. I gasped, cheeks flushing red, as he buried his face between my legs. His fingers splayed across my belly, and his thumb found my apex again, even as his tongue speared inside of me. His other hand came up to cup my breast, and I threw my head back and cried out as the sensation of his thumb flicking across my nipple and his warm tongue buried inside of me made every nerve in my body come alive all at once.

"Mmmm," he murmured as he tasted me. I flushed, spread wide for him with my back against the stone. There was a kind of adoration in the way he explored and claimed these secret, sacred parts of me. "Do you want to sing for me, little dove?"

"Please," I whimpered again. Please, please, please. *Please what?* I had no idea, but I kept saying it because I needed it. I needed *him*.

"So polite." His husky laugh rolled over me. He licked and stroked, and my hips bucked, my thighs shaking. His tongue twisted as he devoured me, and I couldn't help the moans he drew from my lips. It wasn't enough; I was feverish, I needed release, I needed—

"*Sing,*" he commanded, hands clamping around my thighs as he pulled me tight against his mouth.

That was all it took; that new intense pressure, the thrust and swirl of his tongue, and all at once my body came undone. I screamed as waves of fire rippled through my core. My knees quivered, and my thighs trembled, but when he finally relented, he rose, and in one swift motion his fingers tangled in my hair and he yanked my head back so my throat was bare to him.

He kissed along my neck, nipping at my flesh, and a low moan escaped him as his hard length pressed against me. I tried to reach for his belt but his grip on my hair did not relent, leaving me only enough room that my fingertips just reached the first button on his leather pants.

"Is that what you want, my dove?" He grinned as he shifted his hips a little farther from my reach, and when I growled in response, he dipped his head and sucked a nipple between his teeth, making me whine again. Held like this, I was at his mercy – back arched like a drawn bow, legs spread, ready to be speared by this dragon as if he were the one who had come to slay me. I ached for him, squirming as his hands roamed my naked body anywhere they wished.

His fingers slipped out of my hair, and he stepped away. I reached to pull him back, but he shook his head, and then a rush of air and a whoosh of flame engulfed him. I watched his body turn to *fire* – bright, molten flames that billowed and fanned like great flaming wings as the wind caught them. Heat radiated off him as his skin glowed like hot coals, and for a moment in that bright, warm light I saw the dragon's scales forge over his skin. Then his flame leapt away into the nearest empty skull. It licked and guttered from one to the next, lighting up the dark all around us.

I stared. Every scrap of clothing had burned off his body, leaving him bare before me. He gave me only a moment to take in the broad swath of muscle along his chest, those rippling muscles along his stomach, and the thick, hard rise of him between his legs. I craved everything about him, as if each plane of his body had been crafted just for me.

He stalked forwards and caught me around the waist. I wrapped my legs around him, and his lips crashed to mine, burning a searing kiss straight into my soul.

"It won't be gentle," he warned, voice husky. Those dark eyes, bright now with lust, held my own as his thumb brushed my cheek tenderly. "But I'll try to go as slow as I can."

My arms wound around his neck, and I kissed his collar bone. The way he could be soft one moment and hard the next thrilled me. "I wanted the monster, remember?" I teased as I threaded my fingers into his hair, drawing a rough moan from him. Then I leaned up and kissed along his jaw. "I... give you permission," I whispered. I couldn't keep the nervousness out of my voice, but when Morrdryn's eyes snapped to mine, it didn't matter. His eyes shifted and coiled as the serpent inside him swirled around his irises like silver rings, and it held me transfixed.

Lightning flashed against the crack in the cliff above; the macabre skulls flickered all around us. I sucked in a sharp breath as his cock met my entrance. Rock hard. The first touch of it to my skin sent a bolt of fire straight through me. All around us, the hushed whispers of the dead mingled with the howl of the storm, and my hips rocked forwards to meet his as he pushed into me. Our breath united when he pulled me close, groaning, muscles straining as he tried to hold himself back and slowly slide deeper into me.

But I ached for him, and before I even knew what I was doing, I rocked against him. As if the beast in him sensed it and *understood* my need, his hands fell to my hips. He growled as he drove up into me, breaking through my innocence in a sharp, decisive thrust. Thunder broke, and I screamed, arms wrapped around his neck.

"Are you ok?" He held me, unmoving, while I adjusted to him inside me.

"It hurts… a little." The way I stretched around him burned, but it also felt wonderful. Like I was full, whole, and complete. His arms were around me, and there was nowhere else I wanted to be. No one else I wanted to be with.

Concern etched sharp lines in his expression. "Do you want to stop?"

"No." I shook my head and pulled his mouth to mine. "Just kiss me," I whispered.

He groaned and claimed my mouth, even as he lifted my hips and slid home again, slower, taking his time. All I wanted was him. I let myself go, let my body slip into the rhythm he set for us. That first sharp pain was nothing compared to the sensation of how he filled me now, all the way to the hilt. Or the burn of pleasure that engulfed me.

The waves beat at the cliff outside in a fury as Morrdryn lost control. The world slipped away, and all that existed were his starry eyes, bright as molten moonlight, and the exquisite pleasure of his body and mine joined together.

He panted as he withdrew, then speared me again, and again. He scooped me up in his arms and then we crashed against the stone. Flame flickered as the dead watched and the stone bruised, but the dragon took me greedily, hungrily. He split me apart, devoured my heart – and even the thunder above could not drown my screams as my entire body filled with his fire.

I cried out his name, tore at his hair, clawed at his shoulders. My body soared as pleasure suffused me, as my climax exploded through me. And as the last flames guttered out around us, Morrdryn shouted my name as he joined me.

5

"YOU SLEPT LATE, MY SWEET."

Glimmers of morning light danced across the soft, sandy bed where I lay, shining across the golden hair splayed across my bare arms. Gulls wheeled and called outside, fighting over the flotsam left behind by the storm; the restless waves were soft this morning, their fury all played out. A finger of cool air drifted across my naked skin, and it took me a moment, still lost in the hazy, dreaming warmth of Morrdryn's arms, to realise the voice was not his.

His arms were not around me. His breath was not against my ear.

A sickening stench of rot filtered into my senses. I sat up, eyes wide, searching out that decay I knew so well – the sour, musky stink of flesh that had liquefied as it separated from the bone. It led up to that flat parapet that rose above the massive skulls of Morrdryn's dead kin. They were the last dragons to roam this land before the fae had been driven out by men. Before a witch collared their strongest and made him into the monster who would kill them all.

There, atop that monolith, Morrdryn stood in the light pouring from the crack in the cliff above. Bare-chested, his head bowed as if under some great weight, his hands clasped before him and shackled at his wrists. Ringing the base of that flat thrust of rock, outside the circle of dragon heads, an army of Ceritha's dead stood guard.

They were restless, shuffling and growling, their eyes on me.

The Witch scowled as she stood over me. "Cover yourself," she spat, and threw my dress in my face.

"Don't... don't hurt him," I begged, and hastily pulled the shift over my head. "Please. This wasn't his fault."

Her answering laugh struck a discordant note against the rattle of bones and other trinkets she wore around her neck. She'd always been a crooked, ugly crone; no matter how many strands of my hair she wove into her spells, no magic could change how I saw her: gaunt and hobbled from age, with sunken cheeks and limp, stringy locks. Her raspy voice had always made my skin crawl, but there was something more in it now, some sudden change in tone that struck a clarion note of warning in my heart.

I frowned. For long moments I stared at the Witch, and she stared back at me. A slow, secretive smile spread across her lips, expectant, and as it did something uneasy coiled in my belly.

My gaze pulled back to Morrdryn. The way he stood – it was *wrong*. Immobile and stiff, his muscles taut and straining. He was struggling against some invisible force that held him in place. Then I saw it – the shadow of a flat, unadorned band of black iron clasped around his neck. The collar that had been there all along, invisible, was now on full display.

And Morrdryn stood perfectly still beneath it.

A sudden, dark fear slithered down my throat. This wasn't about me. That feeling grew as the Witch lifted her hand like some macabre conductor, and as she did, Morrdryn's cool gaze dragged to mine, as if she wanted me to know how easily she could handle him.

But that mercurial glance was quicksilver, as focused as a beast hunting dark water. Sweat beaded on his temple and ran down into his hair. He *was* fighting. Trying, with every ounce of his strength, to break that iron.

"What are you doing, Ceritha?" I demanded.

"You foolish girl." The Witch clicked her tongue in disapproval. "Did you think I wanted *you*?" She brushed a hand through my hair, teasing out the soft strands, letting them run through her fingers. "Such pretty golden locks. So full of life and magic. But you were just a distraction for the dragon, Liora."

Ceritha pointed a bony, crooked finger at the litter of bones on the cavern floor. They began to stir, to crack and snap as something moved beneath them. A discordant sound of steel scraped against stone; the pile shifted and clanked as a large hunk of metal gathered itself from under the muck. A once-shining knight sat up, armour creaking as he hauled himself to his feet and started towards the rock where Morrdryn stood.

The dead growled, sensing a shift. Waiting for their Witch to give them an order too.

Look at me, I mouthed, willing Morrdryn to meet my gaze again – but he did not. He stared straight ahead, unmoving, but I could see him trembling, body straining as he fought the collar. The undead suit of armour lurched towards him with every step, swaying under the weight of the steel suit that had cooked him to ash when he'd died.

"It's quite a delicate thing to harvest a soul, my sweet." Ceritha fisted her fingers into my hair and twisted this time, yanking my head back hard, forcing my gaze to hers. "You must nurture it. Grow it. Sing to it, perhaps" – she smiled, as her eyes fell back to me – "and then cull it at just the right moment, when it's ripe for plucking."

Run, Morrdryn, I pleaded silently.

The knight's heavy, thudding steps were warning bells clanging in my head, telling me to run too. I needed to get to Morrdryn. Maybe if I could get my fingers on that collar, if I could work a spell, I could free him. But held in the Witch's iron grip like I was, with that ghastly countenance staring down at me, I wasn't going anywhere.

"Then, you distil it. Strip his essence from flesh and bone and bind it into a pretty bauble." She tapped her chest, where jewels of different sizes and shapes hung among her collar of bones – the gleaming trophies of other souls she'd taken, perhaps – all forming a grotesque wreath that rattled around her neck. Her eyes flashed. "But it's a hard thing to kill a dragon. I needed you to get him to take the man's form."

I was going to be sick. I had vowed not to be like those who came before me, like all the other women she'd trapped and goaded into escape just to feed the dragon – but I was. I was the worst of them.

The knight snapped himself fully upright, forming into place with a grind of metal on metal. He dragged the tip of his great sword behind him, the once smooth steel rough and pitted from the relentless corrosion of time. There was nothing left in that armour, nothing human inside that helm. But still the wraith followed a dogged path up the back side of the rock, old, brittle bones cracking under its heavy sabatons. It reached out and slammed a hand down on Morrdryn's shoulder, forcing him to his knees, and the sword made an eerie squeal as the undead knight hauled it forwards and shoved the flat of the blade right up against his neck.

"Whatever you want, *please*, I'll give it to you," I begged, tears rolling down my cheeks.

Ceritha laughed. "You've already played your part, dear. Do you hear how restless the dead are? Perhaps, if you're lucky, they'll tear you apart quickly."

A sick, hollow feeling roiled in my gut. I had been so wrong about everything. That Ceritha needed my hair to work her magic, that Morrdryn was anything I had to fear. Ceritha flicked her finger, and the knight raised his sword high over his shoulder, ready to deliver a killing blow.

A wave of dizziness swept over me, but every moment I kept her distracted was another moment for Morrdryn to fight. "You can't do this."

"I've waited centuries to take this dragon's soul." The crone snarled. I gasped as she pulled indiscriminately against my hair. She was tearing it away from my scalp, but I had no leverage to fight her off. "His power will be mine."

Sweat rolled down Morrdryn's shoulders as his body strained against the bonds, still unable to move. If he could just get his legs under him, or twist away, he could fight back. If I could just get to him, if I could stop her – so many ifs.

My eyes rolled up to Ceritha in panic. "Please… don't do this."

"Oh, look at how she *begs*," the Witch sneered. She twisted my hair harder, forcing more tears to my eyes. "He is *mine.* Mine to do with as I please. Mine to kill."

Tears spilled down my cheeks. She had wasted so many lives. "What will you do when you've taken everything? When will it be enough for you?"

Something flickered in her gaze; a restless shadow swam behind those milky eyes and almost – *almost* – rose to the surface. But it was gone as quickly as it came, buried beneath greed and all the lives she'd ended to get here. Her smile only widened. "Ah, sweet girl," she purred, stroking my hair. "There's always more, and I'll take all of it because I *can*. Because I want to."

That rot in her soul was something I couldn't fight. She was too far gone, too corrupted by the souls she'd devoured to make a plea for her conscience. I didn't have any magic that could stop her; the spells I'd made were simple ones at best, and they'd been lost when I'd nearly fallen in the sea. But a new idea whispered in my mind. I didn't need *spells*. The magic I'd thought was only in my hair lived in me too, and it was just as wild as Morrdryn's magic.

Magic had always been wild. It had always been a living, breathing thing to the fae – before men had tried to tame it into books and words. The Witch crafted spells to focus it, to distil it and make it hers, but my song had always called to the dragon, and he had always called to me. We didn't need a spell to know what was between us.

My gaze slid to Morrdryn. His shoulders shook as he fought the iron that sapped his strength. His face was a mask of pain, of struggle, and he gritted his teeth and tried to force his body to move. A few seconds, that's all we had. A few seconds before that blade fell, before it cut through Morrdryn's neck.

I opened my mouth and sang – to my dragon, to my heart. I called up the melody in that ancient language we shared between us. There were no words, only sounds spilling out of me as if carried from deep inside, and the magic that had hummed between us last night began again. It thrummed like thunder rolling beneath the charge of lightning.

I reached for it, and the brilliant crack of light blinded everything.

Ceritha screamed and threw up an arm to block the light. It popped at the edges of my vision, sparkling with searing colours, but it didn't blind me the way it blinded her. Those fingers of lightning scattered across every surface of the cavern, sending up howls of pain from the ghouls shuffling around Morrdryn's rock. The iron band around his neck glowed, his *skin* glowed, filling up with the fire of the beast inside. That beast could not be stopped now, tuned to the frequency of my voice. The collar turned a dark red as curls of steam rose off him, as the slow-banked fury that lived deep within the dragon caught flame.

The metal heated to bright, fiery orange and broke open.

"Stop him!" Ceritha screeched from her place on the floor.

I leapt at her. We rolled, landing in a clatter of bones and debris and both came up clawing for each other. She slashed her nails at my eyes, but I was quicker; I grabbed that necklace around her neck and yanked hard.

I stumbled back into a centre of chaos. The Witch stared, mouth agape, as I took her jewelled necklace and hurled it from us. She looked so small and frail all of a sudden, nothing but thin, aged flesh stretched over bones without her magic to bolster her. As if that's all she was, just scaffolding under the weight of the magic she had taken from others.

"You're going to regret that," she spat.

I smiled. "No, I don't think I will."

The screams and squeals of dead things turned into a raw, high-pitched whine as their eyes turned to me. They lurched forwards, dragging themselves in my direction, and I took a step back. One step, then another – they did not see the dragon. They ignored the violent smoke that expanded around the man as his form began to shift. Massive horns speared the air as his dark head rose towards the cavern ceiling and his flesh hardened to scale. Those mad cannibals scrambled over the rocks, and just as their clammy, rotten fingers reached for me, the dragon roared.

The deafening noise shook the whole cavern. Rocks fell and waves retreated. I stumbled under the concussion of sound. Ceritha's expression twisted as her head swivelled towards me. A kind of terror I'd never seen on her face, in all the days she'd governed my life, shone bright and clear.

Morrdryn wrapped a clawed talon around me and scooped me up against his massive chest. Heat radiated from every scale, flushing my cheeks as the furnace within him built to full power. His silver eyes slitted down as that massive head reared back, and as he did, I lifted my voice to join his. Like threads of gold, filaments of my hair drifted up in the rising heat. The air in his chest was a deep whoosh as he sucked in breath.

I met Ceritha's eyes a final time as that ignited flame raced back up his throat with violent, explosive fury.

Then, dragon at my back, her world turned to screams and fire.

THE STEALER OF NAMES PROVES HIMSELF TO BE A TERRIBLE DEMIGOD

ANTHONY B.T.

1

THE WORST THING ABOUT MY FAMILY IS that I know my place in it. The firstborn son of the firstborn son, and I know the trajectory of my entire future without question. I know that I will someday be buried in the same dirt as all the Stealers who came before me. The children of the bugs that consumed everyone else will consume me. My mother meant to comfort me when she said that. She always thinks she's saying the right thing, but motherhood was never exactly her forte. But that's beside the point. The point is that my blood is still blood, which means that even the things you need can still make everything dirty. That sounds morbid, I know, but it's one of the first lessons my father ever taught me. He was a good man when the light hit him the right way. On the days that it didn't, we all knew well enough to pretend we didn't notice.

If you ever listen to me, let it be right now. I'm serious. Before She handed me the assignment that would mean the end of everything, She said hope is the truth hidden inside pretty clothing. She probably told my father the same thing when it was his turn. I still resent that. But who am I to resent God? To me, hope was for people with something to prove. The only thing I've ever had to prove up until now was that I still had a heartbeat when the sun rose. It still doesn't always feel true – I promise, I'll try to keep the self-deprecation to a minimum when I'm gone. But even you can't deny that I've always been bad at my job. The truth is that I've never liked it anyway, but you know how the Family Business is. If things were different, I think you would be good friends with Her. You have the same sense that everything will work out, even when all signs point to the fact that it won't.

You're laughing. But do you remember the day that my dad died, when I told you to run in the opposite direction? It was a small funeral because it was a scandal. None of the Big Names could stand to be seen there amongst the disgraced Stealer. You know, he was the first one in centuries to refuse. I still don't know why he did it. He wouldn't explain it to me, but I now understand how he felt.

The few Smaller Names that were there put their hands on my shoulders and told me to take this as a warning. They told me to do better. As if there could have been a better than my dad. He was always so judicious with his Stealing. Always so kind to the people. Always tried to make sure that they were comfortable, that they understood what was going on, that they weren't afraid of what would become of them. I knew that I could never live up to that.

After the whole ceremony was said and done, you sat with me on the back porch, overlooking the lake that sat behind the house. We used to swim there when we were kids, do you remember? My mother used to yell at us about it. Something about never knowing what was in there. But we were too young to care. I miss those days.

You looked good in black, and I remember feeling embarrassed for thinking so. There I was, the day of my father's funeral, and half of my headspace was dedicated to how good you looked in a suit. You wore a red tie and I remember you said that it was a defiance. That you didn't think my dad deserved the punishment. I didn't have the heart to tell you that that's just the way things are. He wouldn't tell me why he hadn't taken the name, or whose it was, but he had told me that he was going to refuse. He had warned me and instructed me on what I was going to have to do next. You called him brave and the Council cowards. I agreed with you.

You kissed me that night, and I could taste the beer on your tongue, and I didn't care. I had been waiting so long to kiss you, and I should have soaked in every second, but instead the pit in my stomach told me this was the beginning of doom. I hate it when I'm right.

You stayed over that night, and the next morning over Cafecito and the pumpkin muffins your mom made, I told you what it meant to be a Stealer and that someday I might be called to take yours and I wouldn't be able to stop it from happening. You saw what happened to my father when he dared to look the Gods in the eye and say "no". I told you this as a warning. I told you this so you could still leave if you wanted to. But I also meant that you walk on glitter. *Obligation* is not in your repertoire. You're going to try and argue with me about that fact just like you did on that day, when you laughed, threw your head back into the golden sunrise. You dared me to try and take your name from you. To make the last piece of you a piece of me too. I called you Icarus. You called it an honour. I call it suicide.

That was five years ago, and I don't think you quite understand. You've never had to see me do it. Not that you've ever asked, and I'm glad that you haven't. I wouldn't have told you anyway. I guess I should tell you now. The first name I ever stole has been haunting my dreams for years now.

I had gotten the call about a week after my dad died. She was older, it shouldn't have been tragic. It would have been me or death sooner or later. I was nervous, but I really wasn't thinking much of it. It was just doing my job. My dad had taken me to Stealings since I was young to see how it was done; I knew what was being asked of me. I had become numb to the practice relatively young. And who was she to me, anyway? I know, that's selfish and sad, but you have to understand where I'm coming from here...

Anyway. I had seen Stealings before. This one shouldn't have shaken me. It turns out, watching someone's name be taken and doing the taking yourself are two different monsters. When I watched the fire leave her eyes... it was a botched job, it shouldn't have taken as long as it did, but I didn't know how to do it well back then. I heard her beg for me not to. Her wailing still wakes me up at night. I thought I might save you if I did – if I just obediently took every name they asked me to they might not make me take yours. Forgive me for that.

She was somebody before I took that from her. Her grandchild had wandered off without her but found her a moment after I had stolen her name. Calling out "Granny!", wracked with fear and then... nothing. I watched as this girl – she couldn't have been older than seven – forgot. She opened her mouth to try and speak her grandmother's name, but all that came out was breath. She cocked her head to the side and looked at this woman. She knew her, though she couldn't put a name to how or why. But she knew she was important. The grandmother was a different matter.

She's one of the Hollowed now. No name, feelings, no identity. Wandering through life with no real purpose, no dreams, no aspirations, just monotony and vague memories of what she had once been. Murky details like sticking your head in a swamp. How do you live like that?

Go about your life knowing you have nothing, that you *are* nothing. That when you die, there will be nothing on your headstone and no one will cry at your funeral.

I think death is kinder than I am. Are you listening to me? Is that really what you want? You want me to scoop out everything good that you are and consume it? You want your mother to weep for you and never be able to talk about why? For what purpose? To satisfy the Gods? I don't give a damn about them. They've never met you.

No one tells you enough how important you are. I know you see yourself as thirteenth in the baker's dozen. There has never been anyone more important than you. Do you think your chickens are aware of their worth? What do you think they'd do or say if they knew? The stars still shine when the sun is up. The point is that you need to talk about yourself the way you'd talk about anyone else. You, with your honey-sweet voice, the warmth you've always had for everyone you meet no matter how temporary a space they hold in your life.

Don't look at me like that. Don't look at me with those wide eyes full of every star that has ever shone. I know you. You'll try to tell me that we can find a way out of this, that there's a loophole we'll find in the books somewhere and you'll be okay and I'll be okay, but you've always been more of an optimist than me. You're the hopeless romantic who still believes in fairytales. That the lovers always get to be happy.

My days are constant funerals. I'm with people, and we all care about each other, but the conversations we have feel more like we're obligated to bring some light into the room, open the curtains, realise it's raining, and shake our heads because we did our best. No one wants to be around a Stealer because they think they might be next. Your sister says I have a victim complex. When you think of me, think Hamlet. Think Ophelia. Think *I'm not sure how much power he had, but he used what he could to the best of his ability.* Think *say what you will about him but at least he wasn't afraid.* I think that sadness resembles peace when you flip a coin.

I think up until now I had mostly gotten used to it, though. Maybe that's a terrible thing to say. But every job becomes routine until something throws a wrench into your plans. My mind is mostly made of fog and good intentions. There will always be shortcomings, and I will probably be the root of them. You'll call me dramatic for saying this. You'll also say something along the lines of this being because Mercury is in Gatorade and the fact that my moon is in Leo and I'll always nod along like I understand what any of this means because I know it means something to you, and that's enough for me. You've always viewed me with an indulgence I have never deserved. I have never deserved you. And when I have to do this, you'll forgive me even when you don't remember what we had.

Once, we were teenagers, and Armageddon was the idea that we wouldn't find dates to prom. You were the only person I wanted to go with, but I hadn't learned the right spells yet. I was afraid in a way you never were – of what others would say, of what asking you to prom would make me. I wish I had cared less back then. I wish that had given us more years.

Do you remember where we thought we would be when we grew up? I understand now what your mom said when she warned us that life always has different plans. We were sitting in her kitchen after prom – we'd ditched our dates we didn't even want to go with in the first place. Your mom made us a whole spread of appetisers thinking we were bringing girls home. It seems kind of funny when I look back at it now. Graduation was on the horizon, and we were talking about our Grand Plans – me, art school in the city. I don't know what I thought I was going to do with a degree in animation, but it made me feel like maybe I could be somebody. I thought maybe if I could make art I might make people feel a little less lonely. You wanted to be a politician back then: world changer, love-bringer. I still hope that you can be.

Your mom smiled at us like we were the cutest little fools she had ever seen and told us to keep our heads in the clouds but our feet on the ground. That we never knew what life would have in store for us. I rolled my eyes. You laughed. You always seem to find it funny when people tell you a truth that you don't want to hear.

I knew my magic was limited, but we still thought we had more power than that. We thought that the universe didn't dictate our lives, that we had control, that we could manifest the futures we wanted as if everyone before us hadn't already tried. We were goddamn fools. I didn't know then, really, what I would be called to do. Sure, I had seen it happen, and I had the sense to know I was next in line. It wasn't like they'd skip over me and call for my sister. Back then I was young enough to think that my dad would live forever or, at the very least, that by the time it came to be My Time that none of this would matter.

How do you explain to someone who has never breathed what it feels like? What is blue without using the word ocean, sky? There are no words. You open your mouth and there is only glow. That is what love is, I think. Love is never knowing the real questions. You help me come close. And here you are, telling me that it'll be okay. That you give me *permission*. I hate you for it. Which isn't to say that I hate you. I'm just saying that you're making all of this so much harder than it needs to be.

It's dangerous to say things you can't take back. Be careful. I refuse to be the reason you lose everything. Close the blinds tonight. Speak only in whispers. I think that sometimes you have to sacrifice ease for clarity. It might be the other way around, but you know what I mean. What I'm trying to say is that I want to keep you safe but there's no such thing. There is no win in this scenario, and I wish you'd stop trying to convince me there is. Just accept that this is what needs to happen. I think I have. I think I know how this goes.

You said once that if you tell stories enough they become the truth. If that's the case, tell the story about how we lived happily ever after. Tell the story of how I kept you safe, and we retired to the mountains like you always wanted. You said Vermont is beautiful in the summer and near insufferable in the winter but it's where you wanted to spend the rest of your life. So tell the story where we get to. It's quiet there, we have no neighbours for miles, and no one ever knocks on our door. The only company we have are the people we invite ourselves – my sister, your mom, maybe your friends from work. I don't leave unless I want to, and I only want to when we're low on food. We have a dog, or a cat, something fluffy for you to hold onto when it's too cold. You'd name it something ridiculous like Captain Ice Cream and I would make fun of you for it but I'd call it Cap and love it nearly as much as I love you. I wish I could say that it would make up for the ache pulsing through you. Tell everyone the story about how we got to be the heroes *and* be happy. I never hear those stories, and I'd like it to be us. Tell it real. Tell it gospel.

When you go to sleep tonight, take a deep breath in through your nose. Don't take that medicine the doctor gave you – I know it's supposed to help, but I'm always so suspicious. I mean, doesn't it feel artificial? You said once that when you took it, you had a feeling you'd sipped death. You felt your body shutting down, a machine whirring to a halt. I don't know how you ever took it again after that. I think if you sip on death once, you've got the taste of it in your mouth forever, and I couldn't live like that. You've always valued your sleep above most things. Just make sure that it never gets in the way of your living. Please make sure that sleep never keeps you from life. I'll come to bed later. Let me give you a kiss, tuck you in. Dream well. Rest easy. Please know that I am so, so sorry.

DEATH WEARS A FEATHERED CLOAK

KRISTEN BALES

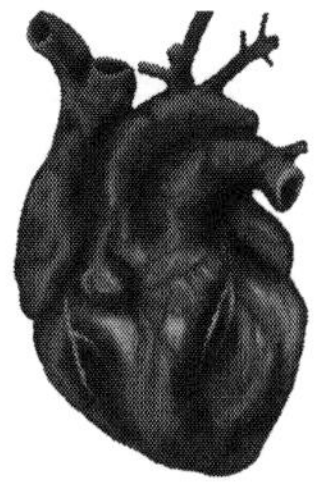

1

W*HAT DOES THE DAWN TASTE LIKE?*

Once, I asked this of a sparrow who smelled of salt and brine. I drank down his heady scent as a clearing tonic; inhaled it in rushed, greedy gulps of relief. I let his essence sit upon my tongue, the mirror of an ocean in my mouth. Salacious and starving, I yearned to savour that bitter thrush of saline tang until my jaw was baptised in ocean water – blessed, by the clinging of condensation. There was no water here, not even rain. There was only the curl of smoke beneath my nose, and the harsh bite of endless dusk.

It had been ages since I'd used my voice. The thing lived beneath my aching chest for so long it came out wooden and unfeeling. What do you call the passage of time when there is no sun to break it? There was only the night with stars, and the stretch of night with the moon. I had assumed I was running out of time. For all things planted must rot, wither. I assume that they, too, are perpetually running out of time.

At the brink of the moon meeting the stars, I called to the bird. "What does the dawn taste like?"

The words were scratchy and hoarse, though this did not dissuade the sparrow, and speaking them came with a cost. Branches ruptured from my breasts. Leaves spurted from my mouth. The moon rose, and I was only a willow. He, only a sparrow. And I was silenced, as all trees are, wishing I could say more.

Chirrup, chirrup, chirrup, the sparrow sang, so far away from its home.

I am far away from home too, I wanted to whisper. *I wouldn't resent you if you left.* Clearly, he didn't belong here. I didn't belong here either.

Chirrup, chirrup, chirrup, he called up to my branches, to the columns of my fronds.

But stay, I wanted to shout back. *Please, just stay.*

The stars blinked, the moon blossomed, and the sparrow never answered, though his head cocked at that distinct, creased angle that told me I wasn't just hearing things. I wasn't just talking to myself, my mind conjuring a flightless bird. No, his tune was real – a sweet, soothing croon. It lulled me into a deep, dreamless sleep.

Though he was but a sparrow, the next morning I awoke with a jolt at the distinct call of his *chirrup, chirrup, chirrup*.

I uncurled from the fetal position, a manner in which my soul so naturally transformed from tree to person, coiling in on its borrowed body like a pill bug. It was easy, to shed branches for arms and buds for fingers. It was simple, to trade that subtle hollow in my trunk for a mouth, to shake off the excess leaves from the canopy of my head. It was strangely natural, to snap off a few branches of my lingering bark spine and situate the column of the twisted candle that had been with me for centuries, the everflame. It was brutally learned, the way I snicked the pieces of myself for kindling. It was necessary, to light the everflame that warmed my exposed skin and shivering limbs.

But it was harder to speak.

I knelt over the flickering candlelight, rubbing my hands together over the emanating heat while the sparrow flitted about. *Don't come near it*, I yearned to caution him. There was nothing as insidious as a flame meant to preserve things in a bitter state of endless death. This was no life, to sit here and rot alone. Perhaps, if I attempted to say all this, the magic that bound me to this forest would stir. It was the sort of magic that didn't like to be rustled. Ancient magic, as fate had taught me, had a penchant for punishing. I clamped my mouth shut at the untested consequences, for I was not awake to be condemned to sleep eternally as a tree.

Chirrup, chirrup.

The sparrow sang at my feet, chittering at my bare, soil-caked skin. I fumbled for words, staring at the thing like he were a ghost.

I sat there for a while, clutching my head in my hands – not in pain, but in rapture. Music is meaningless to those who have heard it thrice over, but when it falls on ears that have only known silence... I grieved for the songs I'd never hear. I grieved for the time until I heard them again.

The sparrow was more than a bird to me – more than music to my ears, so depraved had I been. Birds, beasts, and the sweet beating of the heart of the wood had long abandoned me.

You need no one.

Long ago, my mother had recited those words over the crackle of a wildfire she had started out of maternal rage, those spindly fingers laying the damning kindling of my youth.

None but yourself, my sweet sapling.

She had burned the forest, ravaged the trees, all for the sake of my survival. She'd had a premonition, of a thriving tree with my dying body, still human, beneath it, and she would stop at nothing to ensure death would not come for me. I was no oracle, though I inherited the scars of one. Her resin still lived in my cursed bark, I supposed.

When the moon rose, and the sparrow still skittered about the charred branches and starving lichen upon the cracked ground beneath the everflame, I was mesmerised. It was no simple feat to wander so far, yet alone *live* to fly so long.

It was a rule I made decades ago, that all mirages must be real. In a barren magical forest, things are hardly ever what they first appear to be. I cherished the inkling that beneath the feathers and down, there was something else; under the cloak of wings, a man. For all things enchanted can be found ordinary, if looked upon twice.

He was close enough that I could touch him, and I had fingers until the façade of daybreak. So, touch him I did.

I gently pressed two fingers to the brush of feather where the nape of his auburn shading met the brilliant, speckled crown of his head. *Here, broad shoulders,* I thought. *And a beautiful portrait of ink.*

The sparrow tilted his head in encouragement. I pursed my lips, measuring the length of his neck. Emboldened, I curled a finger to brush it. *There,* I imagined. *Your pulse. Alive, bursting at the seams with mischief that leads you.* He had to be brash to fly such a distance, so far from the sea of which he smelled.

Here, I mused, turning my hand over to further peruse.

I let out an enthralled gasp, then promptly stopped breathing. He had clambered onto my open palm, still and serene.

Eyes as depthless as the night that owns me.

I stared back into them, utterly weightless. He watched me as if he knew I was watching him, weighing his worth in the palm of my hand.

Attentive, I decided, blinking nervously back at him. *If you could speak, you'd tell me everything I have missed – the sun, the warmth, the thrash of sea foam, the shimmering of the waterline as it hits the horizon...*

He shook out his wings, and my tunnelling thoughts dispersed.

Arms, I thought, honed by a sword bound to a warrior of old.

Hands. I smiled down at his claws, hoping they'd leave a mark – small indents, which would sink deep into my bark. Perhaps a huntsman who worked with them often would be capable of such a thing.

"You and I are the same." I finally exhaled, cursing internally as the whistling vines and unruly verdure in my lungs suffocated the sentiment. The everflame winked out, and I was a tree once more.

That night, I dreamt of him. His fingertips brushing the crooked, gnarled branch where the notch of my forearm should bend. They skated down, down, down, caressing the tops of my hands, the juncture of my knuckles. The sweet friction of his skin, so soft and delicate, admired the length of my fingers, which had so brazenly held him. He was teasing, tugging at the cascade of my leaves. In the veil of night, the hunter made flesh was flush against my cage of bark and branches.

"Let me lie here, my love." His voice was a thing of curling shadows, warm and effervescent as the stars above. "Drink from me until the dawn. Then, you'll know the taste of the sun."

When I awoke, there was naught but thorns and thistle. He was gone. And I, a willow in an empty forest, alone.

2

I THOUGHT OF THE BIRD LIKE ALL THINGS I could remember: often, obsessively, endlessly. When there is nothing in front of you, there is nothing better to do but ruminate on what could be there – what *should* be there. Memory worked its cruel shackles on me; time dug in its fangs. Days turned into months, months into years, and I was haunted by a tune I would never hear again – cursed to know the feeling of feathers beneath my fingers. Sometimes I dreamt of him, lying under my trunk. Other days, I slept through the starry night to fantasize what it would be to taste his skin. If it truly would be like summer upon my tongue. Fantasizing kept me sane, even if it was a bald-faced lie.

The everflame sat at the crest of my roots, taunting me. Some days, I wouldn't light it, often without realising it. An apathy bid me to never care, not for heat, not for warmth, not for life. Sometimes I wondered if I would be better off completely sedated, bound to the roots and the bark until the soil beneath chewed me up and spit me out. Many days – many months – I forgot to light the everflame. Instead, I practiced speaking. A tree, though quiet and forsaken, still had language. So, I told myself the story, reciting the work of the cruel, cursed land back to me.

"There once was a tree who loved her forest..."

"No, she was not a tree, but a woman..."

"A woman who was once a child, who called for a sparrow..."

"She called until her knuckles turned blue and her toes a sickening crunch of silver sheen. She couldn't walk, could hardly breathe. She hoped to freeze to death – hoped the unseen hoarfrost would spur her roots and finally usher her into oblivion – but it didn't work. It never worked. She was cursed to live on, just as she always had... alone."

One morning, as time would have it, I found the burden of the cold had sealed my lips with frost. Panicked, I searched for the candle that claimed my days, hoping to speak with lips, tongue, and teeth once more.

"What does the dawn taste like?" I whispered to the vacant breeze on another nameless day. The knobs of my eyes began to wither and weaken. There was hardly any discernible light between the slanted leaves of my waving tresses. My body melted, just as it always did, as the curse loosened its grip on my bark and bramble. I tumbled to the forest floor, tousled out of a listless, dreamless sleep. With a wince, I seized the lingering twigs from my spine in one perilous *snap*. My hands reached for wax, for the thick column of the candle, but they collapsed around… *nothing.*

The everflame, which had not moved in a century's time, was gone. Like a depraved sprite, I scanned the forest for my prize. In the near distance, a pocket of pale white sat idly, tucked among a pile of faded hazel brush. No, not gone. *Moved.*

I scrambled along the empty forest floor, unyielding sinews slowing each armoured step like I was tunnelling through a raging sea. The last time I had used them, I was chasing down a sparrow. Like a moth without wings, it was tricky to crawl over the blank expanse of cracked soil without a branch to steady my arms, nor a cushion for my parched, swollen feet. Still, I managed to gather up enough strength to make it through the mangled stumps and ashen coppice.

The everflame was positioned on its side, as if it had been studied, weighed, and promptly discarded like any ordinary candle among this forgotten hellscape of a wood.

"This isn't possible."

The exasperated sentiment left my lips as I surveyed the carnage, the sole proof that anyone had been here at all.

But no one ventures here, I thought, bending to sniff at the disturbance. Smoke lingered – had someone lit the everflame? The musk of leather clung, as if gloved hands had handled it. And… salt.

My eyes widened to the reverie – the tune of a bird, who smelled of the sea.

No.

I shut down the blissful revelation.

You've grown old, I reasoned with myself. *You're going mad in this depraved wood.*

Gathering up the candle in my hands, I situated it in the makeshift hazel brush casket, which was beginning to look more like a carefully arranged wreath. It was almost as if someone had intentionally braided the shrubbery, taking care to arrange the long-discarded overgrowth.

"Huntsman hands," I mused aloud, feeling the burn of the words against my vocal cords, so chafed with disuse.

I lit the everflame, pinching the tip of it with a wince as the blaze grew soft and persistent. The eight steps back to the black crevice in the earth where my roots dug was less torturous than the first few steps. I glanced back to where I'd left the everflame to bend towards a long-disposed branch in my solitary home.

This branch was the only remnant of the wood that existed long before, other than my own fragmented growth. I pressed my charred fingers to the flaying bark, marking it alongside a stretching pattern of identical bruise-like burns. My mind creaked, stagnant from the impact of counting them. To keep the passage of time was prudent, though I had long abandoned that practice. It felt like abuse, keeping track of the line of supposed days meeting the nights. Each evening bled into the next. It was all the same. It was silt, sifting through my grappling fingers. Still, I gathered the history of my age in my vision.

One, two, three, four, five...

But what of the everflame, disturbed?

I had forgotten, promptly abandoning the fantasy that I was no longer alone. I glanced at the candle, still sparking in the tepid dark. Though it was difficult to see through the veil of the first light when there was naught but stars like budding lanterns on the muted clouds, the everflame still shone like a beacon. Someone had been here; someone had tried to light it.

They had not been successful. There was no wood to ignite it, nothing but immutable thorn and thicket. The only possible conduit to light such a thing was... me. Whomever it was had been cautious – thoughtful – enough to leave my branches be as I slept.

Perhaps my sparrow?

No. The thought retreated, petrified to the branch before me.

One, two, three.

I collected myself again, drawing my focus to the cauterised wood. Trees must know how old they are, even if they cannot unspool their trunks and peruse every ring of their infancy. How little I yearned to display that growth, to keep the memory of my age.

Twenty, twenty-one, twenty-two...

I prattled on, cataloguing each century in the backlog of my mind.

Forty-one, forty-two, forty-three...

Snap.

The stark interruption halted the numbers in my head.

Snap. Click. Snap.

My eyes snicked up, rising to meet the sound. The forest was whispering, murmuring as if something large was moving through it. I rose carefully, like a doe might move in the thrall of an intruder's steps.

And I thought of the bird. I tried to forget what he felt like, but the memory of him felt kind under my bruised and brandished fingertips, soaked with soot.

Snap. Click. Snap.

In the long, endless plain of a cleared, desecrated forest, there was the shape of a man, stalking for me.

3

SNAP. CLICK. SNAP.

Boots crunched on parched ground. Someone – something – had found a path in… and if there was a path in, there was a path out.

"What do you know of it?" I whispered.

I watched the breadth of the horizon bow to him like he was an avenging eldritch god. The smudge of his head turned, tilted towards me as if he could hear the stirring of my words. I waited for my branches to sprout, for my legs to take root – screwed my eyes shut, bracing for the shift.

But it never came. I crouched low, surveying him from afar.

Click. Snap. Click. Snap.

The remains of the wood crumbled beneath his leather boots, and he moved as deftly and swiftly as a predator provoked. Still, I had no urge to run. No such instinct had been taught to me. If this was the end, I would welcome such a gift.

The glow and peck of the budding stars above illuminated his cloak. At first, it was a thing to admire, a gathering of slick, glossy pieces that all fit together as one. The pattern was distinctly jagged but swayed in the evening light. I was mesmerised by the way it shifted with him, a second skin that didn't quite cling but didn't quite weave – a waving of illustrious black sheets in a phantom wind.

As he neared, my admiration soured to horror. Feathers. The cloak was comprised of hundreds upon heaps of feathers. My chest splintered at the memory of my sparrow, severing in two. This was no male; this was a huntsman. So, like all things of the forest spotted as prey, I ran.

"Wait!"

I could feel the warmth of his voice hit between my breastbone as I pivoted.

"Stop!" the huntsman demanded, as all hungry predators might.

His pace quickened, and I began to bolt. It was a clumsy jog – my legs so stiff and atrophied.

He caught up with me in a manner of a few strides, stepping into my path. I stood rigid like a creature cornered to be eaten, my limbs refusing to work.

We surveyed one another, and though his cloak was dark and glistening in the shadows from whence he came, his eyes were bright. They were the sort of cerulean I had never imagined before but had smelled once – for just as the everflame had been doused in it, this man smelled of salt, reeked of leather.

The *ocean*.

Capsized, I drowned in the sea of his gaze. I had never seen such a beautiful, bottomless chasm. It roused a mutilated piece of me, the one that wanted to live, to survive another day to track down something just as beautiful, just as stunning. I wanted to find the dawn, that light that had long abandoned me.

The man began to move, breaking the spell, and my bones remembered that he was a hunter, and I was but a tree. I withdrew, retaining space between us.

He took a step forwards. Another.

My swollen lips moved to scream. *You'll kill me!* As if the hunter heard, he flashed a grim look of understanding, a hand reaching within the hidden folds of his cloak for something silver.

The hilt of a broadsword, laced to his belt.

I flinched back in terror.

He scoffed. "I'm not going to cut you down."

I balked at the tune of his lips. It was effervescent, soothing. The sound was the thing of dreams. It held me aloft in the sort of trance that only a magicked forest could conjure. Perhaps he was only that: another dream.

His fingers laced, gripping near the weapon. I shrank back, the soles of my feet burrowed into the crusted earth beneath, but his fist only curled around the feathers. He shrugged off the cloak, holding it askance.

"Here," he offered.

"I cannot take it." I finally spoke. The words were rusty in my parched throat. Understanding passed over his eyes, as if he had heard the rhythm of my voice before – had known it, in the very fibre of his being.

"You'll freeze," he urged, shaking the thing in his hands with insistence.

"Not here, not after I lit the—" I stopped the words, waiting for a branch to finally explode out of my jaw.

"You lit..." he encouraged, taking three more steps towards me, cloak in hand.

I drew my lips down at the cascading waterfall of feathers, breaking the intense bridge of his attention... and carefully reached for his cloak.

"Allow me."

I wasn't sure what it meant, what he was requesting; I only nodded quickly. The hunter didn't hesitate, moving behind me to wrap the cloak around my shoulders and situate the tie about my neck. Though it was cushioned by the thick bundle of feathers, he handled every motion with care. His hands moved lovingly, a caress upon my weary shoulders. I had never known anything but the weight of a burned forest on my back. All this I had carried, until I had forgotten what it was to have nothing but grief crushing me. My back had never been covered or protected from the elements. Relief coursed through me as the chill of the land in my bones was calmed by the barrier of down. Someone had meticulously constructed this. Had the hunter sheared the feathers? Sewed it together?

Huntsman hands, I reminded myself, looking down at my cloaked body with sickened fascination. I was cloaked in the ancestors of my sparrow, and the trappings of death felt familiar. Comforting, even. How strange it was, to be warm.

"Better?" The man's cerulean eyes were assessing the garment, appraising his work.

"Yes." I shifted on my feet, his intense gaze floating back to mine.

What are you doing out here? his eyes seemed to inquire. Instead, he waited, content to give me space to speak first. Without the burden of interrupting branches spurting from my lungs, I spoke openly, freely – willingly.

"What are you doing out here?" I asked for myself and myself alone.

The corner of his mouth twitched. "Hunting," he said, as if it were explanation enough.

My lips clamped in displeasure. Still, I found my thoughts tumbling out of my mouth. "In a forest full of dead things?"

He chuckled, a still, small thing to himself. Even in the dim light, the crease of his amusement was sunny, pleasing. "It is unseeming and dreary out here."

The statement neither confirmed nor admitted to my suspicions of his huntsman nature. "What are you doing out here, truly?" My tone bordered on accusatory.

"Well, what are *you* doing out here?" he threw back at me with a mischievous grin.

I balked, frozen at the answer in my chest. The spell would not let me speak it, would not allow for the room to explain.

"What are you—" He registered the sorry state of my body, stiffening, and turned on his heel. As if he were leaving, as if he were—

"Wait!" I choked out, anger piercing my sternum. He couldn't leave me here, not after centuries of being alone.

But he wasn't leaving, he was averting his eyes. They trailed off, searching for something.

"Is there something I can help you find?" I asked, unsure if I could even help. Surely, he wasn't hunting for *me* in this forest.

He looked at me briefly, scanning the forest line. "You seem... familiar with this place," he said carefully, eyes slotting through the open space. "Where are the trees?"

My features hardened with centuries of bitterness. "Gone."

He ran a hand through his long, silken raven hair. "Unfortunate."

"Is it?" I gritted out, feeling insubstantial.

"Yes." He turned, still holding the secret between his eyes. "Because I was tasked to retrieve a tree, native to these parts. If I were to return empty-handed, the consequences would be tedious. Futile, if you will."

"Will you... be cursed?" I winced.

He shrugged. "I *am* cursed. Though I'm not sure why you'd care..." He nodded, as if waiting for me to fill in the gap of my title, my name. I wasn't sure what it was. It had been long gone, lost to the thrall of a fading memory.

"Lark," I suggested, thinking of the sparrow. I had never known a name, never felt the belonging of a thing of permanence.

"Lark." He tested it upon his tongue. It was lush, beautiful, and delicate. I wanted him to say it over and over, until my ears were sickened and sore with the sound. All this, I dreamt up until I finally realised he had been asking me a question.

"Would you like to come along with me, Lark?" he asked wearily, as if he'd already repeated it a few times in my presence.

"No."

"Alright, then."

"Wait..."

He spun on his foot, at the ready.

"Yes?" I shaped the suggestion in my mouth and tried to feel the finality of it in my grounded bones.

"Are you certain?" He held up his hands.

Was I certain? The idea of leaving had begun to chafe. How did you leave a place, where the roots that magic flowed through sustained you? But I had feet, and it had been a morning of moving them. Was there a tomorrow for me, outside of such bounds?

"Yes," I said this time, if only for myself.

"As you please." He held his hands in his pockets, patiently poised for me to do something… anything that showcased my commitment. This time, I held my own hand aloft. He snatched it, lacing his gloved fingers through mine. The leather was soft, pliant in my burnt hands. He turned my palm over, categorising every mark upon my skin.

Slowly, we inched forwards together.

"What do you wish to find here?" I pressed, trying to draw his attention from what I knew he was perceiving upon my skin. Those markings were not my story – not the *only* tale my body told.

"I wish for sun and the shade of a tree," he mused, as someone who knew the sun's warmth would mindlessly do.

I was looking at my hands, watching him turning them over in contempt. The soil clung, a layer of filament over the singed skin. I was buried in the filth of centuries.

"I wish to bathe," I countered.

He broke his stare with a mirthless laugh of, "Out here?"

But then, his features softened as he addressed me intently, his mouth a thin line of determination. "We'll search for a spring."

We. The levity of it curled around my gut. I had been alone in a forest of—

"Come on." He wasn't waltzing away, wandering off with me. Instead, he extended his steps, slowly pushing forwards to match my pace. My eyes were glued to the place where our hands met, gloves on skin. At his wrist, his tunic hiked up, revealing a sliver of scar. I marvelled at it. He was keeping a story beneath his tunic, and every bit of his story left me wanting, intrigued.

When I halted my steps, the hunter heeded his. He was waiting again, I realised. Allowing me to lead myself out. When I made no move to continue, he lowered his voice to a reassuring, conspiratorial rake of a whisper. "The trees have ears, but never fear. There's not a single tree out here, and I have nothing to hide."

I laughed nervously and led us on.

"You can stay, if you'd like. I am not your keeper, nor you a captive." He was looking at me curiously, as if when he finally would move to release my hand, I might bolt.

"Water," I said by means of insistence.

"Water," he echoed, though it was calm, soothing.

So enveloped was I in him that I nearly tripped over the everflame. I bucked from his grip, turning and sprinting to grasp the candle in my hands. I clutched it close to my chest, heaving with panic.

"Is something wrong?" He backtracked, watching the scene unfurl before him with sudden veracity.

I frowned in confliction, wondering what it would be to take root elsewhere – wondering if the everflame would burn anywhere else other than where I had found it. "I—" I tried to explain, but the bounds of the curse tangled my lips. Still, he waited.

Finally, I skirted around the gaps of my bindings and said, "It will be difficult for us to leave. This land has limits."

He smiled knowingly. "I am not bound by the rules of this land."

But I was.

"Come, let us go, Lark." He beckoned us on.

I stiffened at the demand but vaguely shook my head. "I'll stay."

His brow arched in a question.

I shook my head again, shrugged, and explained, "I have no need to leave."

His brow arched higher.

He scrubbed a hand down his face, caked in sweat and mud, as if he had been digging for something long before he stumbled upon me. When he opened his eyes, they lit with something I had never had the pleasure of seeing before. His lips quirked, stretching out in the most illustrious smile.

My heart, hollowed and heavy, broke. My cheeks shook, trembled with the impact.

"You're smiling," he said finally, reaching out his hand again. "If you wish it, we can leave this place."

Everflame in tow and his hand in mine, I hoped that the weaving of my fingers displayed what I wished to say aloud but could not voice for fear of the consequences.

I wish it, my bones canted.

4

WHEN I TOOK HIS HAND, I BELIEVED THE curse to be broken, but curses didn't sever so easily, and consequences were still ripe among my branches.

The false dawn came, and the hunter wandered off to forage for any sustenance. I didn't think to ask him where he was going, didn't think to warn him that he would come back to face the night alone with nothing but a willow for company. I wasn't used to speaking enough to know the bounds of the curse, enough to dispense the warnings that mortals so often needed. I wasn't sure when he returned, only that I had already transformed. I was a tree. And he, a hunter.

I watched him keenly from the narrowed, hazy shade of my dreams. Could feel something like a body resting at the crest of my trunk. Something like hands playing casually with the sprouts at the tips of my exposed roots. It was a gentle, knowing touch, but I still suffered the nightmares. Once, a crone had cursed my blood – cursed my mother before me.

"At night you will dig roots into the soil." The crooked mage waved a hand over my naïve, fresh eyes. I was but a child, but I knew when I should be frightened. My mother held me, but she could not shield me from the words. She could not protect me from what she had done – how she had burned the trees, baited the queen of the woods from her smoked-out cavern of old – and so the crone cursed me.

"And by day you will be but leaves, fronds, and branches. A monument never strays far from the place it was meant to mark. You will mark my skeleton forest. You will only sleep to dream of the life that will never be found, and a forest shunned by the one in which I was supposed to abound."

The nightmare was short, vapid. It did not cling as it used to, and the dregs of my waking were filled with a sweet, blissful voice. The terror of my past was chased away by the tune of something new, a sound that whispered gently in my ear. The noise was as clear as the moon, comforting as the call of a sparrow.

"You held my jaw,
Lips to mouth,
And tongue, to teeth
And bone, and marrow.
We were kissing,

Embracing as if
The forest was dead
And the last living thing
Exuded between our lungs,
Exchanging life as vows,
Souls as gold,
And time as its maker.
When it all ended,
We were still there

Kissing as if the forest was burning—
Loving as if the rain was ash,
Cursing as if the sun was brimstone—
Because it was,
It had already burned.

Come morning, you'll drink the dawn from my hands."

I gracefully blinked away the dreamscape, the poem still fresh in my peripheries. As I came to, a body came into focus at my feet. The hunter was there, a notebook clasped in hand. He had been reciting the words on the page, I deduced, as he folded the notebook into his pocket. His cloak was already draped, delicately placed about my shoulders.

I watched him quietly, shaking the sleep from my eyes. How did he know that a tree could hear him so?

He watched me watching him, his raven hair dipping over his face.

"Who are you?" I demanded, doubt clouding my vision.

He was silent, fixated somewhere distant.

"Did you know I was a tree?" There was demand laced in my voice as I drew him to attention. I fixed him with a hard stare. Then, I commanded in defiance, "How?"

For only two people knew, and this hunter was not the crone, nor my mother.

As if he could see that secret there, the bounds of my spell, he smiled warily. He leaned forwards, plucking a lingering leaf from my hair. Without warning, he produced something small and wooden from the depths of his pocket. I scrambled back, but he held his hands as if to say *It's okay.*

In his right hand was a match, and in his left a rock.

He took the everflame, unlit at my feet, and struck the match.

I watched the thing burn, incredulous.

Finally, when the pattern of the fire was well and true, the hunter spoke.

"I have," he said, and then by way of explanation added, "I have been looking for one such as you. I am a druid."

He smiled, and I did not balk at it. "And I speak to the forest, often."

"You lit the everflame." My eyes bulged.

Even caught in the act, he looked bemused. "There's something inside of it that I have use for."

My mouth hung open. "There's nothing but eternal candle wax."

The hunter raised his midnight brows as if to say *Are you so certain about that?*

He muttered something low and audible to himself. As if beholding to his words, the flame upon the candle danced orange, faded to a pallid yellow, and began to burst with a delicious spark of striking, unmistakable cerulean blue – akin to the eyes of its maker.

Then, the wax began to drip. For two centuries, the candle had cast a flame but never melted. I could feel his magic working, incensed by the sweet taste of salt and brine of the flame's curious smoke. The magic of his fire was warm, like silk upon my skin. It did not demand penance. I had only ever known the cost of magic, not the pleasure of it. Magic had never been free. It was bought.

I blinked at the candle, at the puddle of wax beneath it. "At what price do you summon such things?"

He shrugged, though his shoulders tensed in contrast. "Does it matter?"

It did, but I nodded anyway. Even if the everflame were but a useless nub, the forest had bound me, the forest would find me, and I could not leave.

"How *do* you know of my kind?" My focus had become affixed to the capsizing votive.

"I've seen your kind before." He spoke to the fastidiously melting flame, our attention merged. "In a forest by the sea, where the trees are lush and verdant."

"What do they look like?"

"Hm?"

"Do they look like me?" I motioned to my eyes, and his smirk softened to a blissful grin, unravelling in the muted moonlight. "My eyes," I clarified. "Do they carry the same shade of those leaves?"

"They do." His grin widened. "But every shade of you has enchanted me so, whether willow or human your features bestow."

"A poet." My eyes glittered with discovery.

He fished out his notebook again. "My own mother taught me the art of it. She was canny in her dealings, but I'm far more...."

"Charming?" I suggested.

He laughed, a wild and wicked thing. "Yes, Lark. Charming. Shall I read to you as you sleep?"

I nodded, pleased with the idea. *I had a mother,* I wanted to tell him. *She made a deal,* I yearned to say candidly. Instead, I crossed my arms to hide the scars that boasted the crux of that bargain, content to listen to his words. I fell asleep with the pressure of a body against my branches, and a druid singing wistfully in my ear.

5

AND THUS, WE WALKED THROUGH THE forest. By day, we inched forwards through infertile terrain, and by night, I drifted asleep to his endless supply of words. The magicked everflame burned until it thawed to plated silver, revealing an object within. Just as he had proposed, the wax was hiding secrets. An amulet, a strand of silver encasing a sparkling gem of sanguine. When the thing was properly cleansed of bits of clinging wax, he presented it to me, and I hung it thoughtfully around my neck.

It was a cold weight atop my bare breastbone, on a cool day like any other. As we followed the path of his memory out, I finally registered that as he swung his arms to walk, he did so at an odd angle. As if to prevent his skin from blistering against his tunic. As if—

"You're injured," I blurted out.

"Mortally," he supplied, waving away the implications with vapid disregard. "The price of remaining in this human form is steep."

"Let me see!" I cried in protest, stalling his movement with a hand. His jaw clenched at the contact, after which I glowered until he removed his tunic to allow me to inspect the damage. Willingly, he did so.

The wound was volatile, as if a beast had taken chunks out of his spine. It was a vicious trio of lacerations of deep and flaky crimson. The lacing tips edged to his shoulders, rubbed raw by the contact of his loose tunic.

"Let me heal you."

"This cannot be fixed," he replied tightly.

"There are berries, upon my branches," I said by way of explanation. "When I am asleep, pluck them from my leaves. Three should do. I can make them into a healing paste."

The hunter nodded in agreement, settling into a sitting position.

"Is it soon?" he asked as I closed my eyes.

"Yes, it will come soon."

The unseen dawn came and spent, and I awoke to the weight of three delicate amaranthine berries in my palm. I put the fruit in my mouth, chewing it gently. Every inch of my skin was magic borrowed, encased in a form that wasn't wholly my own, but I could still make use of it.

Across from me, the hunter was staring blankly into the void of the fault lines on the fake horizon, settling his mind elsewhere.

A place I cannot go, I realised as he fixated at that point, reliving something I could not see, could not feel. I could only tell that it was just as visceral as the waking world before us.

His cloak had been settled beneath me as a cushion. I shrugged on the feathers, tying the clasp tightly around my neck. It was warm. Soft. Already dispelled of his tunic, the hunter's scars were on stark display.

I traced them openly, following the echo of a barbarous nightmare that he would not disclose. He did not move, did not strain. I mixed the paste in my hands, working it into his skin. He didn't respond, at least not in words. It was the way he didn't recoil from what must have been an unforgivable pain that I knew this was not simply a surface-level ache. My hands worked delicately in soothing circles, a knot growing in the pit of my gut. His features remained unfeeling, unchanged. I had been there too, many times before.

"Once, there was a mage of terrible renown." I drummed the words upon the top notch of his spine. "She stole my voice for leaves, for her forest was taken."

"You burned the forest?" He hissed.

I laughed, though it was a bitter thing. "My mother." I was speaking openly – his magic had loosened the truth out of my chest. Somehow, the spell did not take me under, bury my lungs into the soil.

He turned to me over his shoulder, eyes hardened to agate. "It is not your burden, then."

I frowned. "Not all burdens are so easily placed where they should be, nor curses so easily scorched. My mother thought she could eradicate my fate by destroying the forest, but fate is not so easily erased." I winced at the words. "The fate I was condemned to was worse."

Because of her actions. I didn't need to add it; I could see in his vengeful features that he understood.

We sat there for a while, staring openly at one another. When the paste was caked, I scrubbed off the casing. The skin beneath was new, healed.

When the hunter stretched his arms through his tunic, he let out a long-suffering sigh. "Ask anything of me, Lark, and I will give it."

Immediately, the chain of sanguine gem thumped against my racing heart, and I knew what I wanted. It was but a whisper, as vibrant as my berry-tinged lips. "I wish to see the dawn."

"By the morning, you shall have it," the hunter vowed with a roguish grin.

As all things he had promised before, I entrusted he would bring it to me.

6

"LARK." SOMEONE'S HAND WAS AT MY CHEEK, beckoning me to wake.

"Lark," the cool voice summoned again, a sweet pressure at my arm.

It was the hunter, helping me to my feet. My body ached, as if it had not been a tree. My bones creaked, but not with the crusting of bark. It was a gratified ache, as if someone else had been pressed up against my skin – as if I had slept as a mortal would, bound only by skin and sinew. Like he knew the memory of his body was entwined in mine, he smiled down at me.

"Look." He pointed to the horizon line.

The dawn broke.

It was visible, stretching far beyond the boundary of the forest.

"Brace yourself," he warned, but nothing could have prepared me.

It was so bright. My eyes stung. Tears, hot and streaming, tracked my cheeks.

"Lark," he was saying, but I barely registered it. "Lark," he said again, though it was tender, gentler.

"I wish I could stay here." Forever, I wanted to add, but speaking it aloud felt too fragile. So new that I might lose it.

"Too long you've lived in this forest alone," he murmured, so low I could barely hear it.

I glanced at his face, so tanned and loved by the sun. His hand flinched, as if he wanted to reach for me. Comfort me. *Anything*, my bones murmured. He had promised me anything.

"This is menial." His voice resonated quietly. "You could have asked of me something far more remarkable, Lark. The dawn is free to all."

Anger resonated through my sternum.

"Am I not permitted to ask of you another favour?" I was bold enough to request.

"You are," he said. "But only later, after we've left the forest. Then, you must make your request."

"Are you going to slight me if I don't?"

"Curse you?" he teased.

The blood drained from my face.

"Lark," he enunciated slowly, the dark claim beneath it laced in venom. Not at me, but for me. "You can trust me."

I did not profess my trust, and he did not press me to, but I could see his jaw feather along with his intent. It slowly dissipated as the day wore on and the night was true. Under the stars we slept, and I was not a tree at his back, but a mortal in his arms.

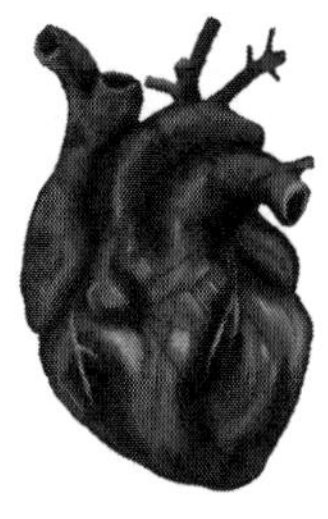

7

"WAKE UP, LARK." HIS ARMS WERE AROUND me, his touch casual and illustrious all at once. He untangled me from his arms, escorting me to a gathering of bushes and—

"A… spring."

Somehow, with some elusively ancient magic, the hunter – a druid as he was – must have conjured it. I was not convinced it wasn't an illusion until I shed his cloak and dipped my toes in. It was cool, and it was bliss. All at once I spun, soaking up the generous, impossible pool of blue in ecstasy. Dancing, spinning, and sighing, I splashed in the water with delight.

At my back, I could feel a pair of eyes watching my pleasure unfurl. When I turned to him, his eyes were heated. My smile turned furtive as I met his darkened stare, then coquettish. He made a study of my body, and the thing blossoming in my chest beckoned me to speak.

"Come here," I said by way of invitation.

"As you please." He was quick to dispose of his clothes, shrugging them off as he sank into the water. His body was magnificent, a thing that should have been etched in marble, encapsulated by stone. His fingers twitched as he kept his distance, eyes alight with fire.

"You've touched me before." I thought of the evening, our bodies bundled together. "Why do you restrain yourself so?"

"You have touched me long before that," he said softly, distantly. Then, his voice lowered to a gentle, grousing of a whisper. "I was but a sparrow."

My pulse ricocheted in my throat. *That's impossible.*

"H-how?" I managed.

"I was cursed as you." He moved in three steps, the water sloshing about. "I was bound by my mother's power to the vestiges of a sparrow's wings, but you welcomed me, despite my sorry state."

We were forehead to forehead, his breath teasing the open air between us.

"How did you break the curse?" I asked in a rake of a whisper.

"Carefully." His smile was lazy. "Just as you will."

I did not care for curses, nor answers. His skin was a flare before me, and the only thing upon my skin was the locket.

"May I?" He drummed his fingers on the chain, itching to remove it. I nodded, and he tossed it to the bank. Then, there was only us – no curse, no crone, no nightmare to be had.

"What?" I blinked up at his silence.

"It's nothing," he said, though his body told a different story. His fists were clenched, his neck trembling. When I didn't stop staring, he let out a long, lavish sigh. "You're resplendent, Lark, but I want to touch you. Touch you, just as you have touched me. Please."

My hair was loose, unbound. He toyed with it absently, arranging it as a shawl upon my shoulders.

"Hm..."

He hung on the sound, waiting, but I did not answer. Instead, my fingers curled around the hem of his hair and pulled. I dragged him down, down, down into the water with me, until we were both doused in it, gleefully drenched to the bone. We drank from one another, as lovers did, until we each had our fill. He ushered me to the bank, trailing behind me like a pup.

"Lark." My name was a warning as the water rivulets fell down my back in revelation. I knew by the way he called me what he was seeing. He reached for me, his touch so familiar now, grasping at my shoulders to ascertain the canvas upon the skin of my back.

"My human scars." I shifted, trying to turn away from his acute attention, but he would not let me budge.

"The only way you found warmth—" His voice drifted to the locket at the lip of the bank, distraught.

"Was to give a piece of myself."

I finished the thought for him, hauling his jaw to look at my face. I knew how it must look, the thin abrasions so white and mangled on my back. It was the piece of the curse that I was forced to suffer through, giving pieces of myself to be burned, just as my mother had burned the forest. I didn't want him to see that. I wanted him to see *me.*

In quiet understanding, he peppered my lips with slow, languid kisses. Backing away, he moved to ask, "And what do *you* like?"

He sounded genuinely interested.

I didn't know, but I did know.

"You," I mouthed into the dip of his clavicle.

He looked pleased.

We were nearing the edge of the forest, the air thick with something foreign and heavy. Moisture, I realised. Then, without any forewarning, it began to rain.

Tears strung my cheeks.

"Lark" – the hunter kissed the crown of my head – "please, tell me what pains you."

"Do you know when you feel so close to something you can taste it, but you're too afraid to want it?"

He sighed, long and deep into my hair. "I do."

The admission held far more weight than two simple words.

Freedom was so close that even the idea that it had been there for so long filled me with anger. All I had to do was leave, a thing I had never thought of before. How had I not imagined it to be so easy? Surely the boundary should have been insurmountable, but this was all but a farce. Unconvinced I hadn't lived in the realm of a dream for the past three weeks, I reached for him – for the friction of his skin, the presence of his corporal form, to awaken my sense.

"This is real," he said, as if he could hear my thoughts, squeezing my hand in reassurance, ushering me towards the forest boundary.

There, the trees were green, verdant. It had been so long since my bones had been a tree that I hardly knew what it felt like to behold one, to feel leaves between my fingers.

"We're leaving, Lark," he insisted, pulling me forwards by the hand. He was speaking quickly now, holding my hand clasped in his as he brought it to his mouth. "It feels like I've been ready to find you for so long that I didn't think to ask you where you've been, what you've seen. It pains me that you've been pained. It hurts to see what I've missed. Do you fault me at all, Lark? For how long you waited, when I was condemned to the curse of my faulty form?"

"No," I said plainly.

When he asked for confirmation, the hunter looked wounded. "No? Truly?"

And then we were there, at the stark divide between grass and lifeless dirt.

He took one step over, and then another. I watched him, entranced. He held out his hand in invitation. I took it, and the forest that I had been bound to was nothing. Nothing but wasteland. Nothing but fiction.

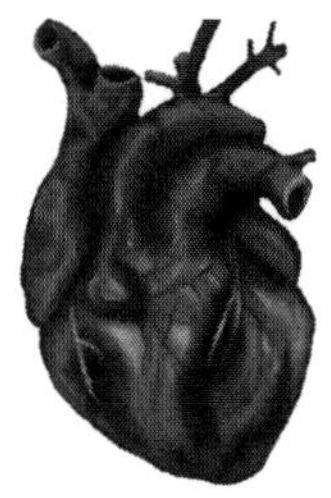

8

AT THE BOUNDARY OF THE FOREST WAS A palace. Large and grand, it towered over the trees. So many trees, so much vibrancy, my eyes stung with the shock of the swath of colour, the depths by which it stretched. Endless. It was endless.

The hunter grew quiet as we drew closer, as if shoring up the words he wished to say. I didn't press him, though my trepidation grew. We arrived at the steps to the asinine structure, weaving through the gardens before it. Taking the first step, he spun to face me.

"I cannot ask you to stay with me, Lark. This is where we part."

"But you were tasked to bring me back!"

"I fear the consequences—"

"Damn the consequences!" I groused.

"Lark," he pressed, "you have been captive for centuries; how can I ask you to stay by my side? You can travel far from here, far from the ground that cursed you so. You should not enter the palace on my behalf, for I fear of the consequences we both will face. I fear what you might endure, my love, at my behest."

"Do not send me away!" I planted my feet on the same step, indignant.

"Go, Lark," he intoned, shaking a hand to the forest. So lush, so alive. "Just leave. You don't need to stay here; you don't need me."

You need no one. The memory of my mother's voice punched me in the gut.

"No," I said coldly.

"Leave." His voice rose. "I'm giving an out. Take it."

"Never." I retreated, letting my steps carry me back to him. When I was in his arms, he shook me, but not with ire. With grief.

"Gods above and below," he sobbed, kissing the crown of my head. "You deserve it more than anything. To be free, to be wild. There's nothing I'd love more than for you to take what you deserve."

"But what if I choose you?"

"You already have me." His grip tightened, rubbing my shoulders as his kisses turned desperate. "You always will."

We ascended the steps of the palace, a solemn air gathering about the druid. He looked torn between the warring consequences in his mind.

Perhaps we could run, together.

I fantasized what it would be, druid and willow, nurturing and caring for a thriving forest like the green against our backs. Every day, a new dawn to taste. Every night, an evening in his willing arms. *What was it that lay within the palace, barring my sparrow from such a future?* All these things and more I considered, flashing through my mind like brush in my ears, but when my senses returned to me, the palace doors had already been cracked open. The druid, standing like a blotch of ink against the towering oak doors, held the door open for me. He looked to the forest, as if waiting for me to turn and run for it.

I did no such thing.

As I crossed the threshold, memory fluttered through my chest like a brick. My blood sang with familiarity – I had been down these halls, toyed with the knob of the door, lived and breathed in this palace of old. I had wandered as a babe, still fresh from my mother's arms. By some illicit magic, the walls hadn't crumbled, the floors still held our feet. As we walked through a smattering of columns leading to the throne, I understood why. There at the dais was a crone, with fingers made of crow's feet.

"You—" I started, surging forwards.

The witch held up a hand, and the amulet on my chest vibrated with a sickening force that stopped the words from my lungs. My toes extended, the soles digging into the grain of the marble as my lungs expanded with leaves and flora. The faint shout of my hunter hit my sprouting branches as he yelled something loud and vicious at the crone, but my mind was already filled with bark, my mouth with resin. Tears of sap dripped down my face. Had my hunter known she would be here?

"You, my darling girl, were a fool to return to the castle of your forebearers."

My eyes, though knobbed, could still see the witch descend the dais. The hunter stood in front of me, as a shield.

"For the crimes of your blood, you shall burn. And you, my son, shall burn with her."

"You will not take her." The hunter snarled, low and deep. Then, he turned to me. "I'll need my cloak back, love." He reached out, holding his hands for the thing tangled about my branches. "But I shall give it back, as soon as I'm finished." Then, with a flourish of a smile, "I will keep you safe. You have my word, as you always do."

Though I could not answer, my branches fell in acceptance. The fabric tumbled down my vines, landing in his open hands. He drew himself up into its cover as a sheath, advancing on the witch.

"Foolish boy!" she crooned, thrusting a conjured ball of fire at him.

The hunter dodged the blaze, his expression murderous. He blinked imperiously at his mother, as if she were nothing but a pestilence. The cornered crone growled, advancing on him in three steps.

"Just as her mother, your lover will burn."

The witch threw a fireball at my exposed trunk. My eyes widened at the flame, entrapped by the ring of fire. The hunter roared, facing the crone. His features morphed, and suddenly he was a scathing gathering of shadows, thorny and unforgiving.

"I am no longer the son you bore," he seethed, circling the crone with a glint in his eye. "I am not the hunter, nor the hunted. I am your reaper. I bargained with Death to vanquish my curse, vowing to take my revenge upon you. I became Death incarnate, and you can no longer cheat me, Mother."

Her crinkled, wrinkled features contorted into disbelief. "That's..." – she gulped, readying her hands – "not possible."

He laughed, but it was cruel and vicious. "Did you truly think you could keep me here, entrapped as a sparrow? I come on swift wings, however small, however daunting. No matter the price, I will still deliver death to you."

He launched at her, a broadsword of shadow suddenly materialising at his side. Before he could strike, I strained to move my hollow of a mouth.

"Death."

Though I was but a willow, he still heard. My lover stayed his hand at the call of his true name upon my lips.

"I would like to make my request."

"Anything," he said, the fierceness in his eyes fading into willingness.

"Do not come for her." My voice was steady. "Let vengeance be mine."

"Anything," he said again, backing away from the witch to face me. "As it pleases you."

His eyes, rimmed in black, faded to a crisp cerulean blue. Empty-handed of vengeance, he turned to face me in full. Giving the witch his back, he said, "Anything you wish for."

"I wish for her to live out her days as she thought I would – cursed to exist forever, bound by the visages of time."

"If it pleases you," he vowed. "So be it."

He nodded, raising a hand, and a fierce magic filled the air. It was thick, paralysing. My vines unravelled, the amulet around my neck snapping in two. I tumbled to the floor, watching the bounds of my cursed overgrowth wrapping around the witch, turning her into a tree.

He draped his cloak of raven feathers around me, helping me to stand.

"You fought well, my love." He kissed me well and true.

Not all endings were vicious; not all hands dealt cruel. I would not be one to burn, not one to curse as my mother once had, but to give to my forest.

"Because you welcomed me" – Death held me tight – "I shall keep you, and you shall taste a thousand dawns, with nothing on the horizon but life, forevermore."

A FIRE REKINDLED

BECCA RYDEN

1

EYES THE COLOUR OF AMETHYST WATCHED me from the dais. My skin prickled with the attention, a subtle gnawing ache lingering low in my belly. It was a hunger for something more than food or wine could satisfy.

Hiding it from my master took a skill I'd cultivated through years of suffering. It wasn't natural for me to be anything other than what I was and what I wanted. It didn't stop me from trying. My body remained stock still, the features of my true form hidden from reality. It was how my master liked me: docile and dainty, as though I were a doll. My purpose was to be wielded, manipulating the emotions of those he negotiated with, keeping them from realising his true intentions until ink met paper. But that side was merely a mask meant to lure unsuspecting prey. The creature inside, the thing I loved most about myself, wasn't allowed to exist in his presence.

To my left, my master sat in a chair at a table with a dozen ambassadors from other empires. Dull, uninteresting conversation passed between them, the drivel of greedy politicians. They were vying for a vandium trade deal – the precious, rare metal that could hold magic for even the most inert user to wield. The Valdir controlled three of five existing mines, making this trade opportunity something no empire could pass up, despite the danger of trading with them.

It wasn't just the trade routes that made the deal dangerous. A Valdir alone could subdue dozens without spilling a drop of blood. Their gaze was hypnotic, and their bite was consuming. They fed off the power of others, as voraciously as most species consumed water. Or so they said. It was a strange dichotomy to be Valdir. Yet, with so little time spent in their presence, it was one I hardly understood.

"*Siren.*" A voice, smooth and melodic, teased my mind. Deep in my thoughts, I moaned. How long had it been since someone identified what I was? How long since I heard that word said with anything but malice?

A soft snap drew my attention away from those haunting eyes. A subtle hand gesture from my master guided me towards the Tree Folk's ambassador. My master required him to become compliant.

The carafe of Menosia brandy was an elegant, crafted thing of gold, vandium, and crystal. An opulent container for the most decadent of drinks, in a palace so refined, it was as though the gods had made it. Or rather, the god who sat in this very room.

I brought the carafe to my master and refilled his drink. More than one set of eyes followed me. Their hunger, their desire, teased the part of me that my master feared, yet enjoyed subduing. I stoked it, drawing my sleeve up as I offered another politician a drink.

Splashes of emotion flicked across my mind. I was always aware of them, but mostly I paid them no mind. Focusing on them would only make me ravenous. Now, my master's command bade me. The consequence of ignoring such an order would fall when no one was to see me for days. I did not enjoy the thought of hurt and humiliation, and he'd long ago beaten the defiance from me.

At least, the part of me he preferred to see.

Drifting around the table, I filled cup after cup. Every movement came with dragging gazes. Only one interested me, but I refused to meet it again. Meeting the gaze of a Valdir was playing with fate. Daring to meet the eyes of their god? That was not wise by anyone's standards. But curiosity was a devil of depraved talents, as was my gift.

A set of emotions, tamed but strong, rose to the top of my list. As I moved, so did my influence. Subtle, teasing hints tainted heated words, dulling the fire behind them.

His anger was like a not-yet-ripe peach. Eating it was only so satisfying. I wanted more, but my master's order demanded temperance. Only the Ambassador of the Tree Folk, and only enough to sway his opinion and not draw notice.

My feet carried me without pause. My hands guided the carafe without spilling a drop. I was the image of perfection, a doll anyone would want at their beck and call. I returned to my place at my master's side, obedient and silent.

Those amethyst eyes continued to watch me from the dais. The awareness of his attention weighed, calling to the predator inside. The defeated part of me wanted to beg him to stop, to look away, to find anything interesting besides me. I wasn't worth a moment of his attention, even if the darkest parts of me wanted to bask in it like the sun.

"*Imy.*"

Despite the word being in a language few at the table understood, the conversation halted at the command. Every member of the table turned to face the dais.

It was too simple to call the being on a dais a man. Watching him rise from the vandium throne was a mistake. Eyes glimmering with power caught mine in a grip I couldn't remove. Words in a language I never knew spun through my thoughts, echoing sweet, terrible nothings.

He released me from his gaze. I sagged with relief and regret, my thoughts racing and my heart threatening to stop.

Searing pain stabbed through the hidden part of me. The sensation was something I knew all too well. Showing it would earn me no reprieve. I forced myself straight, my face and thoughts blanking through the pain. It was far from the worst he could do.

The voice I'd heard in my head spoke to the room, his language smooth and somehow crisp. A Valdir man stepped away from the wall, translating his words into High Speech for the room to understand.

"Osiris has grown tired of these pointless negotiations. We encourage you to return to your quarters to rethink your proposals. Any proposal that includes an exchange of labour, in any form, will be denied. We will allow no one to move about our lands who does not meet the bonding requirements. Tomorrow, we will resume."

Emotions shifted in the room, dancing from annoyed focus to irritation, and even anger. None of the emotions showed on the faces of the politicians, but I felt it. Especially from my master.

Alone in my room, no one could see me draped over the edge of the bathing tub. Blood pooled on the tile floor, growing with every slow drop that fell from my feathers. The plaguing torment limited itself to my predatory features, something I tried to feel lucky for. They were the parts of me I could hide. In days, when we left this palace, my master wouldn't hold back as he had tonight. This was a temporary measure meant to remind me of what was to come for stepping out of line.

A knock at the door drew me from my misery. Feathers vanished with a push of my will, taking with them the blood. Only what fell on the floor remained for me to stumble around as I retrieved a robe.

Beyond the door, a Valdir woman waited.

"Osiris summons you."

My chest expanded with a long inhale, sending phantom fire streaking down my back. "Allow me a moment to ready myself."

She caught the door before it could close. "No. Now."

I hesitated, the damage sparking against my nerves an overwhelming reminder of what would happen if I acted outside my master's expectations. "Have I been summoned... alone?"

"Yes."

My gaze darted to the door across the hallway. "Prime Minister Montevallo will notice my absence. May I inform him?"

"No."

Accepting my fate was something I'd come to terms with long ago. Pulling the robe tighter around my body, I entered the hallway.

Being bound to an ambassador meant I'd been in more palaces than most. The Eternal Palace, the shining gem of the Valdir, had ceilings higher than any I'd ever seen. This was opulent and extraordinary. Only those who could manipulate the world around them could maintain it. How else would they reach a metal sconce twenty feet above the ground? Or polish the gleaming vandium trim tracing the seams of the walls and ceiling?

The Valdir woman pushed open a door leading into a vast chamber. She closed it behind me, leaving me to explore the room with my eyes. The furniture was luxurious, every elegant arch and finely woven thread belonging in this palace of extreme finery.

Pain stole my breath, and with it, any space I might have had for observations. My master knew I had gone somewhere without permission. A noise I regretted slipped from my lips as I fought the urge to bow. It wouldn't make it feel any better.

"*Siren...*"

I barely recognised the word in my mind. Footsteps padded towards me. I tried to force myself to focus and turned. I barely avoided meeting amethyst eyes and instead caught on lips that were far too perfect to belong on the face of a man.

But he wasn't just a man.

Steps as light as a fox's and as steady as a lion's circled me. I remained still, accustomed to being inspected for flaws. My master would have found something to disappoint. Would a god find the same? Because I could not find a flaw in him. Each time he circled me, I noticed more. The first time, it was his size. Broad shoulders and a defined chest were bare of clothing and twice as wide as I was. On the second, it was the vandium cuffs at his biceps and wrists, the shimmering, precious metal crafted into magic-storing jewellery. And after the third time, he stopped before me, looming as a giant facing a lamb. My head tilted back and back, stopping on a straight, somehow perfect, nose.

His mouth moved, and words in another language flowed. He paused, and something I understood came from his lips in a thick, delicious accent. "A man who enslaves a siren begs for death."

I'd heard the remark before, but from those who were lesser. Years of brutal consequences had my mouth opening to deny it, but I paused. This wasn't a merchant or mere soldier, whose sympathies were pleasant and useless. This was a god. If I told him the truth, would he turn away as they had? Or would he do something about it? I wasn't a Valdir. There was no reason for him to intervene, but this situation... It had something I'd long forgotten how to feel blossoming in my chest.

Hope.

"I am bound by a blood oath to serve."

A frown dragged the corners of his mouth down. "By your words, or another's?"

"My grandfather's."

He made a noise, his lip dragging up in disgust to flash a single fang. "Do you like this man you are sworn to?"

My response ended before it could start as fresh pain flared, sensing what I was about to say. There was no hiding my reaction from the god before me.

Large, warm hands cradled my neck and face, dragging me to meet those glowing, jewel-like eyes. Honey soaked my mind, soothing away the sensations of the world. The pain was there, filtered through muslin that held back the worst sensations until I could think again.

"*There is no need for words,*" his voice echoed through my mind. "*Show me.*"

It wasn't a command, but the lightness in my chest had me obeying as though it were. Plucking apart the tie of my robe, I let it fall to the ground. His eyes never strayed to take in my bared body, instead staying locked with mine, his irises gaining an inner glow when mine changed from mortal to serpent.

The predator I held back most of my life shimmered into existence. Mulberry, emerald, and royal-blue feathers covered my hands, the peaks of my breasts, and the apex of my thighs, only to thin into trails that accented the curves of my body in elegant, colourful patterns. Talons as sharp as a chimera's replaced my nails, ready to rend and tear through flesh.

Two feathered wings extended from my back, the peaks rising above my head, while the tips hovered just above the ground. I kept them folded tight to my back, as though it would somehow ease the pain I could not stop.

Osiris' face changed, the steady hold of his gaze narrowing. He inhaled, his frown deepening as soon as he scented the blood that dripped from my feathers once more.

He strode behind me but didn't speak; I knew what he saw. Living wire threaded through each wing, twining around the delicate bones and weaving through the feathers and membrane beneath them. At rest, the wires merely kept me from extending my wings. When active, they bore into my flesh, writhing and tearing.

"Is this how he controls you?"

I opened my mouth, only for the wires to lurch and steal my words. Several feathers fell, their bases cut from the violent movement.

He was quiet for several moments. I didn't dare to speak. Enduring this pain for years taught me how to appear unaffected, to stand tall and maintain the innocent appearance of a doll, just as my master preferred.

"*Vivum filum*, living wire, was made to secure and break a prisoner, providing both a binding that cannot be broken and a device to break one's will," he murmured. "It is controlled by the one who is keyed, both by direct manipulation and by predicting intent. In theory, the only way to remove it is to be released by the key holder, or to remove the body parts it secures."

I didn't respond.

"The oath. What does it bind you to?"

The only answer I could give was silence. Fingers trailed down a portion of my wing untouched by the wire. It was so unexpected that my feathers ruffled and shivered.

"Stay silent if you wish me to remove it."

He understood. A kaleidoscope of emotions warred in my chest. Did he mean to remove my wings? I couldn't let that happen. Despite the affliction, my wings were the part of myself I treasured most.

"My wings—"

He was in front of me so fast my head nearly spun. Those haunting eyes caught mine once more, and his voice echoed in my head. "*I am Osiris. I am the god of the Valdir. The world bows to me. A device as cruel as this will bow to my will. As will you, siren, if I demand it.*"

The challenge in his words set off a reaction. With the predator released, I couldn't stop myself. I stepped into him, our bodies separated by a whisper. "I am more than a siren. I am lust, I am thirst, and I am hunger. I am the creature who deadens men and women. I will no more bow to you than the mountains bow to the sun."

Challenge lit in his eyes, and a hint of a grin was all I saw before his mouth crashed over mine. He dragged me to him, my naked body flushed against his, skin to feathers. He tried to devour me, but I refused. Teeth clacked, lips bruised, and my talons dug into his back, needing more and everything. Pain flared through one wing, then the sensation dulled with his influence. I ignored it, my need guiding every action. But it grew, spiralling throughout every nerve, from bone to follicle.

I hissed when his efforts morphed into agony, but Osiris didn't let me stop. Even when my body locked in place to fight the urge to pull away, he took advantage, his mouth trailing down my neck, his fangs skimming the tendon. I didn't realise he was trying to distract me until the pain hit a crescendo, nearly blackening my vision, and stopped. My wing sagged, even as it throbbed in time with my heart. Something hit the floor behind me. Breathing hard, I glanced back. Wires flailed on the floor, their barbed ends violently striking the tiles. They writhed and twisted, each movement inching the mass towards us.

The wires lifted from the ground and shot across the room, slamming into the door. The door opened a moment later, and the woman who escorted me here stepped in. Without looking at us, she found the wires. They lifted from the ground without her touching them and floated out of the room ahead of her. When the door closed, I met Osiris' glowing gaze. Afraid to speak, I showed the question in my eyes.

"I am a god, siren. Magical tools will not stop me from getting what I want."

Fresh pain blossomed in my other wing. I glanced back, my wing flaring slightly, allowing me to see the end of one wire as the barbed end retracted through my flesh, tearing the puncture wide. It stole my breath, then Osiris stole my attention. His mouth took mine again, conquering any protest I could have had. When the pain grew, my body shook, knowing what I was allowing to happen. As though he knew it would be harder to distract me, his touch wandered. Fingers followed a trail of feathers along my spine, my hip, and farther, delving through thicker feathers to find a wet, neglected part of me.

Caught between opposing sensations, it was everything I could do to stay on my feet. The pain was terrible, but this... it had been years since someone saw this side of me and found me anything but repulsive.

Writhing wires hit the ground, then shot to the door to be retrieved. My knees gave with relief and exhaustion. Osiris caught me before I could hit the ground, then he did something I couldn't have prepared for. He lifted me into his arms, cradling me close. My wings vanished as I took on my mortal form, unwilling to subject myself to more pain. He took me to an adjoining room and set me on a bed of fine silks and soft pillows.

My body shook even as I curled into him, seeking the distraction he'd so readily offered. Perhaps it was foolish. He was a god. I was a slave. Whatever was happening would only be temporary. Was it a sin to want to taste divinity?

Welcoming fingers trailed from my hip to my thigh. "Are your wings affected by the world when they vanish?"

"No. I feel them, but they exist apart from reality."

A low, hungry growl vibrated in his throat. He thrust me onto my back, his body a delicious weight pinning me to the bed.

"Tell me no," Osiris purred against my throat, his fangs dragging down my skin.

"Telling a god no—" My breath hitched when he nipped at my collarbone. "It would be a mortal sin."

His head lifted, catching me in his seeking gaze. Words drifted through my mind. "*This is your chance, siren. Tell me no, or you and I will find no rest this night.*"

I would have no rest without him. Spending a night in a god's arms instead of struggling to breathe from pain? It was an opportunity I would only get once.

"One night," I whispered, making a promise. For one night, I would escape into the embrace of a god. When the sun rose, I would return to my fate.

Pleasant, delicious soreness warmed my belly. It made standing behind my master a tolerable, even pleasurable, experience. My master knew I'd gone somewhere last night. Mistakenly, he thought I'd returned to my room shortly after. I was sure I had Osiris' woman to thank. It kept my master from asking too many questions, and from furthering his punishment. Had he, he would have discovered the removal of his controlling restraints.

Despite the throb of healing flesh throughout my wings, Osiris made me forget my name. He'd satisfied me in so many ways, I didn't think I'd ever felt such bliss, or would ever again. I wished the ache would never go away. But eventually, it would fade. Only the memory of last night would carry me through the dark days to come, and the bleak years beyond.

A snap drew me from my thoughts, the gesture from my master guiding me to the Tree Folk's ambassador once more. Emotion swelled within me, flaring with the fresh memory of last night. I felt so appreciated, wanted… it was as though he revered me. I knew it would never happen again, but I wanted it. And this man who thought to control me – he was the reason I could only dream.

Ignoring the promise I made, I reacted with how I felt. It was foolish, but I forced my emotions on the Tree Folk's ambassador. He stood, his argument escalating from refined but firm to enraged and defiant. He spouted words of war that spread throughout the room, igniting furious passion as they met the ears of those taking part.

My master turned in his seat, his eyes flashing with rage. Despite knowing the repercussions, I glared back. His expression darkened. When I didn't bend, it morphed into something vile.

He shot to his feet, the chair skidding back several feet. With a vice-like grip, he dragged me out of the room of arguing politicians. Rage boiled off him, lapping against my senses in scalding waves. Everything in me wanted to devour it, to steal his rage, his spite, his everything and deaden him until he was no better than a corpse. The only thing stopping me, as it always had, was the blood oath.

He threw me into his bedroom, sending me sprawling across the floor. Years of suppression and helplessness coalesced into fury in my chest. I rose to my feet, unable to force myself to cower before him. Despite knowing there was nothing I could do to defend myself, I stood in defiance.

"You defy me," he sneered, stomping into the room. "I thought you learned this lesson years ago. It seems I need to beat it into you once more."

His hand lashed out. I caught it before the strike could land across my cheek.

He snarled. "I have told you before. Accept your punishment."

My arm shook with the effort of fighting the command. I bared my teeth, my eyes flashing serpent. My soul's fire, once snuffed to embers, burned anew. It spat and roiled, turning the bars of my oath-bound cage molten. He could force me to do anything, but none of it would be willing.

The door to the room slammed against the wall, shattering the wood. For an instant, the compulsion of the oath changed, dragging me forwards. My talons appeared, and my wings tore through the back of my dress. Before I could do more than raise my hand to slash, the compulsion was gone, leaving me stumbling. My master fell to the ground, his head unnaturally bent to the side.

Osiris stood above the corpse. He couldn't have cared less for the body, despite the political ramifications that were to befall him for the death. His focus was solely on me.

My predatory features vanished, leaving my dress to hang off my shoulders.

"You killed him," I said, disbelief shallowing my words.

"A siren should never be allowed to be tamed." He closed the distance, and though we didn't touch, I'd have sworn his hand clutched my heart. "If you had remained his dog, I would have let you go on being as you were. But you fought back. I could not allow him to crush your spirit when you just rediscovered it."

"You're a god. Interfering in my life... It should not be more than a pastime to you. Why bother?"

Amethyst eyes bore into mine. "Stay here, with me."

"W-what?"

"Stay with me. No oath or bonding is required. Just stay."

I couldn't trust the bubbles dancing in my chest, no matter how giddy they made me feel. "What would I be if I did? I have only served. I do not know if I can be anything else."

"Perhaps it is time you are allowed to learn that for yourself."

What he was offering was absurd, and yet I couldn't help but want it.

"Elaine," I said, my voice a whisper. When his brows furrowed, I clarified. "My name is Elaine."

One large hand lifted, cupping my face. He stroked my cheek, then my bottom lip.

"Osiris is my ordained name. My chosen name is Jaeger."

SOULBOUND

STARR Z. DAVIES

1

TODAY'S BATTLE HAD BEEN LITTLE MORE than a skirmish, but the entire camp celebrated pushing back the forces of evil. If all continued as it had, the human and elf allies would soon drive their enemy back past the outskirts of the Kruos territory.

As everyone celebrated around several bonfires, Loralai a'Malik allowed her heart to pull her away from her fellow Kruos Shieldmaidens to seek the company of another.

Loralai was proud to be a Shieldmaiden, an elite force of female Kruos elves highly trained in close combat and brutally efficient at their assigned tasks. Training took decades to earn a shield, and her father insisted it was no place for an elfin princess. Despite his opposition, Loralai underwent the training and eventually earned her shield.

By the time the war began, Loralai had been a full Shieldmaiden for only a few years. Now, her father was both relieved to have her so experienced in fighting – particularly in her own defence – and worried that he would lose his only daughter in the war. As if he didn't have several sons to take up his mantle when he crossed the Great River to the Afterworld.

Her eldest brother, Malikai, heir to the Kruos elf kingdom, often hovered nearby both in battle and in camp. It irritated Loralai to no end to have her brother treating her like a youngling in need of protection. Tonight was no exception. Loralai felt Malikai's eyes following her as she crossed the camp in search of her target.

She spotted Quade near another bonfire, exchanging a few last-minute commands with some of his men. She wove around clusters of human and elf soldiers, making her way straight towards him.

As if sensing her approach, he looked up and flashed her that winning smile that melted her heart every time.

He was not *Prince* Quade, as he was surely called in his own homeland far to the south, where he would serve as heir to the human kingdom of Novavito. Here, among warriors and leaders from all over the world, he was honoured with a title befitting his heroic deeds: Lord Commander Quade Martnarving.

When others ignored the Kruos call for help, Quade had not hesitated to rally his forces and marched them to the far north. His heroic deeds on the battlefield swiftly earned him the respect of not only his human compatriots, but the elves as well.

Loralai and the Shieldmaidens had fought beside him several times in recent weeks, and she could not help admiring his skill. Quade clearly mastered not only the sword, but the bow and lance as well. In battle, he moved with a grace and skill no other human demonstrated. Humans and elves alike would tell stories of his heroic deeds for centuries.

It was not only his battle prowess that drew Loralai to him. Quade Martnarving treated everyone with respect, no matter their station, and easily earned it in return. Pair that with those broad shoulders, chiselled jaw, and sculpted muscles, and she could have easily believed Quade a child of Solisina and Justis, Goddess of Beauty and God of War.

Women flirted with him endlessly – and a few male elves as well. Loralai struggled to contain her jealousy when others asserted themselves. Yet Quade politely disentangled himself from such situations with ease.

No, Quade had eyes only for her. They had walked together and shared stories of their lives, bonding in a way Loralai had not expected. He was as perfect as a human could be, in her opinion. And a perfect gentleman with unimpeachable honour.

The men around Quade followed his line of vision, spotting Loralai's approach. After a quick word from Quade, they dispersed, and he turned his full attention on Loralai, not bothering to mask his interest in her.

She stopped in front of him, and he took an unconscious step closer.

"You moved like the wind today," Quade said, resting his hand on the hilt of his fine sword.

"You *were* the wind," Loralai teased back, and her mind wandered to what it would be like to move in intimate ways with him. Her face flushed slightly, and she hoped he didn't notice. "You're getting proficient with those dragons."

"I have little choice." Though he spoke the words, they were clearly an automatic response. All his attention, all his focus, fixed on her and her alone.

The dragons were a new addition in the war, and the dragon riders had been forced to learn quickly to trust the beasts and fight from their backs. Only a few of the best warriors could ride dragonback. Quade settled into the role as if he were born to it.

"I had hoped we might find some time to speak alone," he said softly. Quade reached up to a hair that had loosened from her braid, tucking it tenderly behind her pointed ear.

She shuddered ever so slightly at the touch. Loralai could think of a million different little reasons she admired the man before her, human as he may be. Not the least of which was the way the bonfire light flickered in his dark eyes.

"Alone?" Loralai teased. "Sounds scandalous."

Quade chuckled. "I would never dream of dragging you into anything so scandalous." His fingers lingered a moment, tracing the point of her ear before sliding down her arm to take her hand.

Without thinking, Loralai inched closer, lacing her fingers around his. "Perhaps a little bit of scandal." Her silver eyes shone with amusement and promise.

Quade chuckled, and the sound lit up every nerve in her body.

"Loralai." The sharp voice startled them both.

Quade immediately dropped his hold on her hand and stepped back. The withdrawal made her heart ache. As his gaze slid to the right, Quade straightened and lifted his chin, every inch the king he would one day become.

"King Malik," Quade said, bowing properly to the elf king… her father.

King Malik stopped beside them, arms crossed over his chest as he eyed the two of them. Loralai couldn't hold his gaze and found herself staring at her boots instead.

"I fear I've let this go too far," King Malik said. "I should have intervened sooner."

"Intervened with what, sir?" Quade asked, cocking his head to the side.

But Loralai eyed her brother Malikai across the bonfire. His hand rested on his sword, his face set in disapproval. Her heart sank. She knew where this was going and desperately wanted to stop her father from speaking the words.

"I respect your skills, Lord Commander," her father said. "It is only because of my respect for you that I have waited, hoping this would stop on its own."

“I’m afraid I don’t understand,” Quade said, but by his tone, Loralai knew her father had insulted him. And Quade knew as well as she what was coming.

“My daughter is off limits,” King Malik said with so much assertive authority Loralai winced.

Quade, however, did not flinch. “I assure you, my interest in Loralai is honourable.”

“No doubt it is, but I cannot allow it.”

Loralai rested a hand on her father’s arm, begging him with her eyes. “Father, he is a good man.”

King Malik’s icy eyes turned to her, and she could see he would not be swayed. “He is. Which is why I know he will honour my decision. You are the Kruos princess.”

“And he is heir to his own kingdom!” Loralai argued. “I fail to see—”

“The Lord Commander is human, Loralai,” King Malik snapped.

Quade flinched at the insult, his jaw twitching.

“Plenty of humans and elves have found happiness together since our alliance formed,” Loralai countered.

“And none of them were the princess!” King Malik turned his back on Loralai and faced Quade in a way that felt so threatening Loralai wanted to push him back. “You are a good human, noble and wise and fierce. You can choose any female you desire, but not my daughter. I will not hear another word of it.”

Quade's gaze slid past her father to Loralai, and she could see something inside of him breaking. Several long moments of silence passed.

Then Quade raised his chin proudly, swallowing hard. He cleared his throat, and his words broke Loralai's heart. "I will do my best to abide by your wishes, King Malik. Perhaps when I win this war for you, your opinion might change."

"Unlikely," King Malik said, bristling at Quade's backhanded comment about winning *for* him.

Quade bowed only as much as propriety dictated, cast one more heartbroken glance at Loralai, then pivoted and marched away.

As he vanished into the night, King Malik turned to face his daughter. "You are not just anyone."

"Nor is he."

"I will not have my only daughter—"

Before he could finish, Loralai barked at him to hold his breath, then stormed away. The pull towards Quade had grown overwhelming in the weeks as their relationship developed, and she was certain that a century without him would change nothing.

2

THE DAYS FOLLOWING KING MALIK'S command had been lonely. Loralai hadn't realised just how much time she had been spending with Quade until he distanced himself at her father's orders. The space slowly ate away at her soul.

Tonight was not about war, but about another victory. Or it should have been.

The Blazing Hearth Inn hardly had space for patrons to move about. Elves and humans alike crowded the common room, sharing drinks and celebrating today's victory in the ongoing war against the forces of evil. In the corner, an elfin bard regaled the heroic feats of the day with tall tales and harrowing songs. Voices bounced off the rafters. Lamplight and the fire in the massive hearth on the southern wall cast a gentle glow off the polished wooden beams.

Loralai clutched at her Murandy Hills wine – a treat brought to the northern lands by their human allies – sipping slowly at the drink as her comrades celebrated today's win. Her fellow Shieldmaidens clustered together only a few steps from the bar.

As the Shieldmaidens chattered around her, Loralai's gaze remained fixed on the back corner of the common room.

A handful of male Kruos and Luthian elves sat at a table alongside the kings and heirs of the human kingdoms of Novavito and Vorovesti. A single woman lingered at the edge of the table, standing instead of sitting like the men, her arms crossed and her face set in a grim line as the elfin and human leaders exchanged urgent, hushed words. These six would decide the tactics for the next day because, despite the victory today, the war was far from over.

Loralai's father and eldest brother sat among them. It was the Kruos kingdom in jeopardy, after all, and King Malik and his heir were willing to go to any lengths to save it.

But it was not her father or brother who stole all of Loralai's attention, nor the handsome human Vorovesti king with his golden hair and striking blue eyes. No, all her attention poured over Quade.

Loralai licked her lips as she stared across the common room, tasting the earthy undertones of the Murandy Hills red.

As if sensing her gaze, Quade looked up from the battle plan spread on the table before the leaders. Those beautiful, depthless pools of darkness pierced her very soul. In the days since her father shut down any blossoming affection between them, Loralai continued to feel that pull towards Quade.

Quade had been perfectly respectful of both Loralai's and her father's wishes, much to Loralai's regret. But despite the days that had passed, their eyes still met across the battlefield or across crowded rooms such as this one. Something still drew them together.

An elbow jabbed into Loralai's ribs, and she gasped, glancing sidelong at Sil, her long-time friend and fellow Shieldmaiden.

"You're staring, Lor," Sil teased. "Don't let your father catch you again."

Loralai turned her attention to her friend, only to find several of her Shieldmaiden friends smirking at her. A blush crept across her cheeks. All of them knew, to some degree, how deeply Loralai's fondness for Quade burrowed. They also knew that her father had staunchly put the notion of the two of them aside and how much it made Loralai ache with misery.

"I just hate being excluded from their strategy sessions," Loralai said, but it was only a partial truth. "If being the only princess of Kruos is so important, why does he insist on leaving me out of such meetings?"

"Because you are not part of the council," Sil said plainly, as if it should be obvious.

"But *she* is?" Loralai argued, shooting a glare toward Kieta, the only woman at the table with the other leaders.

Though shorter than most by head and shoulders, Kieta had earned her place as one of the fiercest warriors on the battlefield. Yet her porcelain skin, silky black hair, and alluring form attracted a lot of attention from the human males. Whenever Quade laughed or smiled with Kieta, Loralai wanted to smash the woman's face with her shield. Not that Quade had shown Kieta any genuine interest to warrant such jealousy.

The Shieldmaidens snickered, reading the envy and deflection easily. Loralai downed the rest of her wine bitterly.

"*She* was chosen by the gods and has brought the dragons to our cause," Sil said, a hint of amusement in her tone. "Can you make any such claims?"

Loralai grimaced, then realised Quade was no longer among the council. Her silver eyes swept across the crowded common room.

A tide of bodies stepped aside to give Quade a path to the bar only a few feet from where she stood. Loralai wished she could be closer to him, even if only for a moment. Her father insisted this was a passing infatuation, and that when the war ended Loralai would thank him for preventing her from making a huge mistake. She couldn't say she agreed.

A few soldiers offered to buy Quade's next round, but he politely thanked them and refused the offer. Quade looked over his shoulder at her and offered a warm smile before leaning towards the barkeep and making a request.

Loralai forced her eyes away. Every part of her was drawn to him, and it terrified her, especially since her father had staunchly put his foot down against any romantic interest between them.

Around her, the Shieldmaidens continued telling a story from the battlefield. Loralai attempted to remain in the moment and listen to the tale, but her heart and mind were elsewhere.

"But the moment that demon saw my shield and blade, he turned and tried to run," a Shieldmaiden said. "Our reputation is spreading, fellow maidens. The enemy knows us well now and knows our presence is certain death."

"You dispatched him quite efficiently as well," Quade added as he nudged his way through the crowd with two drinks in hand, a black and tan ale and a glass of rich-red wine.

The flow of the crowd pushed him closer to Loralai. He shifted the glasses in his hand to avoid spilling, but the crowd had pressed them nearly chest to chest.

No, not just the crowd. The Shieldmaidens at his back squeezed in closer to force him into tighter proximity with Loralai. She loved them and hated them for it.

For a moment, the two of them stood so close she could feel the heat of his body beneath his tunic. Loralai found herself drawn into the dark pools of his eyes. The tension and yearning between them grew so thick Loralai had to remind herself to breathe. Her heart hammered against her chest as if calling out his name, desperate for him to hear.

"I thought you might want a fresh glass," Quade said, his rich timbre reaching deep into the heart of her. She missed him fiercely.

"Thank you," Loralai said as she reached up to accept the offered drink. All around them, she could see the Shieldmaidens smirking.

As her fingers grasped the wine, they brushed against Quade's. What shot through her was not a bolt of lightning but more a vine of light and love and endless hope that wrapped around her arm, climbing up towards her heart. Loralai froze. No, that couldn't be...

Quade's finger shifted, stroking against hers, never breaking his gaze. Was he moving closer on purpose?

Loralai bit her lip, drawing his eyes downward.

A hand clapped down on Quade's shoulder, and the two of them startled.

"Thank you, Lord Commander, but maybe next time a round for *all* the Shieldmaidens," Sil said, her voice slicing through the tension.

Quade nodded as he stepped back. "A mistake I will not make again," he reassured Sil.

Before heading back to his table, Quade cast one more glance at Loralai. Then he returned to the council, where her father stared at her with warning in his silver eyes.

"I think you two just need to bang it out," Sil said crassly.

Loralai gaped at her friend, once more flushing scarlet.

Quade couldn't escape the Blazing Hearth Inn fast enough once the council adjourned. He tried to respect the elf king's wishes, truly, he did. But every time he drew close to Loralai, some invisible force pushed them together as if she were part of his destiny and he could not escape it. No woman had ever consumed him so thoroughly. He would die, old and heirless, unable to take a wife because Loralai would remain a part of him for all his days.

Eager to get fresh air, Quade strode out the back doors of the inn. His steps carried him to the stable where his battlehorse waited – a mount he rarely needed with the dragons to ride now. He entered the stall and began brushing the horse, seeking some distraction. It didn't work.

The way Loralai moved in battle had captivated him more than he dared admit aloud. If her father had any idea how completely she possessed Quade, would he still refuse him even a chance? Quade could give her everything she could ever desire. Refusing him simply because he was human and not an elf felt unnecessarily cruel.

By all accounts, the Kruos elf king admired and respected Quade. He even deferred to Quade's judgement when it came to battle strategy, admitting that Quade had a keen eye for organising their forces and pushing back their enemy.

That admiration, it seemed, only extended so far.

"You really like pushing your luck," a familiar voice said from the other side of the stall door.

Quade smirked sadly at King Tiberis, his long-time friend. He and Tiberis often spent time together during the summers when their fathers would meet in a king's summit – well, along with Tiberis's older brother, Narcisse, who was now their very reason for fighting in this war. Quade and Tiberis always knew how to find trouble, and Narcisse had always been certain to show up and make it worse. Quade had assumed Narcisse was simply jealous of their friendship and wanted to drive them apart. Instead, his antics only strengthened the bond between Tiberis and Quade. Tiberis now called Quade his brother – a title he rarely bestowed on his actual brother.

"I can't help myself," Quade admitted begrudgingly. "It's like no matter where I am, something always pushes me towards her." His brush strokes were slightly harder than necessary, and the horse snorted and turned an eye on him in disapproval. "His reasoning infuriates me, as if being human makes us unworthy. I've only ever protected him and his people. Have I not proven myself time and again?"

"You have." Tiberis leaned his muscular forearms on the stall door. "Maybe it's time to ask forgiveness instead of permission."

Quade snorted and shook his head. Going against King Malik would serve no one. "Is that what you did when you chose your wife?"

Tiberis smirked. "Which one?" He shook his head. They both knew whom Quade meant. The wife from the outlands. The one his nobles refused to accept as their queen. So Tiberis selected a second wife from among the nobles just to appease them, a wife who had befriended his precious outlander. Somehow he made it work, and the two women both cared for one another like sisters. "In all seriousness, my father would turn over in his grave if he knew I gave my heart to a woman from the Western Continent."

That much was certain. "You had the fortune of not having to answer to her father, a necessary ally in the war."

Tiberis shook his head. "Not true. Vanna's father refused to give me permission to wed his daughter unless I named *her* children my heirs. And that was only *after* a lot of arguments. Thankfully, Solfia didn't care about our children being heirs to the Vorovesti throne."

Quade squared his shoulders and turned towards his friend. "So, what, you are saying I should just go for it and beg her father to forgive me for breaking my word and going against his wishes behind his back during a war? That I should just hope he doesn't have me killed for it?"

"It's a war against his people that he would have lost were it not for you," Tiberis added seriously. "I'm here to deal with the black stain on my family name. You are here by your own choice, for him and his people."

Quade wished he could agree, but if the forces of evil won, if Narcisse had his way, not even Novavito would be safe. Nowhere would be.

"Besides, you are not some common human off the street," Tiberis added. "You are heir to your kingdom, one of the most powerful kingdoms. Second most powerful." He grinned and shrugged at the last.

Quade chuckled, tossing the horse brush at his friend. Tiberis ducked as he caught it, then held it back out to his oldest friend, not the least insulted by the playful action. If anything, he fought off a smirk.

"You deserve happiness, and it's so obvious that this distance is making you both miserable," Tiberis said. "Even the great King Malik can see that." He turned to leave Quade alone with his thoughts once more after Quade snatched the brush from his hand.

Beg forgiveness. Quade could do that. He just wasn't certain if Loralai's father *would* forgive him.

3

FIRE BLAZED ACROSS THE SKY ABOVE THE battlefield as dragons swooped in and out of the flames and smoke. Quade adjusted his grip on the lance as Kieta had taught him, sending a prayer to Justis, God of War, for true aim.

A scream made the world tremble. The familiar melody of the voice ripped into Quade's bones, filling him with a battle-terror, the likes of which he had never known. His gaze fell on Loralai on the battlefield below, her sword a blur as she danced with blade and shield with only a few Shieldmaidens nearby.

Quade's dragon banked in her direction as if reading his mind.

But before he could reach her, dozens of shadow demons closed in a ring around her like a cloud of darkness.

Quade launched himself off the dragon's back, lance poised for a deadly strike. A shadow-arrow pierced Loralai's armour, punching through her stomach. Before Quade's feet could touch down on the ground, Loralai's body spun as she fell. Another arrow slammed through her armour. Her silver eyes stared lifeless at the burning sky.

The rest became a blur of motion the moment Quade hit the ground, screaming and using his lance like a quarterstaff. He fought until the last of his strength winked out, until the battlefield was a wasteland of dead enemies.

Then he fell to his knees and screamed as everything inside of him shattered.

Quade bolted upright in bed, nearly hitting his head on the slanted ceiling. Sweat rolled off his body, and his heart raced so fast he feared it might kill him.

A nightmare. That's all it was – a strange composition of his battle fatigue and his feelings for Loralai. But the loss he experienced in his soul felt so real, as if someone had torn out a piece of him and he had lost everything in that one moment.

If they died tomorrow, Quade could not allow it to happen without showing Loralai how he truly felt. Tiberis was right. He would beg forgiveness, because he couldn't stand the idea of another day passing without her.

He threw off his blankets and marched towards the door.

A knock on the door startled Loralai from a beautiful dream where she and Quade sat beside the Great River with their two-year-old son. Light shone over the world, a blessing of Solisina, Goddess of Light and Beauty. Loralai hadn't wanted to leave that beautiful dream, but the insistent knock repeated. Sil hardly stirred in her bed. Clearly, she wasn't getting up. Loralai heaved a sigh and slipped out of bed, padding across the narrow space in her nightdress.

Loralai wasn't sure who she had expected to find on the other side, but as she slowly eased the door open, wary of unexpected attackers, her heart stopped.

Quade waited on the other side, shirtless and covered in a sheen of sweat. What had he been doing? And why was he at her door in the middle of the night with no shirt on?

"I tried," was all he said.

Loralai's heart thundered against her chest as she stared into his dark eyes. Something had rattled this princely warrior. She licked her lips and opened the door to allow him in – a mistake, most likely, if her father ever found out.

"Tried what?" she asked, attempting nonchalance.

Quade's gaze slid to Sil, and the muscles of his chest and shoulders tightened. He opened his mouth, but no words came out.

"What's wrong, Quade?" she asked, edging closer to him.

Sil grumbled something in her sleep.

He ran a hand over his face, took a steadying breath, and let it out slowly before answering. "I had a nightmare. It… I'm sorry." He turned his attention to Sil once more. "I had hoped we might be… alone."

Sil groaned in irritation and sat up, glaring at both of them. She snatched her pillow and blanket as she stood, then marched towards the door. "If I am leaving, something had better happen this time or I swear to the Seven Gods I will lock you in a room together until it does."

The door slammed shut behind her.

Loralai attempted laughing off Sil's threat, but she wasn't sure her friend hadn't been serious. Certainly not after what Sil had said earlier in the night. Just thinking about it, about him standing there shirtless in utter masculine perfection, made Loralai's face heat.

She cleared her throat to try regaining control of her overwhelming desire. "Do you need to talk about the nightmare? I'm a good listener."

"I know you are." Quade rubbed his hands together, then tucked them into his pants pockets, then folded his arms over his chest. The restless agitation and uncertainty in his own skin made Loralai intensely curious. His shoulders sagged. "You died."

Her brows lifted, and she eased onto her bed, gripping the edge. "It was only a nightmare."

He nodded, and something about his expression made her want to wrap her arms around him. But if she touched him, she wasn't sure she would be able to let go.

"It was only a nightmare," he agreed. "I know that. But it felt so real, Loralai. I tried to reach you, to help you, but I was too slow. And when you died, something inside of me broke."

Those words made Loralai's heart stutter. It implied his feelings for her were deeper than she had imagined them to be.

Quade shook his head. "No, that's not right." His expression twisted into pain. "Broken things can be fixed. I didn't break. I was shattered and the pieces scattered to the wind."

Unfixable? How horrible had that nightmare been? Surely his feelings for her were not *so* strong. Not if he had kept such distance between them since her father had insisted they stay apart. Remembering the threads of light from earlier in the night, Loralai pushed those thoughts away.

Before she could process what this meant, Quade crossed the room and kneeled in front of her, taking her hands. Once more, those threads of light and hope wove around her hands and arms and made their way to her heart. Panic set in. What would happen when they finally took hold of her?

"It made me realise I can't continue like this," Quade said. "No matter how hard I try to put distance between us, to stay away, the gods push me towards you. I cannot, will not, go another day without you knowing the truth, Loralai."

Loralai's heart stilled as she spied the pure sincerity in his eyes. Those threads wrapped themselves around her chest, slowly tightening, settling into place. Seven Gods help her. There was no going back now, was there?

"My heart aches in your absence," he said, his voice deepening with emotion. "I can no longer pretend I can live without you. I would rather stand before your father's fury, face every ounce of his wrath, than endure one more moment without you. No punishment could ever compare to the anguish of being apart from you."

The words made that pulsing thread of light and hope around her heart brighter. Then, Loralai understood what it meant, why that thread bound itself to her just as she was sure it bound to him. She understood it, and it terrified her more than any battlefield.

Quade pulled her hands towards his chest, pressing them to his bare skin. His heart beat against her open palm. "I can't fight it any longer. I am completely and irreversibly consumed by my love for you. This heart beats only for you."

The confession stunned Loralai. Her mind went completely blank as she struggled to form some response.

"Please, Loralai," Quade whispered, gliding one hand to caress her neck, fingers sliding into her snow-white hair.

His other hand pressed one of her palms firmly against his chest. "Please tell me I'm not alone with these feelings."

"No," Loralai whispered, the word little more than a breath from her lungs. "You are most certainly not alone."

They inched close to one another, gazes tethered as an unbreakable bond formed between them. Breaths mingled. His musky scent filled Loralai's senses, so completely and utterly human. When his lips brushed against her own, she tasted the lingering ale and the salty sweetness of his kiss. It was slow, tentative, and so tender it made her heart break with longing. The kiss was everything she had dreamt it would be.

For a moment, Quade broke away. His eyes slowly opened, filled with so much love and yearning it made Loralai shudder in delight. She wanted him. Every beautiful piece, whole or broken. Human and all.

If tomorrow was not promised, she wanted to make the most of today. She wanted *him*.

The next time their lips met and passion poured from Quade into her, Loralai knew he felt the same.

All the desire the two of them had suppressed since the moment they met, everything that had built between the two, came to a beautiful crescendo in that small room of the Blazing Hearth Inn.

Quade's touches were gentle, his kisses a caress as he slid her nightdress from her shoulders. They climbed farther up the bed together, clinging to one another as if afraid of letting go. The intimacy began slow, each exploring one another as if attempting to memorise every curve. Loralai was certain his touch alone could undo her utterly.

When their intimacy prepared to cross the next threshold, Quade leaned over her, and she swore she could see the universe in the depths of his beautiful dark eyes.

After spending over an hour exploring every inch of Loralai with his hands and lips, Quade couldn't restrain himself any longer. He braced himself over her, his body screaming for more, for that final joining of their bodies and souls. The way her silver eyes glittered up at him like the light of the full moon made his heart ache with love. His soul pulled towards her as he lingered there, poised between her legs. Loralai's thighs pressed against his hips as if pulling him to the inevitable.

Because he knew now this had always been inevitable.

Slowly, he rocked his hips. Loralai moaned, her back arching, pushing her chest up against him. Her fingers dug into his arms as he pulled back and rocked against her again. And again. Slowly. Quade loved the way her body responded to his, the way she moaned his name.

The pace continued slow but steady as they revelled in this moment, until her hands slid along his chest to grasp at his hips and pull him deeper.

"I am yours, Loralai," he said as he gave in to her urgent need for more. "Only yours. Forever." He leaned closer, gripping her thigh as he thrust harder. Loralai released a glorious gasp. His lips moved along her neck, nipping at her ear. "And you are mine."

Loralai could hardly collect her breath to moan in agreement. He loved that he had that effect on her.

"Say it," he murmured into her ear. He pulled back, teasing at her. "Tell me you are mine."

Loralai moaned, writhing beneath him. "I'm yours," she said, her words a breathless rush. "I've always been yours, Quade Martnarving. And you are mine."

Quade felt those threads of hope wrapping around both of them as he pushed into her again. Something glorious bound them in this moment. He couldn't explain the magic around them, but it pressed them both onwards until they lost themselves in the carnal bliss, locking into place as they fell over the edge in one another's arms.

At Loralai's insistence, they refrained from talking to her father for the time being. She knew it couldn't last. Quade had agreed to give her a few days to warm her father up to the idea of the two of them together, but he wanted to tell King Malik.

The sneaking, in particular, bothered him. Quade had told her as much a few times in the past week.

Loralai lay in his arms, in his tent, after another vigorous late-night rendezvous. His heart steadied as she listened, marvelling at the way every piece of them came together so naturally.

"We need to tell him in the morning, Loralai," Quade said, stroking her bare back. "I can't keep this from him much longer. He watches my every move like he is waiting for me to slip up. The longer we wait, the angrier he will be."

"Soon, I promise." Loralai propped her chin on his shoulder, admiring his strong jaw. She just couldn't tell her father yet. Some part of her feared that once King Malik knew, he would try to force them apart. Loralai could hardly stand being away from Quade for an hour. What would her father do to keep them apart?

"You keep saying that, and I would wait forever for you, but what happens when we are caught?" Quade gazed down at her. "I love you, Loralai. I'm not ashamed of it, and I'm not scared of him. But I *do* respect him and I'm betraying his trust every time we meet like this. I need to come clean."

Loralai closed her eyes and took a deep breath, then let it out slowly. "I'm sorry, Quade. I never meant to cause you this pain." But deep down, she was terrified her father would force her to return home. He certainly would be within his right to do so. "What if he still refuses?"

"Am I truly so unworthy of his daughter?" Quade asked, and the misery in his eyes made her ache. "Perhaps I am. I've been doing this with you knowing how he feels."

Quade untangled himself, pulling away from her as he searched for his clothes.

"Quade, he could send me home," Loralai insisted as he pulled his shirt over his head. She couldn't help admiring the way the muscles in his back flexed with the simple motion. "He could force us apart."

Without glancing back, he slipped on his pants and stomped into his boots.

"Where are you going?" Loralai asked, sitting up on his bedrolls.

Quade strapped on his sword and marched towards the exit. Before opening the flap, he paused, his gaze admiring every curve of her bare body. "Take all the time you need, but until I can approach him with some semblance of my honour intact, I don't think we should do this again. Please, I beg you, find your way back to your tent tonight. And find your way back to mine soon."

Then he ducked out.

Loralai pulled her knees to her chest as tears burned in her eyes. Did Quade understand why this was so hard to explain to her father? It wasn't just that she chose him, and she would give up everything to be with Quade. Something else bound them together. Something she was afraid to give serious consideration. Something even her father could not oppose.

But first, Loralai had to be certain if her suspicions were true.

4

WEEKS PASSED. LORALAI AND QUADE spoke, but only in passing. True to his word, he refused to meet with her in secret any longer. Every day that passed, when she tried to follow him, Quade gave her a look that clearly said, *Tell him first*.

A few times, Loralai had forced Sil to intercept her father or Quade when it looked like Quade was about to take matters into his own hands.

But how could she tell her father the truth when she was not sure how to prove it to herself? This was bigger than the three of them.

Off the battlefield, they kept their usual distance, though occasionally Quade suffered moments of weakness. Most of those moments involved a few kisses or embraces, followed by Quade once more insisting he couldn't wait any longer and Loralai talking him down.

Sil and the Shieldmaidens had noticed the difference between the couple. Of course, Sil knew the truth. Loralai hadn't been able to hide it from her best friend, just like Quade insisted King Tiberis knew as well. Not surprising, considering how close the two men were. Just how much had Quade told his friend? How much did Quade even understand?

They just needed time to sort this out, but time was not on their side. Not when battles raged nearly every day just to hold their ground.

Quade and his dragon dominated the skies, along with a handful of other dragon riders. As the battle raged and fires burned the sky, something instinctual made his gut churn. He turned the dragon and peered over the battlefield, searching for Loralai. At last he found her fighting alongside her fellow Shieldmaidens, their blades and shields a blur of brutality. But the shadow demons drove the elves apart. The Shieldmaidens could fight alone but were much more deadly as a group.

In a heartbeat, Quade and his dragon plunged towards the earth, towards Loralai. Memories of that nightmare from weeks ago pierced him wholly. The dragon breathed deadly fire across the battlefield, clearing a massive span of shadow demons.

The dragon climbed once more, beating enormous wings to bank up for another attack. Quade scanned the battlefield for Loralai. It was several heart-stopping moments before he spotted her. Alone. Surrounded.

Just like in his nightmare.

Quade kicked the left flank of his dragon. Only a half a heartbeat later, they were twisting towards the earth in that direction.

A line of enemy archers prepared a volley of shadow-arrows. All arrows were aimed at the Shieldmaidens. At Loralai.

Quade didn't feel the battle-terror he had experienced in the nightmare. Instead, a surge of pure, animalistic fury rushed through him. He barked the fire command, and the dragon obeyed, but several of the archers remained unscathed.

Quade unleashed a roar of rage and launched himself off the dragon's back the moment he was close enough to the ground. Loralai continued spinning her sword, but the enemy closed in.

His battle-cry caught the attention of the surviving archers as Quade somersaulted to the earth. He gripped the lance in his hands and slammed it into the ground moments before his legs absorbed the rest of the impact. Startled archers loosed arrows.

Blinded by unbridled anger, determined to save Loralai's life, Quade yanked the lance from the ground and spun it like a quarterstaff as fast as he could. It hummed as air rippled around it, sang as arrows shattered against the metal shaft.

Now, he had the dark spawn's full attention.

Quade slammed the tip through one archer and swung it around with enough force to take out nearly a dozen more. But the dead weight of the impaled archer made it too hard to continue wielding the massive weapon. With a howl of pure wrath, Quade launched it with every ounce of strength his muscles could muster. The lance soared through the air as straight as an arrow, impaling three more shadow demons before rolling a few others over and hitting the ground.

The second the lance left his hand, Quade pulled his sword, Nova, from the sheath at his back. Foes attempted forcing their way around him. He cut down those he could reach, becoming a wall between them and Loralai far behind him.

Loralai's scream of pain momentarily distracted Quade. He glanced back, unable to see any more than her armour and a flash of her white hair as she fought her foes.

An arrow slammed through Quade's armour. He staggered, glancing down at the shaft. Then he rushed forwards. If this would be his final charge, he would keep her safe. He cut down three, four, seven, ten enemies.

Another arrow lodged in his shoulder. Quade grunted, stumbling a step as blood dripped from his wounds. His dragon shrieked overhead. Quade gritted his teeth as a jagged knife swiped at him, and he dropped the sword into his good hand. With an upswing, he beheaded the creature, then spun to take out four more who dared get too close.

A third arrow pierced his side, ramming into his armour and deep into his gut. Quade staggered forwards, fell to his knees. Shadow demons surrounded him like a starving swarm of army ants.

Quade howled, twisting his blade up and around him, launching to his feet to take down ten more in just a few steps. But the fourth arrow hit his chest plate, which slowed it but didn't stop the tip from piercing his skin.

Quade fell to his knees once more.

Dragon breath surged around him, clearing the battlefield.

He blinked slowly, his sword falling from numb fingers.

As his vision faded, he heard Loralai releasing her own battle-cry.

She's alive...

Quade smiled.

Loralai and the Shieldmaidens dominated the battlefield as fires burned across the sky. But the dark shadow demons the Shieldmaidens dispatched had somehow broken their ranks. In no time, Loralai found herself surrounded and alone. It took all she had to hold her own in the fight as they tightened around her.

After several gruelling minutes holding her ground, Loralai stopped, peering around her at the decimated battlefield as the Shieldmaidens closed ranks once more and the dark forces retreated. A few human and elf squads pursued to ensure the enemy wouldn't try slipping around their flanks. Fires burned everywhere from dragon breath.

Loralai deftly flipped her sword and shield across her back and spun in search of Quade and his dragon. Her gaze swept across the sky. Neither hovered over the battlefield as usual. She was surrounded by death on all sides.

But Quade was gone.

Panic gripped Loralai's heart. A terrible sense that a piece of her soul weakened. He couldn't be dead. She would know if he were dead. She was certain of it. That sense would be much more dire... wouldn't it?

"Quade?" Loralai called, just as others called for friends on the battlefield, searching for survivors. "Quade!"

The rest of the Shieldmaidens took up the search with her as she sprinted north over fallen bodies and slipped in puddles of blood and mud, scanning the faces of the fallen as she went. Some thread pulled her in that direction.

"Loralai!"

She skidded to a halt, searching for the voice. It wasn't Quade. She would know his voice from any other. She would feel him in her bones as she had for weeks since that glorious night they gave in to their love.

Her eyes fell on King Tiberis several yards ahead, waving her in his direction.

And she felt it. That pull in the direction he indicated. Tears burned in the back of her eyes as she staggered towards Tiberis. For the first time since the panic set in, Loralai realised her Shieldmaidens were on her heels.

Tiberis spoke gently but urgently as he guided her towards a tent. “He took a few arrows when he jumped from his dragon’s back to save you. The healers are working on him now, but he lives.” The way he said those final words made Loralai’s heart stutter. He lived, but by what margin?

Quade jumped from the dragon to save her? But she hadn’t seen him on the battlefield. Why would he do that when he knew she could handle herself?

The Shieldmaidens took up position outside the tent as Tiberis held the flap aside and Loralai ducked in.

Quade lay unconscious on a medical cot. The best elfin healers were already working on his wounds, and the arrows lay in a heap on the floor, discarded. All four of them were nearly as thick as her sword hilt. Blood pooled beneath him. Loralai’s legs nearly gave out.

No… “No…” Her voice cracked over that one word as something inside of her shattered. She rushed towards the bed, but her father caught her in his arms and pulled her back. She hadn't even noticed King Malik in the tent with them.

"Let them work, Loralai," King Malik insisted.

She trembled in her father's arms as the truth hit her swift and harsh. Quade lived, but he hung on the edge of life and death. His wounds still gaped, pouring blood. The healers couldn't save him. He was already too far gone for their skills.

"He can't die like this," she murmured softly, her hand sliding over her stomach like she might be sick. "I won't let him."

Loralai pushed her father off, falling to her knees beside the cot and nudging the healers out of the way.

"What are you doing?" her father asked in a panic.

But she ignored him, weaving her fingers into the charm she had been forced to memorise during her training. A charm no elf used except under extreme circumstances, and only with other elves.

King Malik surged forwards, pulling her back and stopping her spell. "Stop! You can't do this."

"I must," she hissed, jerking away from him and returning to Quade's bedside.

"You can't," he insisted.

"But I must!" Her silver eyes flashed as she glared at her father, desperation pouring from her.

"Why?" he asked, smoothing her hair back from her dirty, bloody face.

"I love him," Loralai admitted. "Don't be angry with Quade. He wanted to tell you, but I was so scared of losing him. So scared. I can save him. I have to, Father." She implored him, gripping his arm urgently.

"It could kill you to do this," he said, his voice cracking over the words.

"It *will* kill me if I don't."

A hush settled over the tent. Even the healers watched her curiously now. King Tiberis cocked his head as he mulled over her words. How much of what happened between her and Quade did he already know?

Her father shook his head. For once, the mighty Kruos king appeared weak and scared. "What have you done, Loralai?" he asked softly, clearly afraid of the answer.

"Nothing. It... it happened on its own. I noticed it trying several times before... Before we..." Silvery tears flooded her eyes. "We are Soulbound, Quade and me."

King Malik reeled, his hands falling to his sides as his silver eyes glazed over with shock. The healers around them softly gasped. Even King Tiberis appeared stunned by the news.

Lovers could cast the spell to become Soulbound, binding them to one another for as long as they lived. But for natural Soulbound mates to happen was rare. So rare it had only happened, to their knowledge, three times in the long history of their realms, and not for nearly a thousand years. Natural Soulbound served a larger, divine purpose that only their union could create.

But a human and an elf Soulbound? It was unheard of.

"I have to save him," Loralai whispered, pressing a hand to her stomach. "It's no longer just about him and me."

King Malik's eyes widened, realising she indicated the child she carried, still so new even Quade did not yet know.

"This was always inevitable, Father. Not even you can defy the will of the gods in this. We were chosen. I don't know why, but our child is important, or perhaps our child's child. Do you understand now?"

King Malik's jaw twitched. He eyed the pale Quade, barely clinging to life, but she could not read his thoughts.

"I need to do this before I lose the strength," Loralai said, raising her hands to begin once more. They trembled. She could feel her magic weakening as Quade died.

King Malik placed his hand on her arm. "Wait," he said softly. "There is another way."

The king rose and glided across the tent, picking up his crown from where he had placed it earlier. With a pulse of his magic, he broke the mounts holding the green gemstone that had adorned his crown for generations. Loralai observed with keen interest.

When he returned to her side, her father placed the stone in her palm then took her wrist and put that palm over Quade's heart until she pressed the stone against his bare skin.

"You do not have to sacrifice your life," he explained. "Feed your immortality into that stone. If you are truly Soulbound, it will keep you both alive as long as he wears it."

Loralai nodded solemnly, grateful for this gift and acceptance from her father. Then she turned all her attention on the stone. Loralai made her offering to the Seven Gods, sacrificing her immortality so that it would heal Quade and keep him alive. So pure was her heart and focus that the green stone glowed, softly at first, then with increasing light.

Minutes passed, or perhaps hours. Loralai did not know, nor did she care. Every ounce of her energy went into that stone, into saving Quade's life with her immortality and magic, with their bound souls.

Sil ducked into the tent as the light intensified, joining the onlookers as they watched Loralai and Quade. The green stone flashed, then threads of light and hope came to life around the two of them, growing so bright the onlookers had to shield their eyes from the blinding rays.

Any who questioned whether they were Soulbound and saw the spectacle no longer doubted. For that light Loralai had seen weeks ago became visible to all around them. It bound her life to Quade's, and his to hers.

When the light at last faded, Quade's wounds had vanished. Colour returned to his face.

And a protective case of gold wrapped around the green stone, forming a locket.

"By the Seven Gods," King Malik murmured as Quade's eyes opened, dark with flecks of silver, and settled on his beloved.

Loralai whimpered in relief and threw herself into his arms. "Don't scare me like that again, Quade," Loralai cried against his neck.

He stroked her hair with heartbreaking affection. "This heart beats only for you," he whispered back. Then he kissed the top of her head. "Forever."

Loralai pulled back, swiping tears from her eyes. Quade propped himself up, his dark gaze sweeping the others in the tent as he wrapped an arm around Loralai. Then his gaze landed on King Malik.

For several agonising seconds, the only movement was Quade's slow, steady strokes against Loralai's arm. Despite what her father had just done, she had to admit she didn't know how he would react now.

Tiberis ushered everyone else out of the tent, leaving the trio alone.

"Your Majesty..." Quade said, at last breaking the silence.

King Malik held up a hand to silence Quade's protests. Loralai was shocked by how effective the gesture was on Quade; she would have to keep that in mind for the future.

The future... with him. And their child.

"Recover and get yourself sorted first," King Malik said. "Then meet me at the central bonfire."

Quade's hands tightened on Loralai as if afraid she would be ripped away when the king laid eyes on her next.

Instead, he excused himself and left them alone.

"I thought I lost you," Loralai said breathlessly the moment they were alone. She nuzzled into Quade's neck, still coated in blood. She didn't care.

"I nearly lost you on the battlefield," Quade said softly. He brushed at the locket and chain around his neck. "What is this?"

"I saved you," Loralai replied. "I fed my immortality into it so that it might heal you. Wear it every day, my love, because that holds a piece of me."

His finger hooked her chin, tilting her face up to his. The love in his eyes, reserved just for her, made everything in Loralai's soul lift. "Then, I will keep it close to my heart always." He kissed her, slowly and gently, as if cherishing every brush of her lips.

More than hour later, Quade strode towards the central bonfire, cleaned and in a fresh elven silk wrap popular among the males. Loralai had smiled so fondly at the swirling stitching over the pale-blue garb that he swore he would wear it forever. Her own icy-blue fresh dress swept the ground. It hung from her shoulders and arms like icicles, glided over her chest and hips like swells of smooth, frozen water. She was the most beautiful creature he'd ever laid eyes on.

And she chose me.

Quade tightened his grip on her hand, ready to walk into fire and face her father. They almost seemed dressed for the occasion.

Fire and ice.

As they drew near enough to the central bonfire to see in the darkness, Quade's steps slowed. His grip on her hand slipped slightly at the sight.

The crowd parted, leaving them a path around the bonfire. Hundreds of elves and humans mixed around the fire, watching the two of them.

"Is he about to push me into that fire?" Quade asked, only half joking as they approached her father.

Loralai just bumped his shoulder and laughed in that way he wanted to hear for the rest of his days.

King Malik and Prince Malikai stood together, hands folded before them, eyes on the couple as the two rounded the bonfire. To one side, Tiberis beamed with his two wives beside him. On the other side, Sil and the Shieldmaidens snickered and whispered to one another.

Loralai's breath caught, but she slid her arm through Quade's and pulled him onwards until the two of them stood before King Malik.

The immortal elf king held up his arms to silence everyone. Quade noticed that all of them were dressed in fine clothes, blood and armour gone for this moment. His heart quickened.

"Prince Quade Martnarving," King Malik said. "I'm afraid there is no turning back. For either of us." He held up his palms.

Loralai released her grip on Quade's arm, and he thought he might fall over without her support, terrified as he was. But she slid her palm over the king's, gently nudging for him to do the same.

Quade's eyes narrowed suspiciously. "I'm afraid I don't understand." Oh, he understood well enough.

"Do you seek Princess Loralai a'Malik's hand in marriage?" King Malik asked, speaking clearly enough for all to hear.

Quade eyed Loralai, the pure bliss on her face, the very face of perfection. "Yes." He put his palm over the king's.

Malikai stepped forwards, wrapping a swathe of silk around Quade's wrist, who was trembling, and the king had to know it. But it was joy, not fear. Not in this moment.

"I bind you heart, body, and soul to Princess Loralai a'Malik," King Malik said. "You and yours are now a part of the Kruos as surely as your soul is bound to our princess."

Tiberis stepped forwards. "Loralai, do you seek Prince Quade Martnarving's hand in marriage?"

"I do," Loralai responded, her voice as clear as crystal waters.

Tiberis wrapped the same silk around Loralai's wrist and said, "In the name of the Novavito king, I bind you heart, body, and soul to Prince Quade Martnarving." He patted her hand gently. "You and yours are now a part of the human kingdoms as surely as your soul is bound to its prince."

King Malik nodded to Tiberis, then folded Quade's hand around Loralai's. "To be Soulbound is no small matter," the king said. "It leaves you both responsible for the safety, love, and care of the other piece of your soul. For without one side, the other cannot survive." He leaned forwards and whispered, "Kiss your wife, you fool."

My wife...

Quade pulled Loralai into his arms and did just that. He kissed her for all the world to see.

As their lips broke apart and the cheers of the onlookers roared into the air, Loralai rested her head against his shoulder. Quade relaxed. He could face anything with her in his arms.

"Soulbound?" he whispered into her ear.

"I'll explain later," Loralai replied. She took his hand, and he didn't protest as she pressed it to her belly. "We have something else to discuss first."

The implication of her words hit him harder than any arrow. Quade froze, momentarily stunned. His hand pressed firmer against her belly.

"Really?" His voice cracked with excitement. He broke from his stupor and spun, cradling her face in his hands as the crowd milled into festive activities, only casting a few smiles at the newlyweds.

Silver tears sparkled in Loralai's eyes. She bit her lip and nodded, glowing in a way he had never seen before.

In a single day, he had nearly lost his entire world.

Instead, he gained everything he could have dreamt of. A laugh bubbled out of him, and he scooped her into his arms, showering Loralai with kisses.

His wife...

And his child.

A beacon of light in the darkness.

ECHOES OF THE LOST

NASTASIA BISHOP-MCHUGH

for Alicia,
and your tender heart,

Nastasia ♡

1

THE UNDERCITY IS WELL AND TRULY alive tonight.

Neon lights cover the dark buildings under a perpetually desolate grey sky. The maze of streets bustle with all manner of creature, faerie to demon, siren to werewolf, and everything in between. Including humans like me. Humans who are bound to the city.

Few humans can reach this place, but the bargain I struck with a demon, a particularly beautiful demon, allows me passage as long as I wear the pendant he gave me. All I have to do is stand at the banks of a river, any river, and clutch the pendant, and a ferryman appears and takes me downstream. All rivers lead to the Undercity, if you know the way.

I navigate through the winding streets, past vendors selling potions and brews, past betting tables where memories are the prize, and past the shifty trader with come hithers to her shelves stocked with vials of dark-green blood – someone once told me that green blood only comes from the darkest, most evil of beings. And that it is traded not with money, but with pieces of your soul, both here and in the human realm. It would make a human very powerful indeed.

Since the coalition of the human realm and the underworld, corruption is rampant. The World President at the time was said to have been partial to the green blood trade. It would make sense – he was a fucking idiot. The type of man one would consider a loser who only made friends with money. There's no way he would have wrangled his way into the position otherwise.

My destination isn't too far, and after a short while, my journey through the undercity comes to an end. I push open the doors to the nondescript building and give a polite nod to the security guard – a gargoyle named Angela – and head for a door behind reception.

The only other human in the building, Dennis, tuts at me as I walk past his desk. "You're late," he says.

"Yes, Dennis," I say through clenched teeth. "I'm aware." Late by two and a half minutes – there was a song on the radio I had to see through.

"It's busy today. New World President takes office – a lot of dangerous riots upstairs."

I roll my eyes. I'm well aware of what happens on the surface, aka the human realm. "OK, Dennis," I say before I push through the door behind him and head downstairs.

I actually think he likes working here. I don't know what bargain he struck, but he doesn't seem to have any urgent need to finish it up so he can be released from his bind to the city.

Once I reach the bottom floor, I head to my desk, which sits on a dais above the river Thele. My desk, along with the three others along the riverbank, is its final destination. I can already see boats queued stern to bow down the river and my colleagues racing to process the souls that line up.

I blow out a breath. I'd like to think that busy days make the time go faster, but in the underworld, nothing works as it does on the surface.

"Hey, Elspeth," I say to the green cyclops manning the desk next to me.

She only responds with a short grunt while she reads through the paperwork of the soul in front of her. I don't take it personally.

Before I sit down, I quickly grab a cup of tea from the break room and take a moment, as I do every day, to reflect on how the hell I ended up here.

Who knew fucking a demon would land me such a boring job?

How was I supposed to know, truly, what I was getting myself in to? I didn't know he was a demon at first. They don't all hang around on the surface, and they're not exactly conspicuous when they do. He didn't have his wings, and there was nothing else to suggest what lurked in his blood. Except for the fact he was the most exquisite person I'd ever seen – he was both masculine and feminine, beautiful and handsome, and he embodied every charming thing about a human. I couldn't look away. And that should have been my first clue. We're told to look out for the most extreme of beauties, and to never let them start asking you questions. Tricksters, the lot of them, they say.

But he didn't say anything about customer service, he only asked if I wanted to change my life. And I was so ready for change. After the worst breakup of my life and just going through the motions for months to keep myself alive and functioning, I probably still would have taken a deal even if the demon's wings had been on full display.

But who uses their dick as a contract, anyway? I was on the rebound. Maybe I missed something. Maybe when I screamed 'yes', he'd silently whispered a question binding me to his service. He was holding my face down as he bent me over and pounded me into oblivion – it's possible I didn't hear everything he'd said.

I slyly glance in his – the demon's – direction. Maron. When he offered – well, tricked me in to – the job, I didn't think he'd be my boss. Today, he's entirely shirtless – a common occurrence amongst demons. Narcissists, the lot of them. He appears to be telling quite the enthralling tale to a group of werewolves, who laugh heartily at his words.

Dickhead.

I go back to my desk to find the next soul pressed up against my table, a little too close for comfort.

"Name?" I ask to the man, who looks like he's about to blame me for everything that's ever gone wrong in his life. I only process humans. Which makes sense, I guess. The rules and cultures vary quite a bit between creatures.

"I demand to speak to someone higher!" he says as spit flies from his mouth.

I set my tea down, push my chair back slightly and say, "Sir, you don't get to demand things here."

"What the fuck are you talking about, you bitch! Where the hell am I?"

Not in Hell, but judging from his demeanour, that could very well be where he's heading. This is more like a holding room, really. Purgatory, I guess some might say. When they cross the river Thele, they go either left or right. Left brings them to me. Right sends them upstairs. Something about good versus bad, but who's deciding that is unknown. Well, unknown to me, anyway.

I pull out his form, stamping the word 'cleared' in big, bold red letters on the form, and send it down a tube to the next level, and before he has a chance to wag his finger in my face, the floor opens beneath him, followed by his high-pitched scream, and he is whisked away to his penultimate destination, where they'll decide what his eternal afterlife will be. I only process them to make sure they're actually dead. And you always know because their soul hovers just above the surface of their skin, painting them in a ghostly white aura. Plus, no one alive has ever made it down here. Maybe except that Dante guy. From what I hear, Virgil was fired pretty soon after the incident and banished from the Undercity.

I go through the motions for the next few hours, mindlessly checking paperwork, glancing at their body to ensure I can see their soul, sending them down the tunnels. I need a break. One more, then I'll head back to the surface for an hour to grab some lunch; the pickings down here aren't all that appetising. Fortunately, my contract still allows me to live on the surface.

"Next," I call out, already thinking about what I'm going to eat. Probably a burrito. "Name," I say without glancing up, my mind busy assembling all the ingredients for my lunch.

"Lucas."

That voice. I stop.

"Lucas Storrow."

Bile rises in my throat.

No.

I force my eyes up. *Lucas.*

"Riley?" he asks, pure disbelief and confusion on his face.

"Lucas? What are you doing here?" I ask desperately.

A million thoughts and scenarios rush my mind. I've been busy, sure, but someone would have told me. Someone would have called me.

"I… I don't remember," he says.

Of course he doesn't. None of them do. Not until they're sent to where they need to be. Something happens when they cross the river, removing the memories of their death.

"I've missed you," Lucas whispers sadly.

Lucas. Beautiful Lucas, with his messy blonde locks, dark-blue eyes, tattooed arms, pierced nose, soft lips. And now, a ghostly white aura above his skin.

I rise from my chair and lean over the counter to take his hand. Years of memories flood through me: trips to the beach, competitive days at the arcade, us in our flat, naked bodies intertwined and tender kisses given.

"No, this isn't right," I say. He shouldn't be here.

I reluctantly let go of his hands. "Maron!" I call out.

My supervisor casually wanders over from his circle jerk.

"What's up?" he purrs as he sits on the edge of my desk, his mighty black feathered wings almost shrouding me in darkness.

"This soul" – I shove the papers into his hands – "he doesn't belong here."

Maron is shuffling through the papers, taking too long to say anything. He looks at Lucas, his eyes running up and down. He mumbles something unintelligible under his breath.

"What?" I ask desperately.

"Riley… You know how this works."

"I know this man. He doesn't belong here!" I protest. "I would have known. Someone would have told me!"

I frantically look between the two men. Lucas looks vacant. He still doesn't comprehend where he is.

"Riley," Maron says again. "You see his soul. Send him down."

I won't do it. My eyes refuse to believe the ethereal white glow that hovers above his skin. Tears rise fast and flood down my cheeks. I reach over the desk to grab Lucas' hand, but it's too late. Maron has pressed the button to open the tunnel beneath Lucas' feet.

"No!" I scream.

In that moment, time slows. My fingertips brushing his. His eyes looking to his feet then back to me. The flash of that smile that tells me not to worry before he disappears completely.

"Where did you send him?" I cry out.

"Where he belongs," Maron says.

Rage overtakes me, and with as much force as I have, I punch Maron square in the face. Then I scramble over my desk and hover over the tunnel.

"Riley, don't," Maron warns as he pinches his nose to stem the green blood pouring out while reaching for me with his other hand.

But I do the only thing my heart tells me, so I plunge after Lucas into the abyss.

2

THE SILENCE OF DARKNESS IS THE LOUDEST thing I've ever heard, and she's an old friend of mine.

After Lucas, my nights were filled with the companionship of oblivion. Time passes in odd waves when you're alone. Hours slip by in taunting echoes, but there is no sun of the day and no moon of the night, only the darkness.

Here, she greets me again, this time in a frigid embrace.

"Lucas?" I whisper, his name tender on my lips.

We met in a sandwich shop. I asked for extra pickles, and he chuckled from behind me and said, "A woman with good taste", and we hadn't left each other's sides since. The love came fast and full. Every moment felt like bliss. The first time he sang to me, all the fractured pieces of me started to glue back together, and I thought we'd be one forever. But the love had turned into addiction, and I realised that although he'd healed me, he'd shattered me in new ways, ways I don't think can ever be fixed. And yet now, here in this unknown place, I would search every inch of it to find him.

I should be before the final decision makers, but there are no desks, no creatures, human, demon, or otherwise. Only fading wisps of white gently float through the air.

The darkness in this unknown place is not black. It is not onyx or obsidian. It is not crow or raven. Instead, it is only a feeling. The deepest sadness I have ever felt. But it is not mine. The souls that wander here gently place a shroud upon my shoulders, then another, and then another, until the weight of them pushes me to my knees. Their darkness is what descends upon me as they desperately try to shift their torment.

I feel every ounce of their sadness, their grief, the unyielding burden of their shame and guilt. It clogs my veins, fills my lungs with fluid; how can I keep breathing while I pretend I'm not drowning?

I need to stand up.

I plant my hands on the floor, and its icy, wet surface splashes through my fingers. When I finally stand, the sorrow of a thousand lives is lifted from my shoulders. I know they want me to help them, for someone to take away what they bear, but I am not here for them. I can't be. Not now.

The walk is slow and heavy, but it gets easier the farther I go. This place is not for me. Darkness will have to come for me another day.

"Lucas?" I call once more, this time a little louder.

There is a response, but it is fleeting. Just a breath on an eerie wind. Nevertheless, I follow its direction, feeling its tug on my heart. He feels near yet far beyond my reach. I stretch out my hand, willing to brush against him, feel his warmth, inhale his sweet scent. And suddenly, there it is. The smell of him. Like raspberry jam and peppermint tea – every single day without fail he'd have toast and raspberry jam for breakfast and a peppermint tea in the evening before bed.

The darkness wavers, and a pinhole of light appears. I scratch at its surface and peel away a layer, the black becoming sticky flakes under my fingernails, then step through to the other side.

A woman is waiting for me. She wears a dress of azure and a crown of sapphires. Her gaze upon me is soft, kindly, as she reaches her hand out to me, and I take it. I don't know what kind of creature she is – some sort of human hybrid, it seems. Her face and body are distinctly human, except her ears are just the slightest bit too pointed, her cheeks a touch too rosy, her hair a shade I can't explain – something like blue, but entirely not blue. It moves as though enchanted by the sea.

"Who are you?" I ask.

She smiles. "I am Afina, and I'm here to guide you on your journey."

"Oh, no," I say. "I'm looking for someone. I can't linger; I need to find him."

Her kind smile remains. "Everyone needs help finding their way." She steps aside, letting go of my hand, to reveal a door. A door I know. She opens it and ushers me inside.

I'm in my flat. A figure lies in my bed. I know it's not Lucas, because instead of beautiful curly blonde locks, there is only the familiar muddy brown of my own hair. I look around. None of his belongings are here. This is after. Me, after.

"I don't understand," I say. "Where are the final decision makers? I followed someone here, and that's where he should be, where *I* should be."

"You are lost," Afina says, neither a question nor a statement.

"Yes," I reply, nevertheless. "I'm looking for someone," I say once more, frustrated now.

The woman seems to consider my words, then says, "In order to move forward, to find what is lost, you must first face the moments that led you here."

Despite her vagueness, I understand what she asks of me. I've been in the Undercity and my job long enough to know that there is a place beyond purgatory, where some souls are sent when they walk the line between life and death. There, or here, I guess, they must face their memories, their most important memories, before a decision is made as to which side they end up on. Lucas must not be dead yet. Somewhere on the surface, he clings to the wisps of life. And I'm going to save him.

I look upon the memory of myself, forced to confront the lowest point in my life. I know what happens next, and I don't want to watch, but if this is what the underworld demands for me to continue on to find Lucas, I'll do it.

My face, not my own now, the one I observe in the memory, is devoid of tears. I remember I was empty, in both mind and soul. Tears couldn't fall even if they'd wanted. All I could do was stare without seeing. In that lowest moment, not even Lucas had filled my thoughts. There was just nothing.

I'd tucked away this moment, tightly locked in a box in the darkest corner of my memories. But I guess deep down I know it's important, and that is why it presents itself here.

The memory of me slowly slithers from the bed, and the duvet drops from my body. Only shorts and a crop top cover me. The temperature was low – it was winter – but I didn't feel it. I walk to the window of my eleventh-floor flat and push it up to open. With a pure blank mind, I step through the window, bracing my weight on my hands on the ledge, until I am sitting in the open window, the world dark and quiet below me.

The love Lucas and I shared had been so deeply embedded in every part of my life, and I'd been devoted to the chaos. But there came a point I realised I couldn't do it to him, and I couldn't do it to myself. So I had told him to leave. And he did. But without him, what else was there?

A job I hated? A flat I could barely afford? A broken relationship with my family?

He was my toxic air. The erratic rhythm of my heart.

What was life without the sun?

So in the after, I was nothing. Could be nothing.

In this moment in the window, the darkness had truly come for me, and I was ready to fall into her embrace.

I place my hand on my memory's shoulder, and in that moment, something had stirred within me. A little firefly sparking. My last piece of hope. I didn't know what had brought it to the surface. Maybe the sharp cold air in my lungs? Perhaps looking out over a night sky full of stars? So, I climbed back in through the window and had slunk down on the couch.

I look upon myself with a deep longing to just embrace myself, say I'm proud of you and things will get better, because in that moment, although I had climbed back inside, I still felt the ugliness of despair.

"Why do you fear this memory?" Afina asks me as we continue to look upon the scene.

"It's not fear," I whisper as I hang my head. "It's shame."

She rests her hand gently on my shoulder. "I see nothing here to be ashamed of. I see a love that burned so deep it could not be quelled. The greater the love, the greater the hurt when it ends. Pain means you are alive, and you survived. It's important to move forward and heal. To forgive yourself."

I shake my head fiercely. "How can I forgive myself?"

"Why are you here, Riley?" she asks.

"To save Lucas. To end his torment."

"Do you think it's possible to take away another's pain if you hold so much yourself?"

Whether she's right or not is irrelevant. To end Lucas's suffering, I would take it all. "I won't let him fade away in this place."

She takes my hand, and we step farther into the apartment.

"It's time for you to move on, Riley."

"But how do I find Lucas?"

She gestures to the memory of me, now back in bed, puffy red eyes staring vacantly at the ceiling. "You need to forgive yourself."

I walk to the bed and look down upon myself, and while I don't know if I can forgive myself as I stand here now, the despair I see in the memory of me breaks my heart. Her, I can forgive. So I touch my hand to my memory's forehead and kiss my brow gently.

The pendant around my neck sends a warm feeling through my chest, and a surge of peace flows through me.

"I forgive you," I whisper, and my memory self finally relaxes into a restful sleep.

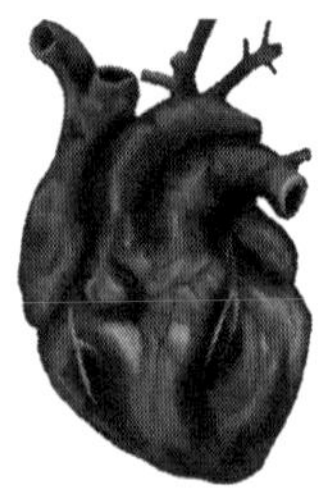

3

AFTER AFINA, I LEFT THE MEMORY OF MY apartment, and once outside, I was somewhere new, and alone. Afina had disappeared.

Warmth does not come here, wherever here is. Instead, an endless icy wind barrels into me. It seeps into my bones, taking over my body, and I shake uncontrollably, teeth chattering, as I walk through a thick fog.

Up ahead, the fog appears to lessen, and something tall and dark begins to take its place.

"Lucas?" I call, hoping he is near.

The smell of peppermint wraps around me. He's here.

I penetrate the last section of the fog and step out into a wide terrain. The ground is spotted with gnarled black roots that lead to distant trees. Beyond them, a large silver gate protects a castle of obsidian. He must be in there.

Overhead, lightning crackles through the greyish green sky, with deafening rumbles of thunder following soon after.

I soon reach the gates and call out, "Hello?"

They open with an ear-piercing screech, and I wince as the sound penetrates my head. No one appears to guide me this time, so I follow the straight, but uneven, cobbled path.

A gust of wind swirls around me as I walk, bringing with it the distant sound of a voice, but then Lucas's voice suddenly tears through the air, like a hurricane made of mimicking crows. They call my name, pleading for me to stay with them, to not leave. The sound devastates me and cleaves my soul in a sickeningly familiar way – those were the last words he cried to me before I left him.

I start running, batting away at the invisible noise, covering my ears, anything to try and escape it.

As I near the doors of the castle, they open out towards me, any sound drowned out by Lucas' relentless cries. The steps up to the doors are few, and I scramble over them and launch myself through the opening. As soon as I am inside, the doors slam shut behind me, and silence finally reigns.

I get to my feet, still trying to fully catch my breath from my sprint. Around me, statues cover the room. Each is crimson from head to toe, with no discernible features, just the definitions of hollow eyes, a nose, and a mouth. Each appears to have been frozen in time, running. But running from what? Or who?

The silence here is stark as I slowly navigate through the sea of bodies, half expecting to come upon another figure like Afina, but there is no one here except me and the bodies.

Behind me, a low rumbling emanates from the darkness. When I look back, the door I came through is gone, and instead this hallway has extended far beyond my view. Should I be going that way instead? But my stomach coils as I realise the bodies are all running in the same direction, away from the rumbling. I start to gently back away, careful to make as little sound as possible.

A deep-orange fog slithers out of the darkness. I freeze, mesmerised by the way it moves, the way it dances down the hall and gently collides with the bodies, wrapping around them like silk. It searches for something. For someone.

I finally snap out of my haze and spin to start running, but I collide with one of the bodies, and just as I'm falling headfirst into the marble tile floor, the body's arms move to catch me.

I look up, breathless, and the empty face stares down at me. While there are no distinguishable features, there is something frighteningly known about this figure. It moves no more, says no words, so I start to untangle myself from its arms, but as I slide my hand through theirs to bolster myself, the air is stolen from my lungs, and I'm suddenly transported.

The memory plays out before me as the last did, except this is not one of misery, but pure happiness. Why does this memory present itself here?

Lucas and I lie on the sofa, naked as the day we were born. We'd just had the most incredible sex, but it's this afterpart where the happiness lives.

We are wrapped in each other – legs intertwined, chests pressed, his lips rest on my forehead. His skin is warm, and sweat rests in droplets across his whole body. I breathe in his scent. It's entirely intoxicating, and I longed to lay in that embrace forever, skin to skin, heart to heart.

"Riley?" he whispers into my hair. "Can we stay here forever?"

I chuckled, traced his collarbone with my finger, gently kissed that sweet spot on his neck. "We can if we want. Who's going to stop us?"

But with my last words, I realise why this memory is here. No one stopped us. And it was the beginning of the end. Where our love blossomed into addiction. There was no world without him. Our lives were lived with utter obsession with one another. He fought any man who dared even glance my way. I sabotaged any woman who dared be his friend. Soon, it was only us, with a love so pure and isolating. The few friends I had left I abandoned. He stopped doing all his hobbies. There was only him, and to him there was only me. The obsession ran so dark and deep within us both.

I had never loved anyone so much, and I didn't know love could manifest in such dark ways. But we were so young. Each other's first true love. Maybe we needed more time. More time to figure out how to navigate such a powerful love.

I'm back in the arms of the faceless body, and with striking clarity, I suddenly realise: the body is me.

I look around carefully. These are all versions of me. Have I been here before?

I look in the direction of where I was running, where all of me are running. The hallway seems endless in that direction too. Escape is not an option.

"What do I do?" I cry out to the statue holding me. "How do I get out?" But it does not respond, does not move again, so I untangle myself from its limbs. "Lucas!" I scream, but the noise only echoes back at me, and suddenly the orange fog stops and appears to focus in my direction.

I start to run, and the fog follows.

As I try and dodge my way through the bodies, I can't help but bump into a few, and I'm plagued by flashes of memories of me and Lucas. Memories that, in the moment, felt happy, endless. But from this side, I see them for what they were: chaos.

In the flat, near the beginning, me heading out for the night with friends. Him saying I look beautiful but asking if I really want the attention of other men. Him suggesting he should come with us to protect me.

Me on the back of his motorbike. We're going so fast. It was thrilling. Dangerous. Terrifying.

His mother knocking on the door, telling me she hasn't seen Lucas for weeks. Me assuring her he's fine. Me telling him she's jealous because of her loveless marriage.

The regret of them slows me down, and I feel like all the versions of me cling to my body, fingers around my wrists, arms around my torso. Why did those moments feel right back then? I believed he did protect me, excited me, cared for me. And I him.

“Please,” I beg to the statues. “What do you want me to do?”

The weight of their expectation is holding me back, but instead of fear I become angry. If this is me, why am I holding myself back? If I want to find Lucas, nothing should be stopping me. And I do want to find him. Those flashes of memories are distorted. I did feel happiness. I loved – love – him fiercely.

The realisation puts me in a chokehold. I’m not supposed to be running. My encounter with Afina runs through my mind. I had to face the past. That’s why I’ve been stuck here. I’ve been constantly running from this abyss inside me.

No more.

So I turn and face the darkness, and the fog rushes towards me and surges up like a rogue wave, and I hold out my arms and let it consume me whole.

4

I'M FLOATING.

A current of sea water rushes over my face, and salt prickles across my lips. The sun is blindingly bright, so I keep my eyes closed.

Someone is calling my name, and my ears are underwater, but the muffled sound is the sweetest thing I've ever heard.

Arms scoop beneath me and pull me up, cradle me like a babe. There are fingers in my hair, a thumb across my cheek.

"Riley, you okay?" the voice asks.

I rest against a bare chest, listening to a steady heartbeat. "Am I dead?" I ask, afraid for the answer.

A gentle chuckle. "Riley, open your eyes."

I comply, and it takes a moment to adjust to the harsh light. Lucas fills my vision, smiling down at me.

"You were gone there for a moment. Where was your mind at?"

I look around. We're on a beach. West Wittering – our favourite beach in England. There're a few dog walkers wandering the sands, but we're mostly alone. Is this another memory? It feels so real.

I look back to Lucas, to his eyes so full of love. "I… I was thinking of you," I say.

He smiles widely, adoringly. "My thoughts are always of you, my love." He kisses my head then pulls the most adorable face as he realises his lips are now covered in the salty seawater.

I feel so full in this moment, so full of hope and excitement for a lifetime with this man.

He rocks me in the water, the gentle waves so soothing against my body. Music flows from his lips, songs of pure love, lyrics that wrap around my heart and penetrate the deepest depths of my soul. I could listen to his smooth voice for eternity.

Lightning suddenly cracks overhead, and I jolt my head back to look at the sky. Where did the sun go? It was here only moments ago. Now, a desolate, stormy grey has crept in. I look back to Lucas. His smile is gone. A sad furrow of his brow has taken its place.

No, this isn't right. I push away from him, kick my feet to tread the water.

"Baby, what's wrong?" he asks.

"We're not here. You're not here," I say, shaking my head.

When he reaches out his hand, it turns to ash, and he fades away completely.

"Lucas!" I cry out.

But the waves drown out my cries as they surge and spin me through the water. I find fractions of moments to break the surface and suck in small breaths, but it's not enough. I swallow a mouthful of briny water, and the burn in my lungs is so fierce. My stomach recoils while a never-ending sensation of gasping for air wracks my body. But my resolve to survive is strong. I reach for the surface and push with all my strength to reach it.

Finally, the waves tumble me onto land, onto the gritty sand of the beach, and I vomit up the water in my lungs. After coughing out everything I possibly can, my chest feels like I've been kicked by a horse.

Around me, the beach has become a barren wasteland. Ship carcasses are scattered across the sands, and up ahead, a tower of broken brick reaches to the sky. At the top of the tower, firelight creeps out, and I know that's where I must go.

The sky has changed from a tumultuous storm to clear and bright, now the sun shines down on me with vigour. The heat is almost unbearable. My lips begin to dry and crack almost immediately, and the strongest thirst I have ever felt overcomes me. It forces me to my knees, to the hot, burning sand.

The crawl is slow and torturous, and it feels like I will never reach my destination. A few minutes into my journey,

I come across a body crawling across the sand too, except it is unmoving, just like the bodies in the castle, frozen in time. I bend a little to look at their face, and like the others, distinguishable features do not exist. But I know. Like the others, I know this is me. When I look up again, I find a sea of crawling bodies, all heading towards the castle.

I navigate through them carefully, as this time, nothing chases me except the desperate urge to save Lucas, and the sun beating down on my back. I wonder if they all perished from the heat of the sun. Maybe they expired from thirst. Seeing all of them only spurs me on, strengthens my will to make it to the end.

Seemingly hours later, I feel like I am on the verge of death. My skin is blistered, my mouth full of cotton, my breath shallow. But I've reached the bottom of the stair that leads to the tower. There is only one body of me that reached this far, and her fingertips stretch for the bottom step but don't quite touch. I edge past her and start my ascent, still on my hands and knees. I don't have the strength to stand.

The brick crumbles beneath my hands, enough to make me question whether the stairs will collapse beneath me. But they hold somewhat steady as I go. Eventually, finally, I approach a door at the top of the stairs, and I vomit over the side in relief and exhaustion.

I use the wall to slide my body up to standing and fall against the door. With little strength, I gently knock, and the door swings open.

I fall over the threshold and splay across the brick floor, but the impact doesn't hurt. Instead, relief washes through me. My vigour and spirit are renewed, my mouth no longer parched, my skin free of blisters. Crossing the threshold of this tower seems to have revived me.

Tears of thanks pool in the corners of my eyes while the cool brick floor is a long-awaited relief.

"Welcome," a voice of deep timbre announces.

My eyes follow the sound. As I look up from the floor, I realise I am surrounded by creatures. Their bodies are of a greyish green colour, and their eyes of obsidian. They are small, no taller than my hip, and appear severely malnourished. Bones protrude from all parts of their bodies, so fragile looking, as if a slight breeze might blow them away.

When my eyes find the voice, the confusion on my face is evident.

"Maron?"

"Hello, Riley."

5

MARON SITS AUTHORITATIVELY IN A chair, no, a throne, of onyx. He's still shirtless, and his wings are spread to their full width, almost covering the wall behind him. They are gargantuan, things of great beauty and terror.

"What are you doing here?" I ask. The creatures halt me from getting too near by thrusting their spears together to form a blockade.

"I am the ending. The final trial."

"You?" He's just my boss in a processing department. "What power do you hold here?" Sure, I knew he was powerful for the fact that I made a bargain with him, but I don't know the hierarchy of the Undercity; maybe all demons, of high and low status, can make bargains.

"Did you truly think someone as magnificent as I was simply a desk worker?" His loud laugh booms around the tower, sending birds in the rafters flying. "Look upon me, human, and tell me what you see."

What I see? I see Maron as I always have. A shirtless narcissist. He inches an eyebrow up, goading me to consider his command. I play along. So, what do I see? I scan my eyes over his entire body. Sculpted muscle, long black hair, a multitude of tattoos, a ring of emerald on his finger, and... the ring. It suddenly dawns on me. When I first arrived in the city, I made friends with a bartender. She told me more about the Undercity, how it works, who's in charge. And about the Undercity royalty. The beings who each preside over a domain. Recognised only by their emerald rings, as they can change form whenever they please, into whatever they please.

"Do you see it now?"

"You're one of the princes?" I ask, already seeing the answer.

"I am Maron, Prince of the Realm of the Lost. You are in my domain."

"Where is Lucas?" I demand.

He gestures to a well in the centre of the room. I move towards it, the creatures allowing me passage, and look into its depths, into its murky waters, and find myself looking upon Lucas. He's in a hospital bed. I'm sitting at his bedside, holding his hand.

"What is this?" I ask.

"A memory," Maron says.

"I don't remember this," I say as I shake my head. I continue to watch.

In the memory, tears stain my face. A woman stands on the opposite side of the bed – it's Lucas' mother. She never liked me. Said I wasn't good for her boy. Said I was undeserving. Here, she sneers as she stares at me.

"You did this," she whispers sharply.

I shake my head, saying no, no, no, over and over while I clutch Lucas' hand.

"He never would have sought out a bargain with those *wicked* creatures if you hadn't broken his heart, left him in pieces. He wished for you to love him again, and look what it did."

"I never stopped loving him," I say, but it's meaningless to her. "How did it go so wrong?"

She hated that I was with him. She hated that I left him. I was never going to be good enough.

"Get out," she hisses.

"Please let me stay," I beg.

"Now."

I reluctantly let go of his hand, but I'll come back. She can't keep me away.

In a haze, I stumble out of the room, follow the long white hospital corridors. Rain ricochets off the windows in the dark of night. I head for the exit, all the while filling my thoughts with Lucas, about the deal he made with a creature who roams the human realm. It's illegal to strike a bargain with a demon, but it happens often. The politicians of this world are corrupt to their core, having only reached their positions because of deals they made, yet they make it illegal for us, scared to have their power taken from them. And because of that, people, desperate people, plea with the creatures, not fully understanding for what they ask.

And now, Lucas lays in a hospital bed, and I don't know if he'll ever wake up.

It's time for me to make my own deal.

Outside, down a dimly lit alleyway, while the rain still pours, I fall to my knees and call out for a demon. I don't know how it works. I don't know for whom I ask. I just hope my plea is heard.

Within moments, something, someone, stands before me.

I look up to the creature, the creature I now know as Maron, to his powerful black wings, which shroud me from the rain.

"You wish to bargain?" he says without introduction.

"Yes," I cry. "Bring him back to me."

Without asking who I mean, Maron says, "He is lost between the realms of life and death, his journey already begun; I cannot bring him back."

I slam my fist into the concrete ground then get to my feet and make myself as tall as I can. "No," I say.

"No?" Maron asks curiously.

"You heard me. No. I do not accept. There is something you can do!" The rain continues to pour without remorse.

Maron considers me a moment. "Listen well, human, for this will be my only bargain. I will grant you passage to the Undercity. But it is up to you to bring him back."

"I'll do anything," I reply desperately.

He holds up a hand to stop me. "A sacrifice must be made. To find your love, you, too, must walk the line between life and death. But beware, the path will not be easy. To gain entry to the Undercity, you must first sacrifice the memory of this bargain."

"If I don't remember the bargain, how will I know why I'm there?"

"If your love is true, you will find your way. With each new dawn, your quest will start anew, along with your memory of any previous journey."

"Each new dawn? It will take longer than a day?"

"Endless days, if you wish."

"I don't have endless days!"

"Time in the Undercity is not linear like on Earth, human. A day there is merely seconds here."

I think for a moment. Every second away from Lucas shatters my heart, but if this is the only way to save him, then it is what I must do.

"I accept," I say, then in a motion faster than I can comprehend, the demon's wings wrap around me, and we are whisked away in a flurry of fire and ash.

I pull myself away from the well and look back to Maron, here and now.

"What the fuck was that?" I cry out.

"Your memories," he says casually.

"I don't understand. Our bargain... it wasn't... we..." I can't even comprehend. "Why do I have a different memory of how we met?"

He chuckles. "All part of the fun."

"So we didn't..."

He scoffs. "No, human. We did not. I bet that got you all riled up though, didn't it?"

I leap for him, but his minions pull me back and force me to my knees. "Why the fuck have I been working a *desk job* here? What was the point?"

He shrugs. "Well, we have been very busy; we needed the free labour."

I am absolutely raging. White-hot fury coils around me. Has this all just been a game? "So you've been tormenting me, tormenting Lucas, and for what? For your... *pleasure*? How many times have I been here?"

"Oh, that wasn't Lucas."

My stomach drops. "What... what do you mean?"

"I must admit, that has been one of my better ideas. The people you've been seeing – none of them have been your lover."

"That doesn't make any sense. I've *seen* him. *Touched* him."

"You saw what I wanted you to see. Haven't you figured it out by now?" His smile is the wickedest thing I've ever seen. "All those bodies of you, you never completed the journey because Lucas was never at the end of it. You *couldn't* finish."

My hands begin to shake, and sweat drips from my brow. "I don't understand. Why?" I plead. "Why would you do this?"

"Why? Because I can. Because humans think they can make bargains with powerful demons and face no consequences. Because they think they can enter *our* domain, as if they are worthy. The treaty between your world and ours should have never been granted."

"So because you have some twisted hatred for humans, we are at your whim at our most desperate?" I spit at his feet. "You disgust me."

"Lucky for you, I do not concern myself with the opinions of humans."

I want to scream, cry, vomit, hack off his fucking wings and throw them to the hellhounds, but I feel so defeated. "Is there truly any way I can save Lucas? Or even go home?"

"Well, you did make it this far, so I guess your lover actually found his way down."

"What are you talking about? You just said those people weren't Lucas!"

"Hmm. I guess the last one actually was. Oops." He laughs with nothing but hate and corruption in his tone. "Want to know something interesting about all of this? You've been surprisingly consistent. Every single time, you followed him down that tunnel without hesitation. You never once didn't believe he was truly there. Poetic, no?"

I clench my jaw. A storm surges in my veins, thunderous clouds of rage and grief clapping through my body, shaking my entire being. With a strength likely only possible in this place of misery, I break away from the creatures holding me down, then grab one of their spears and spin as I let out a guttural scream. The sharp blade slices through bellies and throats, spilling blood across the brick floor, seeping into the cracks; it will stain.

Maron looks upon the scene with an amused glint in his eye – even when all his minions are disposed of and I turn my attention to him. But I drop the spear. I want to feel the crunch under my fingers when I press on his windpipe. And I do. He does not struggle, does not oppose.

He only laughs.

"I guess you don't want to find him, then?"

My fingers loosen slightly, not that they seemed to be having any effect. "Tell me," I grit out.

His eyes flick to the side, and I follow where they lead. A door.

"Where does it go?" I ask.

He smiles. "To the end."

"Can I still save him?"

"Perhaps."

"What must I do?"

He straightens in his seat, ruffles his wings, rubs his thumb across his lips. "One more bargain."

"How can I even trust you?"

"Oh, you definitely can't."

After everything I've been through to get here, I don't want to waste it. Especially now knowing I have attempted this journey hundreds, if not thousands, of times. I can't leave Lucas here. Against any instinct, any voice that tells me to move on, accept what is and what isn't, I'm led by my heart. My heart that pines only for Lucas.

"What's the bargain?"

He stands from his chair and reaches out to me. His fingers weave through the pendant around my throat, then he snatches it away, severing the chain links, which tumble to the floor with a gentle *tinkle*.

"Once you go through the door, follow the way till the end. There, you'll find a pool. The pool of life. Toss this pendant in there, and your love will rise."

I frown. "What has the pendant got to do with Lucas?"

He holds the pendant up to the light, a look of admiration on his face. Then he scoffs. "Humans. So lacking in knowledge. So selfish. If you knew *anything* about this world, took even a moment to learn, you'd know that this is not merely a pendant. It holds *life*. In this case, your lover's. His very soul is held in this pendant. The moment you went through that tunnel after him, his soul transferred into the pendant. He's been with you the whole time."

No.

His smell. His voice. That's why he always felt so near yet so far. He was here all along.

"You have no heart," I whisper, defeated.

His loud laugh booms through the tower, rattling the crumbling walls. "What need do I have of a *heart*?"

He is evil incarnate. He finds joy only in torment and suffering. And the worst thing is there is no reason for it. This is who he is. His role in this world. And there is absolutely nothing I can do about it. I am at his mercy, and I don't think he has any to give.

"I've provided you with your out," he says, almost congratulating himself. "Take it."

"You haven't yet told me what the bargain is."

"Oh, I'd almost forgotten!" he says as he claps his hands together. "Once your lover has been… *revived*, your memory of each other shall fade. To save him, that is the sacrifice."

"Why can there be no happy ending?" I ask. "We'll leave this place, never to return, never to make another bargain."

"I *am* giving you a happy ending." He stands from his throne, forcing me to back up. "Neither of you will remember this place, what led you here. The pain of your love. I'm doing you a favour, really."

"A favour?" I scoff. I'm done with this now. Done with him. Done with this place. If this my final barrier, the only way to save him, I'll do it. I hold out my hand for the pendant.

"You accept?" Maron asks as he reaches out his hand and unravels his fingers to reveal the pendant.

I snatch it out of his hand and stomp towards the door. As I put my hand on the metal handle, I say, "I accept," without looking back.

"See you soon, Riley," he replies.

I spin to face him, to ask what he means, but he's already gone. So I open the door and head to my final destination.

6

THE PENDANT BORES INTO MY HAND AS I tightly clutch it in a fist against my heart.

He's been with me the whole time, and I had no idea. While there's no way I could have known, I feel an overriding sense of guilt. If I did know, would I have been able to do anything about it?

I'm not a magical being; this type of thing is far beyond my knowledge. But isn't that what Maron relied on? Me being a naïve little human so he could play his twisted games.

I wish the coalition between realms had never come to pass. The world is a darker, more cruel place for it.

The hallway comes to an end and opens out into a room of blue stone. In the centre, a pool bordered by small rocks is embedded in the ground, the water only ankle-deep. It ripples in an odd way, in a manner that is enchanting and haunting. Beneath the surface, I'm sure I see moments of skeletal faces crying out before they are quickly swept away. It gives me pause; what if these are trapped souls? Souls who were left behind? Maron said Lucas will rise, but what does it truly mean?

I hold my arm out straight, willing to let the pendant fall into the pool, to trust that this really is the final hurdle, but my fingers won't uncurl. A life without Lucas, without knowing him, feels unbearable. I've come so far to find him, how can I just let him go entirely? Don't we deserve a second chance?

But I'm fighting the inevitable. I'm alone here. And the only other thing I can do is sit here for an eternity, clinging on to a love that needs to be let go. Doing anything to save him truly means anything, no matter the cost, no matter the sacrifice.

So for the final time, I let my heart lead me and open my hand and let the pendant fall into the pool.

The water immediately begins to bubble violently, and soon, a figure emerges.

He is beautiful. The most beautiful I've ever seen him. The ghostly white glow is gone, instead replaced by an invigorating golden aura.

"Riley?" he says as our eyes meet.

"Lucas!" I cry and scramble over the pool's rock border to fall into his arms. "I didn't think I'd see you again." Tears stream down my face.

"I… where are we?" he asks.

I pull back and hold his hands, stare into the depths of his ice-blue eyes. "We're in the underworld, hovering between life and death."

"We're dead?" he asks as his eyes frantically roam my body.

"No, not anymore. It's a long story. Can we just be here for a moment, together?" I press a hand to his face, and he smiles down at me.

"Of course, my love," he says as he pulls me into him and nuzzles into my hair. After a few moments of silent bliss, he asks, "How... how did it happen?"

"It doesn't matter," I say. Because it doesn't. All that matters is now. And I won't tell him this is the end. I want to just stay in this moment for as long as we can.

But he pulls back, holds my face gently in his hands. "Tell me," he says.

My stomach sinks to the floor. I don't want our last moments to be this. To feel the pain and heartbreak of knowing how we got here and what the consequences are. He'll forget all of this when he returns to life; why should these last moments be so hard? But I can't ignore that pleading look in his eyes. It's his life too, and denying him the truth feels like more hurt. So I take a deep breath, and I tell him everything. The bargain he made. The bargain I made. The endless journeys to save him. The final journey. And... the cost.

He sinks in my arms at the final revelation. Says "No" over and over until he's breathless from tears, gulping from the exhaustion of grief.

"A life without you is no life at all," he cries.

I cry with him. "Maybe... maybe we'll find each other again."

And I truly hope we do. We do deserve another chance. He can change. *I* can change.

He finally catches his breath. "Yes. Yes, I'll find you again, my love. In any life. In the darkest depths of the ocean, in the endless stars, I will find you."

He holds me so close and so tight I hope we might merge into one, souls bound together for an eternity. We stay in each other's arms, interrupted only for tender kisses and words of love. But it's not long enough. Will never be long enough.

Soon, he feels lighter in my arms. He's still here, still whole, but I know he's leaving. Can feel it in my core. And he feels it too.

"Riley, what's happening?" he asks. "I feel... strange."

I smile sadly up at him. "We're going home."

"No," he protests and clutches my hands. "It's too soon!"

"It will always be too soon. But you need to go now, Lucas. The world of the living is calling for you. Go, Lucas. Live."

"Not without you."

"I love you, Lucas. Truly and wholly."

He begins to fade, gold glitter slowly replacing his hands and crawling up his arms. "I love you," he whispers as he relents.

"Will you sing to me before we go?" I ask.

Finally, a smile from him. He rests his forehead against mine, for one last song. The words come out as almost a whisper, but they are the most tender and loving words I've ever heard, and will ever hear again.

Then he's gone. He simply fades away, only glitters of gold where he was mere seconds ago. And I'm alone once more.

Where do I go from here? Do I just wait to disappear too?

The answer comes a moment later. Behind the pool of life, the back wall rises up, revealing the banks of a river. A ferryman awaits me.

There is nothing left for me here now, so without hesitation, I step onto his boat, and we begin our journey back to the land of the living.

Rain falls fast and hard, bouncing off the concrete and back into my face. I'm on my knees in an alleyway... but I don't know why.

Where the hell am I?

I stand up and walk to the end of the alley and appear on a main road. The local hospital is to my right. Why am I here of all places? I quickly inspect my body, finding no wounds. Why can't I remember why I'm here? Maybe that's it – I'm having trouble with my memory.

I feel fine in myself, though. And I'm not fond of the idea of sitting in A&E for hours. So I turn around and head home.

The rain starts to let up a little, and I make quick work of the journey, turning onto my street within ten minutes. But hunger pangs suddenly rip through my stomach. When was the last time I ate? Another thing I don't remember.

Instead of heading straight home, I cross the road and make my way to my favourite sandwich place nearby. The loud, robotic *ding dong* as I open the door feels like a punch to the head. Is it always that loud?

It's empty bar the two workers and one person who came in right behind me. Despite the smell of warm bread in the air, another scent permeates the space. It's sweet and fruity, and I suddenly feel a longing ache in my chest. But I disregard it, and the workers quickly make up my sandwich, with me adding "Extra pickles, please" before they close it up.

"Ah, finally, a woman with taste," says a voice behind me.

I spin and come face to face with a man – a beautiful man – with curly blonde locks, icy-blue eyes, and a wide, mischievous smile. I can't help but smile back.

The pull towards him is strong, and I immediately want to know him. There is a feeling deep down in my core that if I do, I'll never look back. Somehow, I already know he'll break my heart.

"Hi, I'm Riley," I say, extending my hand.

If it's possible, he smiles even wider. "Riley. My name is Lucas."

BOUND BY FLESH

LOUISE HEYWOOD

1

TIME IS A TRICKY THING TO KEEP TRACK of, especially with the fickle nature of those who like to determine such things as dates and measurements. For the purpose of a focal point in your history, this tale began around the year 1280$_{AD}$ in a world that now only exists in myth and legend – the veiled realm. It was not always named so; its true name has been lost, consumed, as with anything that faces the Mirror Slumber.

Bael, a powerful but rather lonesome man, had a talent for creating objects that could withstand the chaotic power of magic. He sold his talents across the land, with many coming far and wide to procure objects of great power. Bael hoped he would meet one whom he could love, but his striking appearance and fiery temper further stretched that loneliness. Bael had no problem attracting women to his side, but his volatile emotions were tied to his nature.

A vampiric type of being; his skin would transform to the colour of soot, and his eyes were of fire.

So, Bael remained alone for a time.

He liked to wander the wilderness of his land, and on one particular night, when the moon eclipsed the sun and the nym flies floated in the air, Bael heard something peculiar. Distant voices. There was no rhyme or reason for the voices in the woodland, which no one but Bael and the wildlife that slumbered in their burrows liked to occupy. Two trees almost touching formed a makeshift gateway between them, and this is where the voices came from.

On the date of October three and one, beneath the low light of the eclipse, Bael caught the shimmer of the veil between worlds and was able to watch what transpired beyond, into a world that had never before existed to him. When the night was over, the image and voices before him vanished. Bael returned each night thereafter but found no such thing again. But Bael was the powerful maker of objects. He created a mirror of enormous proportions in a gleaming silver frame with thick, curling legs to hold its weight and imbued its pane with the power to see the world beyond.

There are rules to magic, of course. Magic is intrinsically connected to our worlds, but most cannot see it or have the ability to tap into it. Because Bael created a mirror and captured magic into its depths, the mirror tethered its magic to the reflections of the mundane mirrors of the world Bael wanted to watch. And that is what Bael did.

In the gateway of the trees, he watched the world without magic, without creatures, only beings that he later learned were called humans. Though he didn't know it, he watched the world of the Sublunary – the human world.

Bael found himself visiting the same place over and over, and one night, a woman looked upon her own mirror with surprise when she saw Bael looking back at her. She did not run, cower, or hide from Bael. Instead, a relationship kindled between the two with Bael visiting every night. Though Bael could not find a way to step through into her world, he felt that loneliness starting to ebb away with each conversation they had. They told each other of their lives and worlds. Love blossomed, and Bael tried with all that he knew to pierce through the veil that separated him from his love. Weeks turned into months, months turned into years, until his love beyond the mirror grew impatient and wearisome. Soon, Bael would find her gone from her mirror when he visited, other times, the mirror would be covered. Then came the final blow: Bael heard his love with someone else. Night after night, he would visit, see the cover over the mirror, and listen to them together.

Bael's hurt and devastation turned into malice and rage, and he poured all of his hatred into the fist that he smashed into the pane of his magic mirror. But his fist did not connect, it went through as though the very glass was both fluid and mist. Someone screamed from the other side. Bael quickly removed his hand, understanding what he had just accomplished. He stepped through the pane of his mirror, fully formed in the world beyond. He tore the sheet away that his love had used to conceal her new love and ripped them both from the Sublunary world and into his domain. He ignored their pleas and screams of terror as he dragged them to his workshop – the place where he would no longer create magical objects, but now a new canvas to pour all of his malice and power into the mirror.

After Bael had brought the mirror back to his workshop, he strung his love and her new love to the wall either side of the mirror, naked and shivering, whilst he pondered on how to exact his revenge. The pane of the mirror started to sputter and hiss with each turning cog that twisted Bael's mood into a dark spin. From his time watching them, he had seen how disdainfully fickle humans could be. No wonder his love had so easily cut him away.

Once Bael realised that his anger and hatred fed the power of the mirror, he knew what he would do to make them, and all humans, pay. Bael would extract their transgression from the very skin they allowed to burn in the lust of their false union.

First, Bael peeled away the skin of the man his love had chosen over him. The blood-spluttered screams and gurgles were music to Bael's ears as, piece by piece, he took layers and then inscribed the surface of them over and over with the curse that, in his blind rage, he intended to be the downfall of any human who dared to transgress. His love watched on, screaming in horror until her voice gave out.

She wept until her tears dried up. His love tried to shut her eyes so they could see no more of the horrific scene playing out, but Bael forced her lids open.

"You're next," Bael hissed at her. His love's eyes remained wide and fixed in terror until Bael repeated the same process upon her body. Her screams were loud and piercing until they died away, drowned beneath the wet bubbles of the death rattle song playing along her vocal cords. Bael heaved with triumph, towering over their bodies now lying at his feet in a morbid lump of muscle, bone, and sinew.

The pane of the mirror began to hiss and spit in anticipation of the food Bael was about to feed it. So, he gathered the carcasses and threw them at the pane. Not knowing quite what would happen, and half expecting the bodies to fall in a wet heap on the floor, Bael was joyous when the mirror absorbed them in a cloud of black fog. Bael knew then that the mirror must be fed. He gathered the cursed skin peels from his love and her man, feeding each one into the mirror. This caused the aura of the mirror to alter; it darkened and manifested a presence of the malevolent kind.

Once the last piece of skin had been absorbed, the cursed inscription upon them appeared, etched around the oval frame of the mirror.

"Malleable is my face,
everchanging but firm in place,
for this is a slow race,
to the mercy of my embrace.

Into the guise of my veil,
your pallor doomed to pale,
as your blood begins to ebb and fail,
you must now listen to my tale.

Resting in mist and shadows,
far from light and meadows,
clutched in metal throes,
waiting for cracks in windows.

Receive my poison that seeps,
drawn to your reflection that keeps,
sours, festers from the depths it leaps,
up, up, up your body, it creeps.

Oscillating your changing soul,
until this is your only role,
I scoop every drop from your bowl,
leaving your husk, a darkening hole.

Rendered stricken, you see me moving,
a curse that I have been keeping,
is free and no longer sleeping,
to devour all ripe for the eating."

Bael did not stop there. He began to blame many for his loneliness and decided to research and document everything about his world beyond the Sublunary realm. Once he was done, Bael peeled away the skin from his own body and inscribed all his knowledge bound in words of magic where they would be forever fused into the pages of his skin. Bael bound his completed tome in black leather and scratched the title in red blood magic. *Baelospel*. The spell of Bael, as Bael liked to call it.

Tale origins are often never what we expect, and this one is particularly darker than most. In his blind entitlement, fuelled by his loneliness, Bael created something so dark that would later evolve and mutate into a far greater power than he ever anticipated. From what little I could gauge of Bael, his book, and the creation of the mirror, he intended to ensnare humans deemed unworthy and allow them to be consumed by the darkness of the mirror. For his loneliness, he blamed his own kind in what we know to be the veiled realm. His trap and punishment to them was leaving the Baelospel at the mercy of the humans in the hopes that they should learn about the hidden world beyond the veil and unleash their greed and destruction upon those who shunned him. What became of Bael, the mirror, and the Baelospel remains unknown to this day.

SONG OF BRINE AND BONE

HYPATIA RHODES

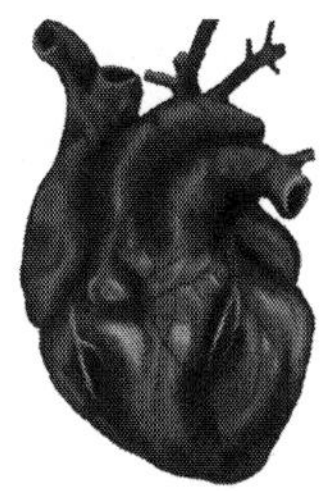

1

I DON'T REMEMBER MUCH ABOUT MY LIFE before I died. Only pure, unquenchable rage in those seconds before I was thrown overboard.

The Buddhists believe in karma. I'm not sure if the Greeks have something similar, but I do know one thing: karma's a bitch, especially when it's at the hands of me and my sisters.

There's something genuinely satisfying about sitting atop the rocks along the Sirenuse coastline, my fin in the water and the sun warming my scales, singing with my sisters. It's satisfying to watch the sailors inch closer, helpless to our allure like we were helpless to their savagery.

Their screams as their ships crunch into the rocks synchronise with our enchanting voices as our song's finale. Then there's nothing but silence. Their voices are drowned in Poseidon's icy domain the same way ours were.

This ship is like all the rest. Some sailors break their trance and abandon ship; their splashes meet with the splash of fins as my sisters drag them to their dooms. The rest are still held under our spell. Their hands hold the splintered wood as they lean over the edge and desperately search for our beautiful forms glimmering under the turquoise water, oblivious to the water now pooling around their feet.

I leap off my perch, my coppery fin propelling me through the current and shimmering like a drachma as the bluish light reflects to the surface. I reach the ship's once-magnificent hull and breach the surface with a shower of water crystals. Blackish hair spreads around my tanned shoulders like serpents spreading across the surface. I tighten my webbed fingers around the boat's edge. Already, a sailor is waiting for me.

His eyes are glazed over, but besides that, he's quite attractive. Black curls and a face rough with years at sea remind me of the men who took me all those years ago. The memory of their cruel faces makes this next part that much easier. I clutch his cheeks and guide his lips to mine, and then he and I sink into the depths as one.

He comes willingly, clamouring over the edge and slipping into my watery home by my side. His chiton ripples under the current from my powerful tail as I drag us below. Once he's fully submerged, our song releases him. His eyes widen in sheer terror, and he begins to struggle, but it's too late now. I wrap my tail around him to keep him pinned. The water churns and froths as my sisters do the same. Nefeli is closest to me, and out of the corner of my eye, I see the exact moment her victim succumbs to the water. His eyes roll back, and he goes limp in her arms.

Mine's a fighter. He thrashes against my grip even as the men around us drop like flies. I look into his eyes. They're golden brown – not unlike other men I've seen – but his are different. They're twisted with anger and something else I can't quite put my talon on. It's as if there's a fire burning within them.

He opens his mouth and screams in rage. Bubbles whip my hair back, but that's not what surprises me. It's when he inhales, sucking in water like air, that my eyes widen. He takes the opportunity to wriggle his arms free and wrap them around my throat. My body freezes at the touch.

Fortunately, Nefeli notices my struggle and hits him over the head with a rock, rendering him unconscious. I hold his limp body in my tail's grip, still frozen. He breathed underwater, just like us. Something that should be impossible, and yet this man somehow managed it. I trail my fingers along his jawline, his stubble prickling my sensitive skin. Such a curiosity.

I follow my sisters into the depths, trailing behind Nefeli's emerald tail and dark-brown curls. White pillars erupt from the sandy bottom alongside mountains of coral-encrusted rock. The flames from torches within the temple break through the dark navy blue. Then, arching up from the castle like a monolith to the gods, stand the golden gates of Elysium. Oceanus' empire – my home.

Typically, we bring the bodies to the barracks, where they are reanimated for Oceanus' army. However, my sailor isn't dead, so I take him to the only place I can think of: the brig. I meet the shield of Oceanus' power that protects the interior from the crushing depths, hardly noticing as my tail is replaced by the soft folds of my chiton and my feet slap against the black pearl floors. Once we break through the water, he's heavy, so I drag him to the cells.

By the time I make it there, I am panting and sweating. I collapse to my knees and take the time to look over the man on the cell floor. I don't usually see human men for this long uninterrupted. He's bigger than I realised. Now out of the water, his shirt is plastered to an impressively muscular chest.

"He's still out?" I look up to see Nefeli standing in the doorway. Her green eyes are narrowed, and her muscular arms are crossed.

I nod. "You hit him good."

She snorts. "He deserved it; they all do. Why haven't you told Oceanus he's here yet?"

I shrug. "Curiosity."

"You know what they say about curiosity," she chides.

I roll my eyes. I have always been too curious. Oceanus calls it my adventurous spirit. He likes that about me, some days more than others.

The man shifts and groans. Both Nefeli and I freeze.

"I'm leaving," Nefeli says. "Keep me out of your curiosities, Dariya."

Meaning, don't get her in trouble with Oceanus. I nod earnestly and turn back to the man slowly gaining consciousness. He groans, and his eyes bat open. I'm surprised again by the light in them. I'm partially convinced if I get too close they could set me ablaze. He sits up and gapes at me.

"Didn't you have fins before?"

I haven't spoken to a human since I died, so I'm taken aback. "I did."

He rubs the back of his head. I'm sure it hurts; Nefeli has a strong arm. "Why do you have feet now?"

"Why wouldn't I have feet?"

"Because you have fins."

I scowl at him. "Those are only for swimming. There's no water down here."

He snorts and rubs his face. "Because that makes sense. Where exactly is 'here'?"

"This is Oceanus' palace, the gate to Elysium."

His eyes widen, and I'm unsure if surprise or fear caused the reaction. He starts patting over his body in search of his sword, as though I would be dumb enough to let him keep it. It belongs to me now. "And why am I in Oceanus' palace?"

"Because you didn't drown with the rest." I rock forwards on my knees and place my hands on the stone bars to see him better. I thought maybe he was a unique type of ocean dweller without any telltale marks, but the more I look, the more human he appears. There are no gills, though I already checked for that. There is no sign of anything particularly remarkable about him either. He's an anomaly, and anomalies pique my interest.

What was that saying about curiosity again?

He looks nervous at my staring, but I can't help it. I forgot how attractive human men are. They are like a particularly poisonous jellyfish, beautiful but deadly to those who aren't careful. I have a hard time being careful.

"What happens now?"

I shrug. "I tell Oceanus about you."

He shifts uncomfortably. "He'll probably kill me."

"Probably."

Suddenly, he stands, his face twisting with indignation. I find myself going to my feet in response. "Why do you want me dead? Why drag my crew into the ocean?"

I cross my arms. That feeling, the important one, bubbles over any fascination I felt. It's easy to forget that they're monsters, but they quickly make their true nature clear. I bare my sharp teeth at him. "It is no less than you men deserve for all you've done."

He steps to the bars. "What are you talking about, siren? I have done nothing to you."

"You haven't? What about my sisters, cast into the ocean by your kind?"

His eyes go wide. "You hold the souls of women lost at sea."

"We hold the souls of women *murdered* at sea," I retort.

He dips his head. "I have endured much, siren, and if I know one thing, it's that a woman is a powerful force. If you have chosen my death, I likely will not leave here alive."

I step back from the cell. "Now you understand your predicament, mortal."

2

"WHY DIDN'T YOU BRING HIM TO ME immediately, Dariya?" Oceanus' voice slithers over my skin like one of his tentacles, seeping in like ink and leaving goosebumps in its wake.

He is slung casually over his throne of coral, wearing a deep-purple chiton covered in a black cloak. His black pearl crown glints from its place on his slicked, bluish hair. His tentacles trail absently through the sea fans and barnacles at his arms and back. He has an entertained grin on his face, but he's irritated. I can tell from the gleam in his ultraviolet eyes as he looks down on me.

I try to keep the fear out of my voice. Oceanus is a titan and my king, holding nearly as much power as Poseidon himself over the underwater realm, a position he would like to strengthen. I owe him everything. He took me in when the gods abandoned me and allowed me to seek vengeance against those who caused me pain. At least, that's what I keep reminding myself as I look to the floor under his crushing gaze. "I was... curious, my lord. He breathed underwater; I didn't know any mortal could do that."

"You and your curiosities. Come here, darling." He beckons me forwards with one of his ultraviolet tentacles.

I comply and sit on his lap. It's not a position I am unaccustomed to. We all take turns with the king when it pleases him. It made me uncomfortable for a time, but he is a considerate lover. Not like when I was alive. Out of anyone, the man who saved me and gave my death purpose is the only one I would ever want to be intimate with.

"If you keep things from me again, you will be punished. Do you understand?" He purrs in my ear, even as his hand wraps around me and pulls me to his front.

"I understand. I'm sorry, my lord," I whisper.

"Don't be sorry. It is in your nature, and you know how much I love your adventurous spirit, little angelfish."

One of his tentacles trails to the hem of my dress. He looks from me to the undead soldiers standing guard. "Bring him in."

His tentacle works between my legs. My cheeks heat in response. We've had sex in public before – after all, Oceanus' throne is one of his favourite locations – but the mortal seeing me like this makes me nervous.

He's brought in by two undead guards, his hands tied at his back. I try to take him in, but the moment he enters the room, Oceanus plunges into me. I moan sharply before biting my lip to stifle the noise. I know Oceanus' game. He's intimidating the potential threat while punishing me for my 'adventurous spirit'.

The man's eyes meet mine, and his jaw hardens. I let my gaze fall to the side, tucking my head into Oceanus' shoulder. I don't want to see him like this. One of Oceanus' tentacles works its way into the seam of my dress and twists my nipple. God, it feels good. I try to stifle my moan, then catch myself. It's wrong that I feel embarrassed by this. This man won't be alive much longer anyway. Why do I care what he thinks?

"What's your name, sailor?" Oceanus kisses my head as he speaks, though I know his eyes never leave the mortal.

"Theseus, my lord."

For a moment, Oceanus pauses. It's brief, but when his tentacle stops moving inside me, I feel it. He's caught something – a weakness he can exploit.

"Welcome to my palace, son of Poseidon."

Now, I'm the one stiffening under his grip, even as he continues plunging into me. No wonder he could breathe underwater. I can practically feel Oceanus' excitement. He would do anything to get under the skin of the gods, especially the one sharing his domain. Theseus may have proved to be his golden ticket, but I'm just not sure how yet.

Why do I care? I hope Oceanus kills him, just like all the rest. I let my eyes roll back at the girth of Oceanus' tentacle and press kisses to his neck. He hums at the contact but keeps his eyes forwards.

"Thank you, my lord. Though, I'll be honest, I hope to not overstay my welcome."

Oceanus laughs at that. Theseus is playing his game, and he does love his games. "My little Dariya here is quite beautiful, isn't she? That cinnamon skin almost tastes as good as it looks." He bites down on my neck and makes me moan. "That hair..." His hands trail upwards until he's fisting my black curls, forcing my head up.

Now I'm forced to watch Theseus' reaction to us. He averts his gaze from me, his jaw working. "Yes, she is."

"My sirens are quite the temptresses. They must be to get sailors like you to die for them." Oceanus drags my head farther back and looks into my eyes, a smirk spreading across his face. "But they are vicious little creatures. They run on vengeance. Do you want the sailor dead, angelfish?"

He's demanding me to prove my allegiance, and I wouldn't do anything to undermine him. "Yes, my lord."

He grins. Without breaking eye contact, he grabs the sash of my dress and tugs it open. I resist the urge to cover myself, not that I have the opportunity to before his tentacles descend upon me. Their grip makes it nearly impossible to think of anything else.

"Good girl," he purrs, soft enough that only I hear.

Theseus is openly staring now. His entire body is tense as he responds. "They are quite the warriors, my lord."

I manage to make eye contact with him for an instant, my mouth gaping. Oceanus would never call us warriors. Oceanus' eyes narrow. Before I can really react, he takes after me with renewed vigour. His tentacles pin my legs open, and he ravages me. The bumps on the underside of his tentacles rub against my insides in a way that builds decadent friction. I can't help it; my eyes roll back, and I moan.

"They are quite something," Oceanus says distractedly.

Then he slithers his tongue over my ear, the ridges of his suction cups making me shiver. "Come, angelfish, let him hear how pretty you sing."

He pinches my nipples, and I have no choice but to obey. My voice sings out into the silence, Oceanus panting into my ear as he drives me there and back again. One final shudder, and I collapse against his chest.

"Good girl. Now, get up." Oceanus' voice is soft but sharp.

Keeping my eyes down and away from my audience, I grab my chiton from where it fell and shrug it back on.

Oceanus turns his attention to Theseus, as though he hadn't just splayed me open for the world to see. "You will stay here until I decide what to do with you."

He glances my way for a breath, his eyes narrowing. "Dariya will see to you in the meantime."

Now I understand. My cheeks heat in humiliation. My king is generous, but he is cruel when angered. I just hadn't realised how upset he was with me. I shouldn't be embarrassed, but I am. I finish wrapping my dress before stepping off the dais.

"Show him to one of the guest rooms, angelfish. No murder attempts." Oceanus winks at me, and I nod before curtsying to him.

I don't make eye contact with Theseus or say anything as I lead him from the throne room. We enter a hallway bordered by coral-encrusted pillars. On the other side, the watery depths are held back only by the invisible force of Oceanus' might.

Along the path are several alcoves leading to gardens of remarkable beauty. Clusters of sea fans, kelp forests, and water lilies alike. I had been enamoured by this place once, but one's cage gets boring after enduring it for so long. Theseus has no such reservations, however. I catch him pausing to gape at fountains and sculptures, though his eyes continually return to me. His staring makes my skin feel tight.

"What, mortal?"

"Do you enjoy being with the titan?"

I pause at the entrance of an alcove and finally dare to look at him. His eyes hold that same fire, now twinged with curiosity and something else I can't quite place. I try not to let the look pique my interest and instead scowl at him. "What do you mean by that?"

"I mean, Dariya, do you enjoy being put on display with his tentacles all over you?" He steps towards me, and I step back into the alcove. I try not to react to how he says my name, but goosebumps spread up my arms.

His questions and demeanour confuse me. "He is my king. He gave me a second chance to seek retribution. I am loyal to him and do as he asks."

Theseus steps in again, and I find myself pinned between a pillar and his massive body. He smells different than anything found in my watery world. The scent tugs on some distant memory, and I must resist the urge to shove my nose into his chest.

Damn curiosity.

He dips to me, his fiery eyes making me freeze. "You aren't answering the question," he says.

He's a sailor, just like the others, and I must hate him. He's also trapping me, a feeling I should not enjoy. I shove him back and twist into the central space of the alcove. The floor is covered in spongy macro algae, and a fountain with a siren sits in the centre. In the clear pools below is a field of bright anemones. Clownfish dart in between their tendrils as I approach.

"I don't know how to answer your question." My voice is soft as I respond, and that tone makes me wince. I am not weak or unsure. I spin to him. "What game are you playing, mortal?"

He laughs. "Just trying to make sure you're okay. You should enjoy it when a man touches you."

I frown. Oceanus feels good, but do I enjoy it? I'm not really sure. I'd never thought about it. It was never about joy; it was about loyalty. Joy was about as irrelevant as the sun down here.

"Let me show you to your room, mortal."

"You should call me Theseus, Dariya."

I grind my teeth but say nothing in response.

We walk in silence for a while more. Other citizens walk by, casting suspicious stares our way, but I walk by without giving them much notice. I'm used to their stares. Sirens have always been considered less than. Second-hand humans – not true oceanic inhabitants.

I take Theseus to the palace wing kept for Oceanus' guests. Armed guards are already stationed outside a door, so I lead him there. The room is immaculate, unlike my own. Oceanus aims to impress or fool, depending on the guest.

"How long am I stuck down here, Dariya?"

He needs to stop saying my name. I don't like how it makes my breath catch. "Until Oceanus releases you."

"You mean until he kills me." I say nothing, and he sighs. "It's so unfortunate. I don't do well trapped like this, you know. I am an adventurous spirit."

I am halfway to the door but turn around. I hope he can't interpret my expression, but based on his smirk, he does.

"Well, escort, is there much to see here for an adventurer like me?"

This is what men are good at – they tempt women like me. I know better, yet I find myself curious to see where this goes. Oceanus told me to see to him; I would merely do what he asked. "I can show you my favourite spot on the surface tomorrow, if you like."

He blinks in surprise; apparently, he didn't think I would be so easily convinced. I shouldn't be. "Are you not worried about me escaping?"

I smile softly. "You can't escape."

3

AFTER BREAKFAST, I LEAD THESEUS TO the halls. Fortunately, it is easy to swim from Oceanus' palace; one just has to push through the invisible forces holding back the water. Theseus strips his chiton and places it in a neat pile near a pillar, leaving him naked save for his sandals. I can't help but stare. I follow the line of his chest and torso, seeming to have been carved by Pheidias himself. His torso ends in a beautiful V that leads to his remarkable cock. I blush at the sight. Citizens of the court swim naked all the time, but they also don't look like *that.* Men that beautiful should remain clothed for the sake of a person's sanity.

"You're welcome to touch," he says with a wink.

My cheeks burn, and I immediately turn away from him. Before he can say another word, I step into the icy depths. The benefit of being a siren is that I don't need to disrobe before entering. My dress melts into my body, replaced by my mighty tail. Its black stripes ripple through the water as it thrusts. It's like returning to my own skin, the feeling of that tail propelling me through the water.

To Theseus' credit, he doesn't hesitate before leaping in after me. He cuts through the water with the agility only the son of a sea god could have, though I still loop back several times so he can keep up.

I lead him along the bottom. It's my favourite way to travel, enjoying the bright corals and the company of the reef fish to the abyss of blue above. I grab Theseus' wrist to stop him in front of my favourite fish in this area – a pair of nesting clowns. I wiggle my finger in front of the female, who swirls around my hand before nipping me. I visit them enough for her to know I'm not a serious threat, but she's still vicious, just like my sisters.

She lunges at Theseus, biting his knuckles where I hold his hand. I can't help but laugh at his incredulous expression before tugging him along.

The ocean floor slopes sharply upward, and before long, we reach the stone pillars that mark the spot. I wait for Theseus to catch up then guide him upwards. The water warms and brightens as we approach the sun-drenched surface until we finally break through.

We're still surrounded by water as far as the eye can see, but a small cluster of rocks jut out of the water in front of us. The central one – the largest – even holds a small lotus tree. It's heavy with fruit in late summer and has a sweet aroma. I grip the ledge and heave myself onto the rock.

Theseus joins me a moment later. He shakes his hair and splatters water over me, then lays a muscular arm over his knee, thankfully blocking the view of his distracting cock. Those honey-brown eyes glimmer, and he tweaks his head to make his dark curls shift and catch in the beating sun. A dimple pops with his infuriating smirk. "This is an adventure to you?"

"This is as far as I can go from the palace." I lie back, the lotus bush shading my face. I grab one of the ripe berries, slicing it in half with my sharp teeth.

His eyebrows furrow. He pops a berry in his mouth and lies back beside me. "You're trapped here? That's unfortunate."

I splash my tail, showering us in droplets that catch the light like crystals. "That's the deal. I can seek retribution, but I belong to Oceanus."

"Is it worth it?"

"That's a strange question," I answer.

He hums thoughtfully. "Do you mind if I ask what happened?"

I flick my tail once more. Before answering, I grab another handful of berries from a low-hanging branch and bite into one, tearing into the soft flesh. "I lived in a small town on the coast of Persia. After the war, a group of soldiers sailed back to Greece. They stayed with my family and invited me to go with them."

I finish off my berry before continuing, though I can feel Theseus' gaze burning into me.

"They attacked me then threw me overboard right before they reached the coast. Couldn't have their wives see me." I laughed, the sound broken and harsh. Even with decades to numb the pain, it still felt as genuine and raw as a blistering wound. To be hurt by someone who had shown kindness, who I'd trusted.

Theseus shifts to his side, resting his head on his hand. I try not to pay attention to the very full view of his body from this angle. "I'm truly sorry, Dariya. Men can be monsters."

His sympathy makes my anger bubble. There's humility in lying beside this man, admitting my hurt and failures. It's too revealing, and I don't like it. I flip over to stare back at him, my teeth bared. "Men *are* monsters. Only now, I'm a monster too."

He reaches out and brushes a hand down my cheek. The touch makes me stiffen, and I watch him warily. He sighs and pulls his hand back. "Can I tell you a story?"

I say nothing, and he takes this as agreement. "Once, I was sent to rescue a group of kids from a mighty beast in the centre of a deadly maze. Though I feigned confidence, I had no idea what I was doing. I met an incredibly bright girl along the way. She helped me escape the great maze and saved my life when the beast knocked my sword from my hand. You remind me of her."

He looks over me with sadness. “I have met many mighty women in my time, but she will always hold a place in my heart. Now you will too, brave siren warrior Dariya.”

“What happened to her?” I ask.

He looks away then, and I can’t help but notice the flinch. “I didn’t deserve her, so I set her free from a life at my side.”

Before I can tell myself it’s a bad idea, I reach out and touch the well of his eye. It’s damp and warm, though it doesn’t light me on fire as I initially expected. Where is that sadness coming from? I could ask, but I doubt he would be forthcoming. Instead, I go a different route. “Can you tell me more stories?”

His smile returns, and I am transported into the world of his adventures. I’m enraptured by each one – his mighty defeat of a centaur, his capture of a great bull to win his father’s heart, even his conquering of the Six Labours. I’m drawn to him like an anchovy to an anglerfish, and now I understand why. I always desired his life of adventure, even more than vengeance.

Through each story, he discusses the ‘mighty women’ who helped, or hurt, him along the way.

“The strongest opponents I ever faced were the Furies. They had monster-like tails that cut at the flesh and leathery wings they’d use to get the upper hand. They guarded the underworld, and in the end, they defeated me.”

I munch on a berry, visions of monster women just as vicious as my sisters flying along the river Styx dancing in my mind. "Why were you in the underworld?"

The silence between us is deafening. I look him over, and though he still lies with his arm behind his head in a picture of relaxation, I can see the tension in his jaw and darkness in his eyes. "I was young and stupid. My best friend told me the goddess Persephone loved him, and they could be together if only he took her from the claws of Hades."

His eyes close. "I should've known something wasn't right, but I was blinded by my friend's love. So much so that I refused to see what was right in front of me – what he was trying to do to her. The Furies came after us to save Persephone. They killed my friend and chained me in the underworld to suffer for an eternity."

He releases a breath, and those eyes reopen. "Persephone chose to release me. She claimed I had paid my penance and learned the error of my ways. I'm still not sure she made the right choice, but I've spent the rest of my life trying to repay her."

I stare at him with wide eyes. Kidnapping women was not uncommon, as proven by the number of sisters I have. Yet, he seems truly bothered by his actions. If Persephone had released him, it would have likely been because she had seen the same thing I had: regret. I let my fingers brush over his arm in some semblance of comfort. "I bet Persephone is glad she let you go."

He says nothing in response. Silence stretches between us for a while, then Theseus finally speaks. "Did you travel much?"

I understand. Talking about the darkness within only makes it hurt more. I shake my head. "We didn't have much money, and then there was the war. That ship was my chance, but you know how that went."

Another bout of silence, then, "What if you travelled with me?"

I sit up and gaze at him. "What?"

He follows my lead, sitting up and looking at me in earnest. "If I ever escape here, I mean. You could come with me. We could see what this world has to offer."

"You would bring me along?"

He nods. "You don't have to say yes, I understand if you don't, but I would be a happy man if you did. Maybe I could repay some of my mistakes by helping you."

For decades, I've felt adrift at sea, clutching to every meagre piece of flotsam that swirls by while I slowly drown. Theseus has thrown me a lifeline. Before I know what I'm doing, I wrap my arms around him and press my lips to his.

At first, Theseus is frozen with shock, but his body quickly moves to respond to mine. He grabs my hips and tugs me to his front, and the instant my tail leaves the water, my legs and dress return. His lips are gentle but demanding against mine, and I feel myself sinking into the taste of saltwater, lotus berries, and him. The only emotions I feel this strongly anymore are anger and desperation, but this is neither. I feel like my soul is full of joy, making my chest tight.

Theseus must feel it too, because he hums happily against my lips. He lies back against the stone and pulls me on top of him, his arms rubbing up and down my sides. Every point of contact is like a jellyfish tendril sending bolts of electricity through me. Goosebumps rise on my arms as his tongue swirls with mine. I twist my fingers into those beautiful curls, still wet from the swim, and relish in their softness.

I gasp and sit up, choosing to ignore what presses between my legs as I straddle him. I stare at him with wide eyes. "What was that?"

He gives a genuine, dimple-popping smile, and I don't think I've ever seen anything more beautiful. "You kissed me."

His hand rubs up my thigh, and all I can focus on is that touch – the warmth of his mortal life against the cold I am so accustomed to. I want to sink into it and forget everything else, but then he says, "Do you enjoy this, Dariya?"

"I'm... not sure." Do I enjoy this? I forget what the emotion feels like.

"We can stop if you aren't sure."

I shake my head. If there's one thing I'm sure of, it's that I definitely want to keep kissing him. His eyes spark with that heat I can't help but lose myself in, and then I descend upon him.

At first, he's gentle, his lips learning the movement of mine and his hands exploring my curves, but that is burned away by his heat. His hand buries into my curls, and his other arm wraps around my hips. He's caging me to him, but I've never felt more free.

I know what to do; I've just never wanted to until now. I reach my palm between us and grab his cock, pumping once. He's already hard, but now he's squirming under the touch. "Gods, yes, Dariya."

I grin against his lips, then slide him home.

I inch farther onto him until he's buried to the hilt. Our eyes meet, and I am sucked into his energy, his *life.* I feel full and warm in a way I never have, and I love it. I'm… enjoying it. He tightens on my hips and rises to meet me in a way that has my fingers curling, then he holds me to the spot.

He groans. "Fuck, you feel so good."

One hand holds me steady, but my other trails over his chest. I want to feel every inch of him. "I love this."

He chuckles distractedly. "You mean, you're enjoying this?"

As he says it, he begins to pump into me at a steady, languorous pace. I moan when he buries himself in me, pinning us together like we're one. My words come out in whimpers. "Yes, Theseus, yes."

He freezes. "Say my name again, just like that."

It takes me a moment to understand, but then I lean down and brush my lips over the shell of his ear. "Fuck me, Theseus."

Those fiery eyes roll back, and he moans, and I relish how my words make him come undone. I press kisses to his neck, marvelling at the steady thrum of his heart. It's everything I've ever wanted – life, vitality, and freedom incarnate in this absolute wonder of a man. I never want it to stop.

The only sounds are our breathy moans and the slap of water on the stones around us. It's mere minutes before I'm falling into bliss in his arms. My nails dig into his skin and stone alike, desperate to find purchase as my reality falls apart around me, leaving only him.

He follows me shortly after, his cock throbbing as he fills me until I'm dripping. We lie like this for what seems like a blissful eternity, but too quickly, it's over, and he's pulling out of me. He presses kisses along my jaw until he reaches my lips, then his hand cups my cheek, and it's like he's drinking my very essence.

"My miraculous Dariya, I think I could breathe you in for the rest of my life and be a happy man."

I'd let him, too, and that thought is as terrifying as it is exhilarating.

4

"WHAT DO YOU WANT, LITTLE ANGELFISH?"

It's evening, and Oceanus has retired to his chambers with several sirens. We are taught to worship that spot on his lap at the end of the day. It's a privilege to share his bed. Now the idea makes me queasy.

His eyes are half closed, and one of my sister's heads is bobbing in his lap. I try to ignore the sight as I walk up. "I was curious about your plan for Theseus, my lord."

Oceanus' eyes narrow at Theseus' name, and I realise I've made a mistake in speaking it. He coats his words when he speaks with that casual curiosity meant to hide his intent. "Why is this your concern?"

I dip my head. "I'm curious how long I will be responsible for him, sir."

His eyes soften at that, then he smirks. "I will be killing him, angelfish. He is a hero child of Poseidon, and I do think it is time to rock the boat a bit. Our armies are ready to take back our world from the gods."

"You can't do that!"

The entire room comes to a halt. The canopied bed creaks as my sisters turn to me, their eyes wide and mouths open in horror. Oceanus' eyes darken, and he stands. His chiton falls over himself as he steps over my sisters and stalks across the space between us with all the intensity of a shark that has caught the scent of blood. Even in his humanoid form, he towers above me, his titan power radiating from him like his body just can't contain it. He runs a hand through his bluish hair and stops inches from me.

"You want to run that by me again?"

I gulp, resisting the urge to cower in his shadow.

He smirks. "What did he say to you?"

My eyes go to my feet, but he yanks my chin up, forcing me to stare back at him. "He promised to take me with him," I whisper.

Oceanus' laughter cuts through my soul like a knife. "Oh, angelfish. You know I love your adventurous spirit" – he dips to me, his lips barely brushing against mine, and I'm frozen by the terrifying intensity in his eyes – "but this borders stupidity, even for you."

I feel like I've been punched in the gut. I know Oceanus can be cruel, but that cruelty has never been directed at me. I barely choke back my tears enough to say, "I want my freedom, my lord."

He bares his teeth and pulls back. "And you think this human will give it to you? Have you learned nothing? He'll take you until he gets what he wants, then he'll drop you right back where you belong." One tentacle curls up my leg and tightens down. "With me."

I shudder. My willpower is crumbling. He has a point; I'm just naïve...

No.

I square my shoulders and stare back at Oceanus, refusing to flinch from the smug anger there. "No. You're wrong."

There's a collection of gasps at Oceanus' back, and I briefly look at the horrified faces of my sisters. Nefeli is here tonight, and her eyes hold a level of fear I've never seen from her. My attention is drawn back to Oceanus. His body grows until he towers above me, his skin taking on a bluish hue and his eyes going black. His ultraviolet tentacles stretch to either side, and he bares shark-like teeth, razor sharp and ready to sink in.

"Oh, angelfish, you will regret those words."

He slaps me hard enough to send me reeling. I look up at him in horror. Never has he hit a siren. He doesn't seem bothered now as he bears down on me. I curl in on myself as he punches me over and over again. I wouldn't dare fight back against a titan; I'm not strong enough. Past the blood dripping from my nose, I see his glossy shoes as he approaches my crumpled form.

"Get out of my sight, siren. And rethink how you speak to your king."

I don't know how I manage past what is most certainly a cracked rib and broken nose, but I get to one of the alcove gardens in the hall leading to my room. My bleeding leaves a trail behind me. If I were in water, I'm sure the scavengers would have found me by now. I get to the central fountain, surrounded by pillars of water lilies, and manage to get one arm over the edge before my knees buckle.

My mind wanders in the quiet, broken only by the hiss of running water. Maybe Oceanus is right; I'm just a naïve little girl repeating the same mistakes. I fall from the arms of one man into the arms of another.

Theseus' arms are quite nice, though. They carry the warmth and life I so desperately want. They would be nice right now instead of being alone in the cold and dark. I look at the angelfish spinning through the water around my fingers, muddied with blood. Seeing their striped fins makes my heart ache. It reminds me of my misplaced trust yet again.

"Dariya?"

Theseus stands at the alcove entry, Nefeli at his shoulder. Her eyes are wide, and she keeps looking down the hall nervously. The second she makes eye contact with me, she turns and scurries away. I understand – every second she spends here, she is in danger. Yet, she risked leading Theseus to me, and for that, I am grateful. Theseus darts forwards and comes to his knees by my side.

He runs his hands over my sides and tugs me to face him. I lift a hand to my nose to staunch the bleeding as I meet his worried gaze. One hand cups my face, the touch tender – so different from what I'm used to.

"Who did this to you?"

I shake my head, the tears picking up with renewed vigour.

"Dariya, tell me."

I gulp. "Oceanus. I told him I wanted to leave with you."

Now, his eyes are burning with an entirely different emotion: anger. He grits his teeth and stands. His words come out in an unchecked snarl. "He will pay."

Then he's kissing me, the fire of his touch bringing clarity to my muddled mind.

The kiss ends as quickly and desperately as it begins, and before I can react, Theseus tears out of the room to find Oceanus. I stare after him, my hand still up as though I can still feel the fabric of his tunic.

This is all wrong. I was killed by a man, and now I am enslaved and abused by a man. Being rescued by a man won't give me my freedom. No, it just cages me with a new sentinel. I must choose differently.

I wipe my nose with the edge of my chiton and force myself to my feet. Stumbling from the alcove, I make my way to my room. It's a small dorm-style room shared with several of my sisters, although it currently sits empty. I'm grateful for that as I feel around under my mattress and find Theseus' sword.

It's heavy, but I force my arms to lift the blade and watch how it glints in the deep light of the sea. The time for asking for permission and waiting for a hero is over. It's time I save myself.

I run from the room, blade in hand.

I enter the circular throne room, only to find Oceanus and Theseus already there. They are locked together in a snarling brawl, the rest of the world holding its breath to watch their deadly dance. Theseus holds his fists up even as Oceanus holds a blade in each hand. It's hardly a fair fight, but that doesn't seem to deter Poseidon's hero. He's already bleeding from a cut on his forehead and his knuckles, yet that never-ending fire still burns in his eyes like a lighthouse in the middle of an unwieldy sea.

Oceanus swings, but Theseus dives to dodge the attack. He narrowly avoids the titan's tentacles and hurls his fist into Oceanus' chest. The move sends Oceanus stumbling backwards. Both men are too distracted with each other to notice me creep along the edge of the room. As usual, they underestimate the women in their presence.

A group of my sisters huddle on either side of Oceanus' throne. I see Nefeli among them, and we nod to each other. We don't need to say anything to understand the need for vengeance against the men who hurt us. My other sisters seem as resigned to the titan's – and my – fate as I feel. Either way, one of us won't be standing at the end of this.

Oceanus' blade manages to cut into Theseus' side. My stomach twists as blood pours from the wound like ink on paper, soaking his tunic red. Theseus crumples, but Oceanus doesn't let up. I lunge as the titan raises his sword to take the killing blow.

My muscles scream as I swing the heavy blade, but I ignore them and hack into Oceanus' neck. The blade goes halfway through before coming to a gruesome halt. I yank it back, intending to swing again, but as I do, Oceanus turns to me.

"*Siren,*" he snarls.

He steps towards me, his black eyes narrowed and fangs bared. "How dare you? You pathetic little female. I am a titan, and you are nothing but my whore, designed to kill and please. You dare attack me? I will fucking *eviscerate you.*"

I open my mouth, but someone at my back speaks before I can. "*How dare you?*"

Behind me, my sisters have stood. Their rage is palpable in the salty air. Their features have angled, and their teeth have sharpened to fangs. Though they don't have their tails, they've never looked more like sirens. Nefeli speaks, though they all step forwards.

"Nothing but whores? We are born of brine, bone, and the souls of women who seek vengeance. And we will find it against any man that underestimates us."

Oceanus stares at them, his indignation clear on his face. I take the chance to swing. This time, my blade swipes clean through, and his head goes flying. It smacks into the floor with a sickening thud, splattering blood across the black pearl finish. Then my sisters descend.

5

A TITAN CANNOT BE KILLED, BUT THEY can be torn apart. As long as the pieces are kept separate, he cannot reanimate. There are many ways to do this, but one we are surprisingly familiar with.

I stand by as my sisters' talons tear chunks of his flesh from his body, and they consume it, their hatred turning them savage. Instead of joining them, though part of me wants to, I turn to Theseus. He's crumpled on the floor, his breath shallow and ragged. I run to his side and curl him into my arms. His eyes are heavy-lidded, and those torches are mere embers, but he smiles despite his dissipating life force.

"You beat him. I should've known you didn't need saving."

I'm not smiling though. I'm about to lose the first happiness I've felt in my death. I don't want to let go. "Don't leave me, Theseus."

My free hand rubs over his chest to feel his heartbeat, and as that once-steady thrum slows and eventually stops, I press my forehead to his. Tears streaming down my cheeks, I close my eyes to pray.

I haven't prayed since my death. There was no point; if they didn't listen while I was abused and murdered, they simply wouldn't listen at all. But now I'm desperate. I let my tear-filled thoughts scream into the abyss to any god who will listen.

As the seconds tick by, I fill the silence with my screams. Where my heart once resided feels like an empty pit threatening to suck me in and swallow me whole like the depths of Tartarus.

At first, I think the shaking is my feeble body reacting to my hopeless sadness, but then it's joined by a bright teal light. I freeze in awestruck terror. A figure appears before me made of raging currents of water. His beard is a mighty cascading waterfall, his maw an estuary. His eyes are the lava pits held under the ocean's surface, held back by the endless depths but never quite let out.

I see where Theseus gets his eyes from.

I knew that Oceanus held a humanoid form for his people, but I never expected a god's raw, extraordinary, terrifying power. Poseidon is the manifestation of the seven seas, and his mighty trident is the force holding that power at bay like a dam, keeping it ready to strike.

"What has happened to my son?" His voice is the crashing of waves against a jagged shore, the caw of seagulls, and the bellow of a hurricane.

I shudder and bow my head to him. Even my sisters, blood-soaked as they are, go to their knees for the god. "Oceanus killed him, my lord."

The ocean around us shudders and groans, and then the walls protecting the palace come crashing down, and we are consumed by tonnes of water. I clutch Theseus to me desperately as the tidal wave crashes down on us. My gown disappears, only to be replaced by my tail, which I use to bat desperately against the force.

"But you have made him pay, little siren," Poseidon says. His voice rings clear as a bell, even through the raging water.

"I have, sir."

The god stills for a moment then shifts form. He descends as a man, his silvery hair and beard cascading like waves down his bare shoulders and chest. Even like this, he is magnificent. "I thank you, little siren, for your bravery. Many men do not have the honour you do."

I bow my head in gratitude. Then I feel hands touch me, and I jerk in surprise. Poseidon looks at me with gentle eyes even as he attempts to pull Theseus' body from my clutches. "In gratitude, I will give you what you so desperately desire. The sea will no longer trap you."

I don't care about any of that right now. I don't want to let him go. "What about Theseus?"

"He will journey to the domain of Hades. I'm sure my brother will be entertained to see him after his last visit."

I let out a ragged sob. His soul has left. He will no longer have that fire in his eyes or that warmth to his touch. The life force I had been drawn to would never exist again. My grip tightens. "Is there no way you can bring him back?"

"Unfortunately not, little siren. His soul has left him."

"Could you not reanimate him like Oceanus did us?" I gesture to my sisters behind me.

Poseidon pauses. "Oceanus was able to reanimate you using the drive of your vengeance. My son has no such drive."

My heart nearly cracks in two, but then… "What about the drive of his love?"

I don't mean his love for me, but rather his love of life, that unyielding fire that burned brighter in him than any mortal. One look at Poseidon's eyes, and I know he understands.

"If I do this, Dariya, he will not be able to leave. Elysium needs a ruler; as my progeny, it will be his duty."

"I don't care. I will stay with him."

There is a softness to Poseidon's eyes as he nods. Only once he does do I release Theseus. Poseidon holds him tight, and when they touch each other, the water begins to bubble with a glowing orange heat. Off in the distance, underwater volcanoes erupt in violent explosions. The cries of the native creatures echo through the churning water, making me shudder.

Then, there is only silence. Poseidon lays Theseus down, and I hold my breath while I watch that beautiful face. Then Theseus shifts, and he groans. His eyes bat open, and I gasp at their utter beauty. They still burn precisely as I remember. I feared that his light would be gone, but he wasn't fuelled by vengeance like I was. He was driven by *life*.

"Dariya, you're alright," he breathes. He pulls me tight and presses his lips to mine, and things feel right for the first time tonight.

I'm surprised by how long it takes Theseus to notice the god of the sea. He meets his eyes and says calmly, "Father."

"Theseus," Poseidon booms, "I have reanimated you to preside over the gates of Elysium. To protect and guide the souls that find their way here."

Theseus dips his head. "I am grateful for the second chance, sir."

Poseidon nods then turns his attention to me. "Dariya, I give you the freedom to walk the earth as you once did. Use your freedom well."

I shake my head. "That won't be necessary; I will stay here."

Theseus looks at me in abject horror. "You will do no such thing."

"I don't want to leave you," I argue.

He shakes his head. "I would never forgive myself if you gave up your freedom for me. I had my chance at adventure; now it's your turn."

My heart is breaking all over again. Of course, I can't have both; I don't know why I ever thought I could. My life never worked like that, so it makes sense my death wouldn't either. Reluctantly, I nod. Theseus died for my freedom – I won't dishonour that sacrifice by not taking it.

"On the solstices, the barrier between the land and sea is at its thinnest. You may re-enter on those dates, but you will be trapped forever if you are not back to the surface by the time the solstice ends. Do you understand?"

I'm hardly paying attention to Poseidon. My focus is on Theseus. I feel like he's already slipping through my fingers. Theseus, however, looks to him. "Thank you, Father."

He turns his attention back to me. "Do you hear that? I will see you on the winter solstice. It will pass before you know it."

The winter solstice... four months away. Right. I've existed for a long time, but those four months now feel like an eternity. Before I can respond, Theseus kisses me. I allow myself to sink into the contact and try not to think about how long it will be before I get to again.

"Go, Dariya. Live."

So, I do.

Epilogue

Theseus

I SIT ON THE THRONE ANXIOUSLY. MY PEOPLE stand around me with the same nervous energy, awaiting the return of their queen. The sirens stand to either side of me as my guards, but also in the place of honour for their sister's return. I know they deserve access to her as much as I do, but I wish I could spend the next day alone with the love of my life.

It's been six months since I last saw Dariya. I still cling to the memory of the last solstice, when her body was tangled around mine, and my cock was inside her. Her in my arms is the only time I feel alive anymore. Six months is a long time to feel like a shell of a person. It's worth it, though. Knowing that my love is enjoying all the world has to offer is all I need to continue enduring decade after decade of loneliness.

The door to the throne room opens, and the tide brings with it the smell of summer flowers. My beautiful Dariya walks through, the epitome of life and adventure. Her black curls swirl in the waves, and her cinnamon skin has darkened with the summer sun. Little freckles litter her cheeks, something new since she regained her freedom. My breath catches in my throat just as it does every time I see her. She is *remarkable.*

She smiles at our people but scurries across the hall to me without delay. I hold my breath until her arms wrap around me and her lips press to mine. Warmth and life flood into me through those miraculous lips. I don't care who's watching; I grab her and pull her close.

"*My Love,*" I whisper.

"I've missed you, Theseus," Dariya says breathlessly.

"Tell me about your adventures, my beautiful Dariya." I adjust her in my lap. Clearly uncomfortable with the groping, most of our people begin to disperse. Even the sirens meander off, though Nefeli gives Dariya a squeeze before disappearing.

Dariya wastes no time going into the story of her travels to the city of Minos. She wanted to see the statue they erected for me, and the thought made me blush. I settle in and allow myself to be lost in her stories until she finally says, "My next adventure is going to be my best, though."

"Where do you plan to go?"

She gives me a guileful smile. "I'm not going anywhere, Theseus."

She must see my confusion because she laughs. "I want my next adventure to be here, by your side. I want to spend the rest of our days together."

I scowl at that, even though my heart leaps at the words. "I don't want you trapped here, love."

She laughs again and shakes her head. Before she responds, she kisses me deeply. I lose myself in the sensation, just as I did all those decades ago when she pulled me from my ship. It's still the same sensation now – like wilful drowning.

"I'm choosing this, Theseus. Besides, what greater adventure is there than loving you?"

Then she silences me with her lips again, and I find myself agreeing with her. A life of love just might be my greatest adventure yet.

EVEN THE WEEDS SAY LET HER GO

SAM TRATHEN

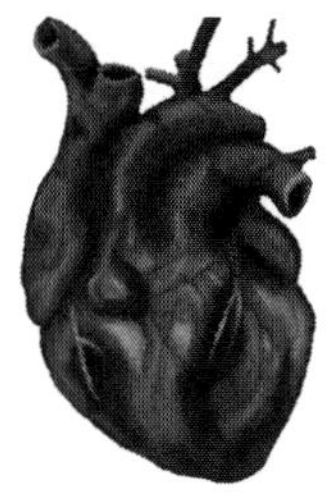

1

THE BONNY BOY IN THE WOODS WAS hunting again, Myre dreamt. Chasing wild deer through purple Wildwood – fleet as any hound, quiet as any hare. He took his kill with careful ease, shut the deer's eyes, kissed her head like a mother laying her child down for a nap, and dragged her away like a lioness with cubs to feed. Myre followed him from a distance so he wouldn't see her, wouldn't know that she was watching him.

A fey breeze picked up his muddy-brown curls and tousled them with love. The deer was laid out in the open field, where a bit of sun could peep in and give him the light he needed to butcher her properly. He took out his belt knife, a simple iron thing with a single engraving she could read: *May all your wounds be mortal.* The knife licked the deer's white belly from neck to tail and slit her open. Her bonny hunting lad turned his strange eyes her way, his narrow body twisting like a sailor's rope, making her heart swell. The heavy, copper scent of blood turned Myre's stomach, but she knew, instinctively, he wouldn't nick the intestine and release that fouler scent. She trusted him, even as her belly squirmed.

"Worry not, I'll leave you your share," he whispered to her, with a heart-wrenching smile. And then he went back to his business, using a bare hand to scrape out the offal.

And Myre? She closed her eyes and went back to her waking, walking life.

She awoke to nothing.

Well, there was a cottage, to be sure. There was food in the pantry and thick, heavy furs on the bed. She wore a nightgown made of soft red linen. No more wool. No, wool was from before. Boru did everything to make her feel comfortable now, and that included getting rid of the wool, which made her hot and itchy. *Comfort*. The linen was lightweight and comfortable, sure. But it also reminded her that she was here – far away from home, locked in.

Sick, perhaps?

No, not sick. Just missing half the time. Sometimes, more than half. Last night, she'd wandered the hundreds of miles home, back to the Hunt and the Wildwood. She'd seen her bonny hunting lad. Too sweet-faced to be her sweetheart. Not like Boru.

When she thought of Boru, her heart swelled, and she brought clean, sharp air into her lungs. But the instant her head began to spin, she had to stop it. She flopped backwards on the bed.

Feel the earth beneath your toes, her father would say. *Don't get lost. Find your body, listen to what it needs. Food, water, comfort. Then find your emotions and tend to their needs too. Small, brief steps back to Myre. Don't go all the way down the path, no matter which way it goes. Don't follow them forever and get lost. Don't get lost.*

Where was Boru?

Hunting, said one train of thought. Not just for meat, either, but the herbs that kept her head from swimming away. And more furnishings for the cottage, probably. They needed another chair, he had said last night. Was it last night? Some blankets too.

He's fed up with you and left forever, said another. She didn't hear them as voices in her head, no. They were both thoughts that came from her, from somewhere deep inside that she could not control. Myre struggled to figure out which one to listen to, just as the door opened.

"Love," said Boru, seeing her awake. "Alright?"

Tall and handsome, like a sycamore tree, was Boru. With neat dark hair, too thick to curl, and nearly black. His eyes were so deep a blue they, too, nearly seemed black. Unlike the bonny hunting lad, his face was made of strong, neat lines, his nose large and proud – he hated it, he'd told her before; she rather liked it though. There was a bristling of little hairs on his cheeks and chin, and when he stooped to kiss her just now, they scratched Myre's lips and brought her, tingling, all the way back to her body. He smelled of the rain and of the world besieged by it. A nice smell.

She smiled into his lips, narrow shoulders deflating carefully. "Yes, alright."

"Good. There's coney drying on the racks outside. And that nice fellow from the town, remember him? Uh" – he was always bad with names, and he chewed over a few possible ones while she watched his broad face work – "well anyway, he brought us some ruffage in exchange for the pelts. Reckon I can cook up a stew, keep you nice and warm."

"You know how to cook?" she asked. But a look of pain crossed over Boru's face, tightened his wide lips until they were nearly invisible. "What's wrong?"

"You ask me that every day," he said, finally closing the door behind him and walking back to sit on the bed next to her. "I'm not mad. I just wonder what else you are forgetting. And why we can't seem to make it stick." He reached forwards and took her tiny, pale, and pointed chin in the crook between his thumb and forefinger, then ran that forefinger on the bottom of her chin, tickling her neck. "Myrebird."

He always made her feel so small. Not like a little girl, but like something precious and fine. Like a dragonfly's wing. Or a fiddlehead. Too perfect and precious for this world. She curled to his touch like a cat in search of a scratch and shut her cucumber-green eyes.

"I'm trying," she whispered. "I remembered why we're here."

"Oh?"

"Surely you know!"

"Of course I know." He moved his hand to her ear and then ran his long fingers through her tangled hair. When it caught and snagged, embarrassment flared in her heart, but he merely reached over to the bedside table and withdrew the prickly brush. "Come here, little bird."

She turned her back obediently, and he knelt on the bed. When he set to brushing out the snarls with such tender care, she felt nothing. Myre was never this kind to her own hair, knew you had to struggle and fight to get it to the state it was supposed to be. Her mother's blood had blessed her with such thick, curly, copper locks – the sort that every girl in court once envied, but Myre doubted any had the patience needed to put up with them. She certainly didn't.

"But it seems the more you say things, the more they stick. So, say it, love."

"It's too warm for stew," she whispered, closing her eyes and relishing in his touch. "It's summer, for the sake of the bones beneath the hills! Time for fresh greens and cold bread, butter sitting in ice and salt. *Oh!* And huckleberry mead. Your favourite!"

If she could have seen his face, if she could see the sadness on his dark brow, she also might have seen the snowflakes melting from his hair. But she didn't.

2

THE NEXT TIME MYRE AWOKE, BORU WAS lying next to her, bare-chested and warm. In his hands was one of the old books her father had given him – one of those ones about war. About tactics. He had a mind for such things. The book's spine made an indent on his chest, pushing the thick dark hair to the side, the skin growing redder and redder. Myre sat up to get a better look at him, and he spared her a glance. The smell of damp was gone, replaced by the musk of man. Once, she'd liked that scent, especially the smell of Boru. But now, it seemed oppressive and dank. Too heavy for her little nose.

"How are you feeling?" he asked, before turning his eyes back to her.

"I dreamt of him."

"Of your bonny lad in the woods?" She nodded, and her hair, which she noticed was either still snarled or had gone back to snarling in her sleep, bounced up and down. "Hm. What's he up to now? Staying safe in these trying times, I hope?"

"Oh," she whispered, then nodded, childlike. "I think he's alright, I do. He's smart. I can see it in his eyes. And he's always got a big dog with him." She grinned. "One of your dogs. So you know he's safe."

At the door, a massive black hound thudded its tail against the wall, pleased to be acknowledged. She looked up at Myre with big brown eyes and shook her head so that the curling horns on her scalp wobbled back and forth.

"Safer than us. That's something, I guess." Boru turned the page of the book, and Myre felt a strange burst of giddiness at the noise the paper made against his skin. "But how are you, my girl?"

"I'm fine. I feel... happy. Every time I see him. I can't explain it."

Boru set the book down on its front, using his bare chest as a bookmark – a crime that would make her father shit his trews. "You love him, you do?"

"Yes."

"You want to go to him?" There was no sadness in his voice. Just a query. They both knew these words were footsteps on thin ice over rushing water.

"I wish I could. But I think I can only do it in dreams." She sat back on her knobbly legs, the red linen nightdress catching around her belly. She tugged it straight. "It's not like you." *Not like I love you, I mean*, she finished in thought, forgetting he couldn't hear those. "It's different. I want to *hold* him."

"You know we can't leave here, Myrebird," Boru whispered, and now he was taking the book up again. But instead of returning his eyes to the old, yellowed page, he untied the yellow ribbon around his wrist and set it between the pages, then set the book on the crooked bedside table. Myre had never realised when she was growing up in the Hunt's keep how lucky it was to have nice furniture. She wondered if Boru had made that little table, or if it was a relic, a leftover of the peat farmer from whom they'd purchased the cottage. Sure, Boru was never meant to be a carpenter! He was a warrior. A hunter! A protector!

"We can't just up and go, seeking your dream lad, bonny though he might be." He said it so gently, so without jealousy. A lesser man would scowl at the very mention of another. And then there was the *we*, too. Other men wouldn't consider the *we*. They would think the very mention of another, handsome love meant that *we* became *she* and *I*. But Myre thought nothing of it, either.

"I know. I have to get better."

"We have to keep you safe." Boru whispered his careful correction. He reached over and took her hands, pulling her onto his lap. "There's big things going on out there right now."

"There's a war," she whispered. He sighed and nodded. "Because of me?"

"Your sister—" No, that wasn't the right word for her. Myre saw it in his eyes. "—the queen. She wanted to sell you off to Carren. Remember?" The name of the place made Myre's belly hurt. "And take me as her champion." Jealousy. That's why there was no hint of it in Boru. The emotion now turned his stomach, made him as nauseous as she'd been, back in the beginning.

"She wanted to make of me a bride. To a king," Myre filled in, sliding her bare thighs around his hips. She felt the heat of his body beneath the blankets. "Not to you."

"If you want to go back to that, my bird, my ghost, I'll take you. In a heartbeat. But it wasn't what you wanted. Not then. Say the word, if it is now. If it's changed."

"No," she whispered. "I want to be here with you." Her voice cracked. Boru and his dark stag's eyes. He was incapable of even thinking a lie. She trusted him with every ounce of her being. And yet, why did the bonny hunting lad speak to her so? "People are going to die for this. For me."

"Yes. But not you. They're choosing to die. Your father wouldn't march them if they didn't. He'd storm the Hold all by himself if he had to."

Myre reached up and touched Boru's thin line of a mouth. He wanted to be there with him, she could see. Didn't want to be stuck here with her – but someone had to keep her safe, didn't they? She couldn't do it by herself anymore. She thought again of the tousling breeze that rustled the bonny hunting lad's hair. Thought of his fey eyes, the dappling of freckles all over his cheeks and nose.

"I don't want him to die," she whimpered.

"He's strong, your father. And fast as a fox," Boru whispered, putting their heads together. Dark blue met silvery green. "You know he's far too clever for Death to catch."

He was sleeping beneath the stars. His long, graceful fingers curled into the fur of his massive black dog. His bow and hunting knife were within arm's reach. But even as Myre tiptoed through his little camp, her bonny hunting lad didn't startle, wake, and attack. He slept on, peaceful as a baby.

Around him, even in the moonless night, she saw little red flowers growing like a wreath. Butterfly weed. That's what they were called. She recalled it like she might have recalled her name in a previous life. *Butterfly weed.*

This was as close as she'd ever gotten to him. Usually, she'd stand on a bluff or plateau and watch him and the hound – who was almost shoulder-height to him and he was far from small! – wind their way along the hills and highlands, bow in hand in case a coney managed to dart along, or a lone witch's horse stalked out to threaten them with teeth.

Myre's red linen nightdress was gone. In place of it, she wore a stark-white sheet, wound about her body as if it were a curtain rail. Her copper hair, long and freshly washed and brushed as it never was in life, lay over her shoulders like a cape. Her feet were bare, but the bracken hurt them not. She seemed to know just how to step to avoid their prickers and stickers. The hem of the shroud didn't even catch them as she approached at a near-run.

"I just want to see your face," she whispered to the sleeping lad. "I want to see it up close. I have this silly notion, you see, that your freckles match the stars above. I want to see if I can find the hunting cat constellation. Then I might find my way home. Or, at least, to you."

The boy didn't move nor respond. Myre took that as permission.

She approached his side, searching out the heat of his body with her small hands, as she often did when trying to find Boru in the dark of their bed after a nightmare. But this one, he was so pale his skin seemed to absorb the starlight and reflect it, like a mirror hit by a sunbeam, almost too blinding to look upon. She found the girth of his ropey arms, found the smell of his leather and wool kit, and beneath it, nearly hidden beneath the smell of the wild that clung to him, that alluring scent of man. She found a sigil of a one-horned stag, embroidered in the Hunt's own colours, pinning his woollen cloak like a blanket around him.

Funny. There'd never been a one-horned stag in the Hunt. Not that she knew of.

"Are you one of my father's warriors?" she asked the sleeping boy, reaching down to touch the red and white emblem. Sure enough, it was cold with the night air. "Did you earn this merit in some battle recently, for me? Do you not have a mother to tell you there's no use going to war over a woman who will never hold you? Never kiss you?" The sleeping boy said nothing. He was on the cusp of manhood, maybe. But still, he seemed so young. She touched the wool then, felt its tiny fingers cling to her own.

And then she saw it. He turned his head, and where there ought to be a left ear, there was nothing but a hole and the tiny, pink worm of a scar.

The black dog rolled over and kicked its long, powerful legs, chasing a dream tomcat, no doubt. The boy gave a sleeper's hum and went with his pup, snuggling down closer into her ruff, pressing a cheek to her belly fur.

"Is this how you got your sigil?" she asked, brushing his long hair, warm and kitten-soft, aside to get a better look at it. "Did this happen to you because of me?" Grief overcame her, that so rare a lad should suffer in her stead! All because she didn't want to go over the sea and be a bride? Because she didn't want to surrender her Boru to the queen, who demanded his loyalty and love? As was her right, as queen of all the Isle?

"A champion's contract is but three years," she told the sleeping lad, in a cracking voice. "He could be home before long, my Boru. But I…" A marriage contract, whether to Boru or to some unknown, foreign king in Carren, was forever. Just like a missing ear. "You've given this up in sacrifice to me," she told her sleeping friend, "and yet I am no goddess, no queen deserving of it." Her voice hitched in her throat, and she began to weep, not as a woman grown weeps but as a bairn weeps, for the want of mother's arms. Desire for the comfort that comes in being set down in a crib, to sleep the night through with the worries of tomorrow left to just that – tomorrow.

Her tears speckled his upturned cheek, adding texture to his freckles. The boy hummed again in his sleep and brought a hand to his cheek, brushing away her tears without any concern, then went back to his own dreaming.

Just like the months in the cottage, time passed without count. And eventually, Myre's sobs subsided. Strength came to her again, and she drew herself up, puffing out her narrow chest, bringing herself, step-by-step, back to Myre.

"Who are you? And worse, who are you to me?" she warned him. "I love Boru more than I love my own skin. But you're enchanting me. Like one of the Old Folk from the hollow hills. Why must you haunt me? Am I not tormented enough?"

The sleeper murmured a wordless agreement.

If he were a ghost, she thought she'd heard somewhere he wouldn't have a heartbeat. He might be able to hum and murmur in his sleep, but he'd have no heartbeat, surely? Myre drew her hand back then set her own glowing, pale hand on the middle of his chest, on his sternum, searching out the heavy and comforting thuds beneath the wool.

Several things happened then, and all at once:

She saw herself, from the boy's eyes. Felt his waking, the clasping of his hands down on her own, saw her own stricken face; her wide green eyes; her stringy, lank hair. She felt the punch to the chest that knocked him, sitting, into a breathless wheeze.

Then, she saw the two of them from the point of a mysterious third party – felt the kindling in this one's arms, felt the heart-stopping terror at the sight before them. She felt the kindling fall to the ground, hit a knee on the way down, felt herself spread strong legs into a run across the little camp. She even heard the thoughts of this interloper: *get away from him!* And, *we'll deal with your kind no longer! Haunt him no more!*

And Myre, for her part? Why, she did the only thing she could do: she turned into a barn owl and flew away.

3

AFTER THAT, MYRE DIDN'T DREAM OF HER bonny hunting lad for some time. How long, she knew not, for the days no longer had any meaning. Time no longer had any meaning nor measurement, save in the form of a beard. Boru's chin scruff came and went. For a while, it grew into a full beard – not as it'd been when they were younger, patchy and stringy like sprouts, but full and thick and beautiful. When they made love, she tangled her fingers in it, kissed his sweat away from it.

And then, one day, it was gone. He was fresh-faced and beautiful, and she kissed the bare chin over and over, like a friend she hadn't seen in a long, long time.

But that was all Myre knew of the passing of time in the cottage. All she understood.

One day, in some unknown season, Boru came home from his daily rovings with a package for her. He'd been gone all day. Lately, he'd been able to do that. She no longer thought he'd left her, had gone home to the Hunt empty-handed, to tell her father she was no longer worth the effort of a war. He'd eased those thoughts away from her with careful love, contented her with his long looks and warm hands on her thighs and belly. Sometimes, she might hear her own voice in the back of her head, warning that he was gone. And yet, somehow, as if it just wasn't loud enough anymore, she was able to dismiss it without so much as a wave of her hand.

And that was a far better gift than any that could come wrapped in parchment paper and a silk, woven bag.

Still, she beamed when he brought the gift out, and she tore at the paper like a wolverine.

"Paints," he said, as she revealed the tiny clay pots. "Keep your mind busy. I didn't even think it, but you must be going stir-crazy in here while I'm out. Maybe you could make something nice and pretty for our little home here."

Home. This wasn't a home. It was barely a house. Myre fingered the handful of brushes he'd managed to scrounge out of the nearby town. And she smiled. "I could do that, then."

"There wasn't much," Boru said, taking off his boots and pausing while down there to ruffle the dog's ears. "But you're creative. I think you can manage just fine, right, Myrebird?"

"Right!" she said, closing the pots and setting them aside, then led him to the bed for a proper thank you.

She didn't start until the next day, when he was off chasing coney for stew – she remembered now, that he could at least cook a passable stew. Myre unwrapped the pigments from each of their parchment wrappings and set them in a line on the ruddy, wooden table, then realigned them according to the limited rainbow – red, yellow, blue, black, and white. Enough to get along with, sure. They smelled of egg yolk, charcoal, beeswax, and more. And though the smell was powerful, it didn't turn her sensitive guts. And that was something.

And that's when she realised the problem.

He hadn't bought her anything to paint on.

No vellum, pot, or tile. The parchment paper was too ripped to be of use. Instead, she turned her eyes around the cottage. The shoddy bowls and cups they used for their sup were creamy with glaze. No paint would stick to them. The furniture was made of rough, uneven wood. It would tear her precious brushes to pieces.

There were the walls, of course – for a moment, she saw the flowers and greenery she longed to cover them in growing and crawling all over, filling them with colour. A hazy memory of the butterfly weed crowded around the bonny hunting lad's sleeping form came to mind. That made her smile, made her heart swell all over again. She had always loved growing things.

She'd always loved creating things too. There was a time when she may have even called herself an artist. All she had to do was apply her clever little hands like swooping birds and even the lowliest place would flare with light and beauty. The Hunt's keep, Fallowfall, was covered with her work, from floor to ceiling. Paintings, woodcarvings, leatherwork, engravings on their drinking horns. Anything she turned her mind to, and all of it growing with the flora and fauna she loved so much, she had to preserve it forever.

One summer, long before she'd ever had to go meet her sister and queen at the Hold, Myre took it upon herself and her pottery wheel to re-do all of the dinnerware in the keep. What had been boring but utilitarian clay plates and bowls became sweeping works of art – green, white, and even a touch of gold. A memory of when the Hunt's folk had ruled all the Isle. Father sent special, all the way to the Stone, for that gold. And he'd done it not because he knew her skilled hands would make it stunning, but because he knew the joy of simply crafting it would make her smile. Yes, that was right. She'd been in a funk then too – bad dreams and spitting fits – and the pottery project raised her above it.

Whenever she'd get into these creative fits, Boru would simply sit back and watch her. He was clumsy with anything that wasn't a dog or a bow. No matter how she encouraged him to dig into the paints or the clay, to try his hand at bringing something to life, his confidence defeated him every single time. "*You can make beauty enough for the two of us*," he'd say, after every failed attempt. "*Maybe*," she'd reply, "*but I wanted to make it together. I like making things* with *you*."

There had been a time when every inch of Myre's life was covered by that which she created. And that was when she had been happiest. To be of use. To bring colour to the red stone walls of Fallowfall Keep. Her home. To make her people smile, and her father scruff her hair and say, "*My, my Myre! What's it you've done now?*"

Why hadn't she done it for so long? Where had she been all this time, wasting away without paints and clay? Maybe that was why the dreams came? And the fits? Maybe it was simply all that juice rotting inside of her, forcing itself out through spit and bile? Like the blood backed up behind a boil.

Either way, it was time. Excited, Myre put the pigments into a wooden box, ladled some water from the basin into one of the misshapen clay cups, and crawled, barefooted, over to the bed. She found her spot against the wall, made a back brace out of pillows, and surveyed her surface.

Where to start?

Trees. You always started with the green, she knew. Even flowers knew that. For they, too, started off as green shoots, springing from the ground, eager for sunlight to bring to life their true colours.

Small pines sprang up first, their long, narrow trunks buffeted with arms in hunter green, shamrock, asparagus. All mixed by her loving hand and careful eye. When they dried, she tipped them with sweet whites and blues. Around the bases of her trees sprang up moss; from that moss, the long, skinny necks that would become flowers.

But what colour for those?

The butterfly weed!

Now, near gleeful, she mixed red and yellow, pulled the reddest bits out first, then the orange, then the yellow highlights on top of that. Her little scene was soon speckled in those dream buds.

When she drew away, she found she'd painted herself into a corner. Just like in her dream, there was a wreath of little red buds. But the middle was empty. Perhaps, Myre yawned as she thought it, she could put a little one-horned fawn lying there.

Maybe later.

The bonny hunting lad whistled a song Myre swore she'd heard before. A jaunty little festival tune, one of those ones that everyone knew. She mouthed the words alongside his whistling but didn't dare say them aloud. Not after what had happened last time.

"She set out milk for me, my brother,
Thought I'd grow wheat in her field,
Once glance, I'd not love another,
More than wheat, this love will't yield."

He wasn't hunting today. Not for meat, at least. If he were, the whistling would've scared away any catch. Instead, he sat and waited upon a bluff, with the big dog behind him to brace his back. Myre watched from above this time, lurking in the trees. Her focus was as narrow as his hips.

In his hands, he held an embroidery hoop stretched with burgundy linen. Half the loop was riotous with colour: a barn owl with wings spread wide. And his hands were skilled – the artist within her recognised and appreciated. She could make out every perfect feather illustrated with looping thread.

The whistling stopped. After a moment, he half mumbled, half sang the chorus. He was not a good singer:

And when she laughs, she rings like bells,
And when she sings, my heart beats red,
No home there'll be for us to dwell,
The road's our house, the earth our bed."

Someone was coming up the hill.

"You know how I hate that song," said the stranger, coming into sight. Myre couldn't seem to register his face.

It was like it was hidden half behind a cloud. And then she realised why. *You're not here for him.*

"Too bad. It makes me think of you," said the bonny hunting lad, with a clever grin. He got to his feet, abandoned his hoop, and crossed the scant space between them to embrace the newcomer, kissing him fully on the mouth.

For all the cinders in her chest, Myre couldn't look away. And yet, it wasn't jealousy that burned in her heart. A fierce joy. An infectious pride. *You love like I do!* The thought bubbled around the space between her belly and her loins. *You love like Boru loves me!*

And that, somehow, was enough.

"Did you fall asleep painting, Myrebird?" Boru's deep voice set her dream to wings, and she opened her eyes, finding herself in the bed at the cottage, with the four close walls all around her, standing guard. As they always did.

"Maybe," she said blearily, locating the brush. It had dried against her cheek, sticking there, thanks to the paint. She tugged it loose then used it to gesture to her face. Boru snorted. He set his own things down – more food from the village, it seemed, as well as his bow. If there was meat, it'd be in the smoking shack outside. Her stomach grumbled.

"Well, you deserve it. Looks like you wore yourself right out." He took off his coat and kicked icy mud from his boots then took those off as well. "You haven't been this busy in quite some time."

"Come, have a look," Myre said. She eased herself up from the bed and went over to wash the stiff brushes in the basin. Boru hummed in agreement then finished taking off his outdoor clothes. He pulled his hair up into a ribbon behind his ears – it was getting long – and went to inspect. Myre busied herself, making roses blossom and fade in the water with the brushes, until his voice called her back.

"Is that him?"

"Who?"

"Your bonny hunting lad?" Boru tapped the wooden plank with his hard fingernail. She set down her brushes and crossed the cottage to join him on the bed.

"I was going to paint a fawn?" The question was more for herself than for Boru. And yet, there he was, nestled between the butterfly weeds, just as he'd been in her dream. Neat and simple was her style for painting people – and neat and simple, he was. No brush stroke ever wasted. She knew it was her brush that had made him, brought him to life – from his strange eyes, to his splattered freckles, to his long fingers clasped over his chest, like a corpse waiting patiently upon its pyre. Even his missing ear. All there.

"Don't look like a fawn," Boru mused. "I mean, don't get me wrong, love. It's very pretty. But it's kind of strange to have him watching us, don't you think?"

"I don't..." She stopped. There was no sense in telling him she didn't remember painting her bonny hunting lad. He wouldn't understand. Boru tried and tried to understand her, but he never did. He just loved her, and somehow, that wasn't fair. "...I'm sorry," she whispered. "I can paint over it."

"No need. If seeing him makes you happy, then I'm happy with him joining us here." He raised an imaginary drinking horn to toast to their new companion. "I mean, seems like he's been here the whole time anyway, doesn't it? Might as well join us in the flesh. Welcome, bonny hunting lad! I've heard so much about you." He chuckled again.

"You're trying to be nice," Myre whispered, her voice cracking. "But this upsets you. I don't know why I painted him."

Boru's fond smile turned concerned, but it felt mawkish. "Do you love him?"

"Yes." The answer didn't strike Boru as it might have struck another man. His face stayed perfectly still, but in the shining depths of his eyes, Myre sensed his grief the same way an aching bone augurs a coming storm. "Not like I love you. It's different; I told you. I don't know how."

"Do you wish you were with him?" He asked the question so carefully, so measured this time. "With him instead of me?" Few men are brave enough to break their own hearts in a whisper, but Boru was one of them.

"I wish we both were with him." At this, Boru snorted. "Not like that!" Myre tittered at him, offering a playful slap to the chest, which he didn't bother dodging. "It's just, I feel peaceful when I dream of him. I know you're not at peace. I don't… I don't know all of it. But I mean, *of course* I can tell, my love, that your heart is breaking every single day, cracking more and more like a baby bird hatching." She took his large calloused hand in her own and wound her fingers around it. "I wish he could give you the peace he gives me. That's all."

"But… I'm the only one in your heart? In that way?" he clarified, just to be certain. He had never been the jealous sort, not Boru. For the way they both saw it, they had chosen each other so young. Who would waste those years spent longing and loving? They had defied a queen to be together, for the sake of the bones beneath the hills!

But then, too, they were *young*. And the young tend to think that way. That things will always be as they are. Her father had warned them of that.

"Of course!" Now it was her turn to snort, indignant. "How could there ever be anyone else?"

"Prove it."

She grinned at him like a little cat eyeing the cream and brought her nose up close to his. "I'm sorry, sir, but I don't know what you mean."

Boru nuzzled her. "A simple kiss. If my lady would permit, would do just the trick."

"Only a kiss?"

"Well…" She smiled at this, then gave him what he so desired – a kiss, but far from simple. The memory of her bonny hunting lad and his faceless stranger shot briefly into her mind, but she shooed them both away with her hand then turned it and lifted her linen nightgown above her head. *You have your kisses, one-horned stag, and I have mine.*

"*Whoa*!"

"What?" *More paint*, was Myre's first thought. But Boru pushed her back, surveyed her lithe, nude form. His eyes focused on her middle.

"You're showing so much!" he said in surprise. "I… you've been wearing naught but that gown for so long, it was hard to tell. I guess" – he laughed again, and Myre sensed tremors of excitement and nerves in that laugh – "it's actually happening, isn't it?"

"Oh!" She giggled and set a hand on her belly. "I haven't even thought about it in a while, it seems." A memory, from some other life. *We're going to have a child. Together*, she'd told him. *She'll have to let us marry now!*

"I was worried," Boru admitted, a breathy sigh easing itself into his shoulders, "with all the stress going on, and your breaks and fits, I thought maybe—"

"—I didn't lose her," Myre said. She reached over and took his hand, then set it on her belly. Inside of her, the baby kicked at the warm weight of its father's hand. Myre had grown used to the kicking – it didn't seem novel anymore, just seemed to be a part of her, the same as her heart beating. Tears sprang into Boru's eyes, and he laughed, throwing his head back. He grabbed her and baby both and pulled them into a bear hug, wrestling them into the blankets. She shrieked a giggle and struggled to get away, but he engulfed her, held her down, and kissed every inch of her, until she was so overcome with the tickling of his chin hair she could barely breathe. "S-s-stop! *Boru*!" He did, at long last. "You thought I'd lost it and was hiding it from you?"

"Dogs do that, sometimes. Bury it in the yard. Eat it."

The giggles shook her body. "I'm not a dog, Boru!"

"I know, Myrebird. But you've given me not a single complaint this whole time. And... things being what they are, I figured you had more to worry about." He laced their fingers together and kissed her neck. "My mother always said it was a nightmare, carrying me. Even after having my brothers. Said she couldn't sit up straight without yakking all nine months."

"That's because *you're* a pain," Myre teased.

"Excuse *you*, my lady. I just thought if I was such a struggle, surely my bairn'd bring the same to you."

"Well, this one isn't a pain. She'll be sweet as honey and calm as a sunny day."

"It's yours, so maybe I could see sweet. But calm? No, lady. You're brewing a wild child in there." Their smirks met one another over her bare shoulder, and he kissed that too, just to be certain. "I may not be a seer. But even I can see that."

"Oh *hush*!"

But neither of them found any quiet that evening.

4

THIS TIME, IT WAS MYRE WHO WAITED AT the top of the hill. Her white winding sheet billowed in the wind behind her. On her shoulders, her heavy hair tried to restrain it like ties holding back curtains.

"There you are," whispered a voice she knew. She turned.

Her bonny hunting lad stood as if he'd always been there, tall and beautiful, dressed in the copper red and white of the Hunt. Not a soldier's leathers. His dark hair played in the wind. From how he stood above her, he was powerful – not the meek, little creature she'd seen creeping through the brush and bracken so many times. No, this was the kit and fly, the gait and glower of a prince. Fear trembled through her heart. Instinctively, she touched her belly but found it flat. And that? That amplified her fear, told her bones to run, *run*, and never look back. He knew she was his voyeur, his watcher, his hunter, and he'd come for justice. She tried to rise but found she couldn't.

But then he sat down, cross-legged, right next to her. Their shoulders nearly brushed. There was a red gladiolus behind his remaining ear, blooming like a wound. And behind that, a lover's braid tucked, hidden. Both he wore without care. Boru would've blushed and shied like a nervous pony if she'd tried to do that to his thick locks!

"I've been waiting for this," he said, with a shy smile. He was older than she was. Not by much. How strange! His smile was broad, as though he'd just grown into his teeth.

"You knew it would happen? That you and I would meet?" His face faltered, and that smile faded. But she reached out and took his hand. "I didn't even know you knew I've been dreaming of you." A question darted into his mismatched eyes. "It's alright if you did! You don't have to tell me how you knew. Not if you don't want to. You don't have to tell me anything about what happens." A darkness came into his eyes. "In fact, I think I already know, but the thought is too heavy. It's not like silence – saying it aloud won't banish it, will it?"

They were quiet together for a long time, each simply daring themselves to look at the other. Eventually, after several passes, their eyes finally met, and Myre realised what made his gaze seem so strange to her: one of his eyes was a deep, dark blue, nearing black. The other was silver-green.

"It was a painting," he said, in his surprisingly deep voice. "A painting of me you did on a pine chest. Sleeping in the flowers." He smiled sheepishly. "He told me that you did it on a wall. After you went back, he took an axe to the whole place, burned it down. But he couldn't do it to your painting. He brought it to the Hunt and my *grandfather*" – the way he said the word was old, the inflection implying that the word held the utmost reverence and love – "made it into a chest for me. For me to place the things I love."

The things he loves. She sat up straight.

"Who is he? The one who rings like bells to your ear?" Her voice cracked as she grinned at him, like two children sharing a secret. "I saw you singing to him," she admitted, blushing. "And I'm not sorry for watching! You're *not* a good singer."

He smiled, crookedly. "I don't think you should be sorry. He is only my heart," said the bonny hunting lad, and a pink blush crept over his freckled cheeks and his pert fox's nose. "My healing salve. My seahawk. The one they must look to if they wish to see the whole of me." He looked away. "He's funny and tough. And when he's mad, he bites down like a bullhound and doesn't let go. Boru says you and he have that in common. Says you're both half-storm. I think you'd like him."

"I think so," she agreed, laying her cheek on his shoulder. He turned and set his own atop her head, then, with a careful hand, reached out and touched her hair, combing the snarls away with his long fingers. Just like when Boru did it, she felt nothing. No pull, no snag.

"Do I have to go to Carren for all of this to pass?"

He startled and pulled away, and Myre looked up at him in shock. There was a desperate, hopeless look in those queer eyes, try as he might hide them from her. His broad lips hung open, and she could see the curve of his too-big teeth "No. You don't go to Carren. She sends Winnie instead."

"*Winnie*!" Myre's heart nearly shattered in two. She leapt away from her bonny hunting lad, as if he'd struck her. "My niece? Why her? She's too young!"

"I..." He faltered. "...I don't know how to answer that. It seems I've spoken too much already." He hung his head and licked his bottom lip. "But how do you tell a hart not to catch the loosed arrow in its breast? The bow is already pulled back." Myre felt as though the breath had been choked out of her. She touched her own throat, as the lad's eyes watched her, too careful to betray anything else.

"You sound like my father when you talk," she said, folding her bottom lip between her teeth. "All proverbs and poetry."

But the bonny hunting lad continued, for his message was too important to delay. "She makes a promise and she has to keep it. That's what queens do. For you? No, she has other plans for you, when she finds out that you can do this." He held his hand out flat in front of him, and she met it with her palm, which only made him frown. "And she has other plans for me too." A silvery tear puddled up in the crook of his green eye, then fell in a long line into the earth beneath them both.

Myre could see it now, as easy as if she were floating above the Hunt, looking down at the rivers and roads and laying them out on a map in front of her.

And yet, she found a gentle peace in the acceptance of what her life was going to become.

"Will you suffer without me?" she asked, after another long while. "Don't lie now. You must never lie to me. I'll know if you do!"

He drew her clasped hand carefully up to his face, unrolled one of her small fingers and pressed the tip of it to the point of his nose.

"My boy, he does this. He says if I smile, I am lying."

She pushed her finger down and looked him dead in the eyes. "Do you suffer?"

"So much." His voice shook in his chest and cracked like a rotten fruit, right down the middle, exposing the pit. "But I survive. All of it. You're going to think I won't, but I do. I promise." She lowered her hand then put both her small cold hands on top of his warm ones, and he turned them up to take her palms in his own. The butterfly weed wrapped itself between their fingers. "I survive. And I am happy."

"Good," said Myre. She leaned into him but didn't let go of his hands. The wool of his cloak caught on her dry lips. "That's all I could ever ask for you." They both fell silent again – the lad to shameless, shaking tears, and Myre, to her peace.

How much longer did they sit there? Again, time had no meaning – not to Myre, and seemingly not to her bonny hunting lad. But he stilled after a while and breathed deeply. And she kissed his head.

"You have to go," said the boy at long last. There were tears in his eyes. "I don't want you to. He doesn't want you to. But that's how it happens, isn't it? You can't not go any more than Boru can't not grieve you."

"Yes," Myre whispered. She touched his sad, wet cheek, cupped his face in her hands, the way his mother never would. "I love you. I always will. Isn't that silly? I don't even know you. I don't know if you're kind or cruel, if you're clever or foolish. But I love you more than anything in the whole world."

He took her again into his arms, pulled her close to his chest. The effort knocked them both from their sitting position, into the grass, but neither fought their topple. He pressed his lips against her forehead, then her nose, then her own lips. The muscles beneath his red and white kit were ropey and hard. They lacked Boru's bulk. No, he was built more like Myre's father: lean and long, powerful as a cracked whip. He smelled of aloe, chamomile, and willowbark. *My healing salve.* But what did he need to heal from?

Nevermind. That was not a question for her to know. There was no answer she would ever know. *I survive. And I am happy.* That was all Myre needed. That was all that was left for her. She breathed in deeply again, filled herself with him one last time. He smelled of Boru – of dog, sweat, and grief beyond knowing. He smelled of her – honey and salt and the deepest part of the Wildwood.

"I love you too," he whispered into her hairline, as wakefulness tugged at the edges of her mind, threatening to pull her away. "I'm with you, and I will be all the way until the end. Now go, and be brave."

She did.

She was.

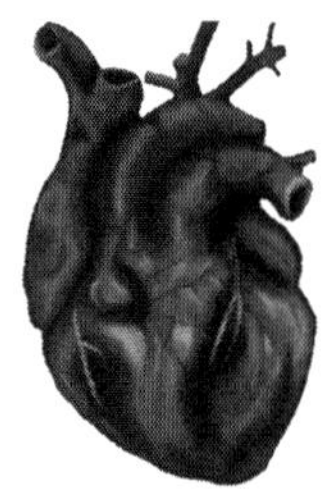

5

SPRING WAS COMING TO THE KARST AND to the cottage. Boru saw the beginnings of greenery peeking up through the grey stone. Soon enough, the rains would come, and with them, a handful of bright, sunny mornings.

Inspired by the reception of his last gift to her, Boru had spent the morning in the village seeking seeds. Not for flowers, but for food. Myre would like that, he thought. To grow things. To fill their bellies with rutabaga, carrots, maybe even a fruit tree eventually. Apples, probably. She liked apples. It would be new to her, sure. But everything she did, she did with purpose and skilful cleverness. The act of doing these simple things brought her back to herself more than anything Boru had ever tried. How happy she'd been with the paints! The silliness with her strange fawn in the red weeds aside, it made him happy. Why hadn't he thought of that before? But then again, Boru faulted himself; he had never been a clever man. Simply a man in love. And love? It makes all men idiots anyway.

They could be happy here, alone. Until the baby came. A girl! She'd been very insistent about that last night before bed.

He opened the cottage door and tossed the seed packets on the table.

Myre wasn't at her most recent painting – a series of gladioluses and ospreys twirling in flight beneath the window. But she wasn't huddled up in the bed either. It took a moment for Boru to realise the totality of what this meant.

She was gone.

"Myrebird?" he asked the empty cottage, dumbly. "*Myre*!" Not under the table. Not under the bed. She'd never left the cottage before, not since they'd gotten here months ago. Still, he burst back out the door, expecting to find her prodding at his lame attempts at a garden. But no, she wasn't there either.

"Myre!" he shouted to the karst, which answered him only in a mocking echo. *Myremyremyremyre...*

No, she wasn't walking the road back to the village. She wasn't hiding behind the boulders that lined out their land, nor any of the small tree copses nearby. A million directions she could have gone, and yet it was as if she'd taken flight – a little white and copper owl against the grey sky – and flown away.

When night fell, Boru, whose throat felt bloody, returned to the cottage. He knew he had to eat, even though he couldn't stomach it. It'd be no use, searching for her without taking care of himself. But while his belly begged, his mind screamed. He knew he had to sleep, otherwise, he'd start seeing her in the bracken, the shrubs, the wind, everywhere she wasn't.

And that's how he found it. The note on the crooked bedside table, written on crumpled and torn parchment paper. When Boru lifted it, several tiny orange flowers fell out.

My dear,

I had to leave. I have to go. I have to confront her and put a stop to this before she can hurt anyone else. She's going to send Winnie in my place. I can't have that. Not my girl.

I don't know if you knew this, if you were keeping it from me or not. If you were, then, well, I know you did it because you love me, but Winnie cannot be held responsible for my cowardice. She's just a child. And the rest of them? Of the Huntfolk? My father, and all the others who march and throw themselves against the queen's walls? It's not their fault. It's time for me to pay my dues. We can't wait any longer.

I'm not angry with you. I know you did it for love. I do. I would have done the same to you, but you need to trust me. Am I so far gone that I don't deserve trust?

Go to my father. Wait there for me. I will settle everything with my sister, and then we can be together again.

Just know these things from me and me alone:
We will survive together. We will be happy together.
I was wrong. We are having a son.
I love you.
Myrebird

He crumpled the note and threw it to the ground, then kicked the leg of the table so hard the whole damn thing came tumbling down.

THE JERSEY DEVIL

RAE WINDSOR

1

This story could be true.
Only the Devil and the Pines know.

The New Jersey Pine Barrens, 1742

I STAND, STARING DOWN AT THE BODY OF A woman I know well. It is the third such body this week, but the first that I've been unfortunate enough to discover.

She stares at the early-morning sky with sightless eyes. Lips parted and neck a constellation of blue and purple bruising. She wears a white dress, not the kind one might sleep in but instead the kind meant for a wedding.

Beside her, in the mud, are hoof prints. Cloven, like a goat's, but much larger than any goat.

The shock of this discovery partners with a bone-deep dread. I know what this will mean. I consider hiding her. It's a ridiculous notion. I can't prevent what will come next.

"Ack, what have you done, woman?"

A hand on my elbow, yanking me back.

My husband crouches beside the body.

Standing up, he wipes his hands on his trousers. Disgusted.

"I'll tell the goode pastor." He turns to walk towards the village.

I want to stop him. Want to reach out and tell him no!

But I do not.

Instead, I walk to the chicken coop and continue my task of collecting eggs.

I try not to think of the body on the ground behind me, or what the pastor has planned now that there has been a dreaded third death.

"The Devil is here! He creeps through our village in the night, seeking a bride to steal and bring into the darkness with him. Lo, he chooses those women who have evil in their hearts. The sorceresses and witches, those who conspire and think wicked thoughts."

The pastor paces. Shouts. Sweats.

The Holy House is sweltering and reeks with the hot tang of bodies. It's been hours, exactly how many I do not know, since this village exorcism began.

Beside me, my husband nods fervently, his eyes burning with an inner light that he would claim to be God.

"We must purge ourselves of this evil. Cleanse the souls of the wicked women in our flock. Rid ourselves of any women who would be a temptation to this devil. Aye, with his cloven hooves and leather wings, he swoops into our village to snatch a bride. He flies her to the Pines, where he prepares her to be wed, but lo, no human woman is evil enough for him. He returns her to us, but not without first taking her soul.

"The Holy Text says that the husband is the head to his wife, and so, men, it is your duty to purify your wives. Ensure they are free of all contaminates of the spirit. We must remember what Our Lord says:

"'I will inflict upon you the punishment of women who commit adultery and murder, and I will direct bloody and impassioned fury against you. I will deliver you into their hands, and they shall tear down your eminence and level your mounds; and they shall strip you of your clothing and take away your dazzling jewels, leaving you naked and bare. Then they shall assemble a mob against you to pelt you with stones and pierce you with their swords. They shall put your houses to the flames and execute punishment upon you in the sight of many women; thus I will put a stop to your whoring. When I have satisfied My fury upon you and My rage has departed from you, then I will be tranquil; I will be angry no more.'

"Let today be the day where all shall be stripped bare. Let those women who continue to harden their hearts against their husband and their God know the penalty for their sinful ways."

"Amen!" the men shout.

My husband looks at me, hungry for his ounce of flesh, and I know it is too late to divert the course of what's to come.

Our home has been ravaged, every drawer upturned, every corner investigated. It's no thief or criminal who exacts this punishment on my home, but rather the man to whom I am bound. In his frantic searching, this purging of impurities, he has discovered items of great evil.

"Is this what you do, when I am out toiling for you?" A book, leather bound and thin, used as a weapon against my skin. Wielded like a mallet, it collides with my cheek. I crash to the wood floor.

"A grimoire? A book of spells?"

"No." My protests are too faint, and even were they not, he wouldn't hear them. "Recipes. Tinctures."

"Why has Our Lord yoked me with such an evil, disobedient woman?" He's loud, raging, slamming into every surface he encounters.

Tears wet my cheeks as I cower.

"I will be rid of you. The Lord will exact his penalty upon you, the penalty of death for your sins. Tomorrow, you will be laid bare before the village, and The Lord will send you to the fires of Hell where you belong."

"Please," I whisper, words wet with sorrow.

"Do not plead with me, demon." He spits. One large calloused hand tangles in my hair, yanks me to my feet.

"Please." I can't hold back the word.

Pulling me higher, until my feet no longer touch the floor. My scalp burns. Will it hold, or will my hair surrender to the tension and allow me to fall? I won't find that answer, as now he wraps a hand around my throat. Squeezing. Pressing me against the wall. Now, I can't plead, even as my mouth frantically forms the word.

Please, please, please.

But I have no air, no space to make the sound. Black spots dance before my eyes. His angry face before me pulses and fades, and I don't think I'll make it to the Holy House tomorrow. Suddenly, a lightening of pressure.

He drops me.

In a heap on the ground, I cough and wheeze and try to breathe.

He spits, a glob of saliva splattering on my face.

With the key around his neck, he locks the front door. This is usual. Every night, we're locked in together. No way out. I know, because I've tried. The windows are locked with a key I don't have. No other doors.

Once again, he grabs me, this time by the arm, shoving and forcing me to the room we'd built for children.

"A fitting place for your final night. You can reflect upon your greatest failure." His words, even more than his violence, send pain through me.

And then, the door is locked, and I am alone, and I thank God for small blessings.

Pacing. Weeping. Trapped.

I follow his instruction unwillingly, looking at the empty room and reflecting on my failure to fill it. This will be my greatest regret.

A movement at the window. A cold chill overtakes me.

The Devil?

I look.

A woman, or at least the idea of a woman. Long hair hanging like vines from her head, edges indistinct. Skin pale as moonlight. Eyes shining like burning coals, blue and full of heat. She is framed in the window, inches from the glass. She is staring straight at me, straight through me. Into my wicked soul.

I approach.

She raises one moonbeam hand to the glass, pressing her fingers to its cool surface.

Is she real? Is she a dream?

I'm her mirror, my hand rising to meet hers. Pressing against the glass.

It shatters. Not in an explosion or a cracking. Raining softly down, landing with quiet tinkling. Our hands collide. Combine. And then she's gone, leaving an open window behind. And I know what I must do.

I run. Silent on bare feet, through the village and to the Pines. A deer path reveals itself, taking me deeper.

I don't know where I am. I don't know where I'm going.

Run.

My own thoughts or a whisper on the wind?

I run.

My body, broken and tired, begs me to stop.

I refuse.

Grabbing hands made of branches whip and sting.

Rocks and sticks underfoot and I press on.

Where am I going?

There, a small clearing. I reach it, stopping. Gasping. Pines in a circle, and the woman is at the centre.

"Welcome." Her voice, like pine needles in a breeze. She stands bare, adorned only by the light from the moon. Dark hair and pale skin. A small smile invites me closer. A step forwards, my feet with a mind of their own.

Am I in a dream?

"You're the Devil." It's a statement of fact from my lips.

Her chin tilts, hair a rippling waterfall.

"Hmmm." A sound like cicadas as she considers my words.

"They say you seek a bride." Another step forwards.

And now she laughs, birdsong in the darkness. The sound electricity on my skin. "Well, I seek no husband." A concession.

A final step brings me to her.

I'm entranced.

A hand on my face, touch featherlight. Warmth rushing through my body. I'm safe. "My husband would have me dead."

"Yes" – a sympathetic smile – "your husband is a man of many demons. He is hunted and does not resist."

I don't understand.

She brushes sticks from my hair, leaves and pine needles falling, floating. "I am wicked." Tears join the leaves, falling.

"There are worse things to be."

"I don't want to die."

We are close, my thin night dress barely a veil between our bodies. Her heat penetrates. I feel it on my skin. I crave more.

"Then, don't." An opening.

Her eyes swallow me. I drown in her gaze. I smell the forest on her, the heat of sun and the cool of shade. She glows in the moon's rays.

I'm intoxicated.

It overtakes me. I must touch her, must know if her skin is smooth as stones or rough as bark.

I cannot.

"There is nothing wicked in womanhood." Her fingers trace the bones of my face. My neck. I'm vulnerable. I'm safe.

Can this be true?

Fire burns inside me; my skin is hot with it.

My fingers long to brush her skin. I mustn't.

A hand on mine, grabbing, lifting, placing. My palm on her breast and my heart is wild. "There is more to this life" – her voice a whisper on the breeze – "than serving men and their gods."

"Please." Again, I'm pleading. But for what?

Blood is rushing to places I've never felt. A burning in my loins that screams to be satisfied.

And still, I don't move.

Can't move.

"What do you want?" A question I've never been asked.

I'm lost in her.

"You," I breathe. The answer is obvious.

She smiles.

My heart skips, stutters, stops, then speeds.

"You can have me," is her reply.

A dizzying, heady feeling.

I can't.

But.

But.

But if I am already wicked, what, then, would it change?

I am transcending.

My hand moves, cupping and squeezing, and I think my head might fall off. My other hand in her hair, soft and silky as river water. A moan escaping her rosebud lips has me foreswearing all other gods for her.

She pulls the fabric of my night dress. The heat of my body may turn it to ash. I remove it, and we stand before one another, naked and glittering.

"I will worship you until the day I die and beyond," I whisper.

"As you should," is her reply.

A tangle of limbs. Mouths joined. Tongues searching. She tastes of honey. She stands, tall as a pine, as I supplicate myself before her. Hands adoring. Tongue praising. Between her legs, a forest floor of exquisite beauty. She tastes of sweet tree sap. Her fingers in my hair, soothing. Healing. Her cries of ecstasy devoured by the pines.

Her attention turns to me. Her focus on my body. Her fingers bringing me joy in a way I've never felt. I cling to her, nails in her skin. It's not bark. It's smooth and fragile as a spring leaf.

I feel a release, a wave crash through me. I can't stand. I slide to the mossy floor. She joins me.

We are tightly bound. I cannot let her go.

"To your husband you must return." Her words, softly spoken, an arrow through my tender heart.

"He will have me dead."

"If you let him."

As if I have a choice. "I want to stay with you."

A pause.

The Pines heavy with the waiting.

"Is that truly what you wish?"

"Yes." Desperately.

"Then, there's something you must do."

"Anything."

Again, I run. Silent. Back through the Pines. They are friends, standing sentry. Something is required of me. A sacrifice. An offering.

One I'm willing to give.

The sight of the village is like stepping into another world. Is this truly where I've always lived? It feels so alien now.

The houses are sleeping, though soon they will wake. Soon, they will gather at the Holy House. Soon, the men will make offerings of their own.

My home is quiet. Locked. But no matter, for what I seek is in the outbuilding. Silently, I approach. I look and see no one. Unlatch the door. It opens with a painful squeak.

I cringe. I wait.

Nothing.

I move in, hands fumbling in the dark.

I feel tools. Spades. Bits of wood.

This is where she said I'd find them.

Hands touch leather, map their shape in the darkness. Boots. I grab them. Hands touch my waist. I freeze.

"What in the Devil's name are you doing?" Growling words from an enraged husband. He shoves me forwards, deeper into the dark outbuilding. I hit the wall. *Thud.* Tools rattle on hooks.

"The evil in you is stronger than I feared." Hand around my throat, pressing my face into the wall. "I must do the Father's work and rid myself of you."

I buck. Kick. Fight.

But he's too strong.

My lungs burn.

My head throbs.

I will die.

I see the woman in my mind's eye. I feel the safety. The joy.

Blindly, I reach. The wall is bare before me. Until.

With fading strength, I swing. A wet *thunk.* A loosening around my throat. I gasp, pull away.

Blood drips.

His silhouette staggers in the frame of the door. Falls. A spade in the side of his neck. The blood comes fast. I approach, watch the light leave his eyes.

I spit on his body. It feels good.

I crouch. Pull off his boots. First one. The other.

With difficulty, I replace them. The boots from the outbuilding. Normal brown leather boots.

Except, look more closely.

There.

Metal on the soles. Cut in the shape of a cloven hoof.

This is the Devil they seek.

I stand. I look towards the Pines. On the wind, I hear a sound. Barely indistinguishable from the rustle of pine needles. But I hear her call to me.

I turn.

And I run to her.

THE ARE OF SUMMER

ONIKA HOWDYN

1

Wind

THE DAY I SIPHONED THE WIND FROM Spryng was the day I found eternal love. For as Sumner burst from Spryng's dying branches and weathered petals, I knew my spirited heart belonged to him and only him.

I had witnessed countless seasons, each one born from the bones of their predecessor. The winds I commanded were my instrument in their passing. None born were the same as the last. And none were meant to live past the time Nature's laws had dictated.

Laws were not meant to be broken, but changed.

I was lost for all time when Sumner's brilliant amber eyes discovered the turbulent storm of my own. His smile bloomed like a flower in the chaos of my heart. One that remained firmly rooted, despite the harsh toll of the winds.

He stood before me in the ashes of Spryng. How I could not bear to be parted from his eyes. He looked at me as if I were everything and yet nothing. And when his hand reached my face, flickering against my greying flesh, I knew he had fallen just the same as I.

"What is your name?" he asked with a note of wonder in his melodic voice.

The vein of confidence I possessed had gone dry, for I had never been so awestruck. Turbulent chaos rose above me through my stormy locks. They ebbed and flowed in tandem with the embers of his crown.

"I am Aré," I replied, "the wind keeper."

Sumner smiled, so brilliantly I could barely breathe. "You have granted this season life."

I laid my hand against his pulsing gold skin. "The winds are meant to be abstract. Indifferent. But you have opened the confines of my stagnant heart to something the winds could never hope to part from me."

His thumb trailed down my jaw, running the flickering flames deep into the edges of my clouded locks. The other hand settled on my waist. "And what might that be, beautiful keeper of the winds?"

"You are Sumner, the second season of Earth and...." Our eyes locked as our lips came together to seal our fate.

He had become my purpose. My reason for being. A purpose I could not be without.

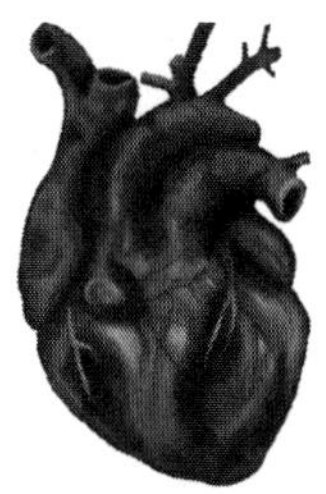

2

Sumner

"SPRYNG," I WHISPERED INTO SUMNER'S ear. "She was kind. She was beautiful. Her song called the birds from Wynter's slumber. So beautiful it pained me to carry out her death."

Sumner glowed with pale-yellow light as he lay across a whipping cloud. It carried us across the blue of the sky, shedding his rays down upon Earth in a blanket of warmth. Each day he lived, our love grew. But Sumner was nearing his end. The winds stirred with the notion of taking his final breath.

I lay beside him, running my wispy fingers over the harsh molten glow of his pointed ears. His blazing eyes were trained above us. His hand on my shoulder left fiery trails of gold across my swirling grey skin. It warmed the winds of my heart, battering and bending the green of the forest below.

"You relish in this story of my seasons coming. But all seasons must pass." His voice rang like a dull bell, deep and meaningful. "It is what Nature demands of us."

Raising my head, the cold strands of my thick grey hair caught in the winds that carried us across the sky. "She demands too much."

He rose to lean on his elbows. The glow cast to my storm-riddled eyes. I clutched the fires that danced with life at his chest, already willing him to stay.

"I will not witness your flame wither and fall to Autum's first breath."

A frail smile tickled his face. "You are as defiant as you are brave, Aré. But you mustn't defy the laws of Nature. There is a reason for them. One we may never understand." His hand guided the violent lashings of my hair behind my rounded ears. "I am not afraid to die."

His hand came to rest on the back of my neck, beckoning me with his molten lips. I turned to place the cool of my own upon the fire, my spirit winding into a turbulent frenzy of song. Each chord struck enacted violence upon Earth. Trees cracked and bled from their bark. Creatures huddled in quiet fear as the wind beat against their mortal frames.

Our kiss deepened, the fires of his burning flesh upon mine. His longing moved to cover my neck, igniting the rushing turmoil beneath my skin.

"I have only ever been grey, the colours of the seasons a passing melody I had learned to ignore, but now, I not only hear, I feel the brilliance of your song. The notes fill me with vibrance." I breathed as my eyes closed to his dominion over me. "How could I ever be parted from them?"

Sumner broke from my skin and laid his palm on my face. "If the laws allowed, I would want nothing more than to remain. But we cannot be selfish spirits." I grasped onto his wrists as he continued to speak. "You must promise me you will not move against Nature. Not for my life or any seasons that have yet to come."

My heart yearned to concede, if only to grant me the pleasure of him upon the clouds. But I knew it would be a lie. A clever trick, so he would be satisfied. That I would never move against what he longed to uphold. But this love was not of Earth. It was otherworldly. A phenomenon never before felt.

If given to me by chance, could I truly abandon such a rare and precious gift? Despite what chaos it may bring. But what chaos could arise from something so pure? It could only be of light and happiness. That is all love could provide.

"I promise," I whispered before kissing him again.

This time, I would not give him cause to speak. Holding on to him, our bodies pressed into one another as he guided me. Feeling the softness of the cloud on my back only heightened the power of our shared destruction.

I braced my legs around the wildfires, begging them to burn me from within.

Sumner branded my neck with his mouth. Each pass upon my skin shook the wild winds from my lungs. My screams of longing evaporated the moisture from the soil, building the cloud that carried us. A storm of our love, each pulse quickening the whirlpool that grew to coat the sky. Thunder echoed, and the sparks of life threatened the ground below.

With vigorous longing, I welcomed Sumner's desire. Waves of heat echoed from the passion leaking from my lips. He threw his head back, seeping deeper into the frame of my immortal spirit. He breathed his fire into me, turning the winds numb and allowing them to flow freely and do as they pleased. No pleasure had been greater than his. No love as strong.

Darkness flooded the clouds as I inched towards the edge. The sombre glow of the pulsing winds melted with the amber hue of his passion. It passed over me and ignited the clouds. With one final breath, lightning sparked from my eyes, tensing my body into a beautiful arch as the waters hurdled towards Earth.

Nothing was spared from our love. Nothing was not soaked nor battered by the rains of the storm that had been born from us.

Collapsing into the cloud, I breathed in the moisture. Sumner leaned over me, the wisps of his burning touch tickling my rain-drenched face. Breathless elation escaped me as I turned to offer him a weak smile. He returned it, leaning down with a soft delicate kiss on my cheek.

"This..." I breathed, "... must be eternal."

"It will be," he said, "even as my celestial body fades."

Sumner came to settle beside me, his fingers caressing the soft contours of my breasts. "I love you, Aré."

"And I you, Sumner."

I nestled against his pulsing flesh, listening to the sounds of the storm as it passed over Earth. My body was exhausted, but my mind was sharp.

I could not steady the winds of change under my own will. It was not in their nature to abide by my heart. Though I commanded them, they knew their purpose, and it was not to love. There must be something I could do to resist. Something that would allow Sumner to remain. The answer could rest in but a single place. A place one needn't enter without cause. For our love to survive, I must discover the secret Nature kept greedily to herself. So that Sumner may live for all time.

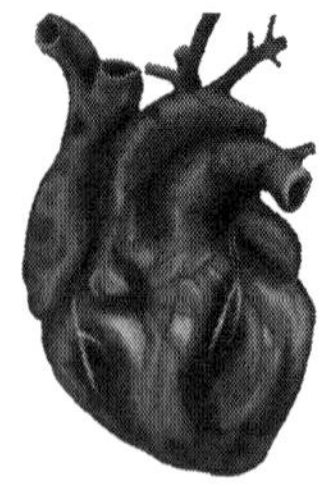

3

The Door

THE DOOR TO NATURE REMAINED WELL hidden. It moved as Earth turned, finding someplace new to keep itself out of mind. If one were keen enough to seek it, it could be done. And I was more than keen.

Following the curvature of the clouds that lay atop the Earth, I glided in perfect synchronicity. Scouring in all directions, marking each path, both beginning and end. As I reached the vast stretches of sand without sea, I scanned what was beneath me with careful precision. Tides of Sumner's song breathed across my face, bringing me to touch down on the amber glow of the desert.

The winds acted differently here. A subtlety that only I as the wind keeper could detect. And with subtleness, came the whisper of a door. Nature was close. The only way to find it now was with patience.

Sand tousled the neutral hue of my frame. As I moved forwards, shadows swayed and flickered, each step carelessly disturbing the ground beneath me whilst the air thickened with the dangers of my presence. Though I wished to halt the death of my deepest love, I did not object to how easily I could deliver it. There was grace in the turmoil. An awe that creatures either feared or embraced as one of the rare beauties their brief lives offered.

I walked and walked and walked. Across the dunes. Through tented villages now ripped from the roots from my stride. Between heated rock faces and caverns that offered salvation from the dry, unforgiving land, there wasn't a step undisrupted.

Not for miles. Days.

Still no sign of Nature's door.

Until I came upon the seam in the sand before sprinkling into signs of green. A dune flowed down into a valley of civilisation. Flickering streetlights and the bleating sounds of life rose from the valley. Clay rooftops protected the dwellings of the city's inhabitants. They would not withstand the winds if I chose to pass through their streets in my search. Would that be callous of me? Immoral? Spirits did not abide by these words. But if all living things eternally shared love, then why not empathy?

A concept I did not fully understand.

My next step proved peculiar. As I passed before a heaping graveyard of stone, the sands did not lift from the ground. I looked down at my bare grey feet. My toes dug deeper into the warm grains as they remained undisturbed. Shifting my foot to the left, the sand stirred. I returned it to where the sand remained steadfast before moving to the right, towards the stones.

I looked into the bowels of the towering boulders before me and continued forwards. Though the winds still flowed through the tall locks of my hair and kissed my face, all else was unaffected. I passed between a gap, sliding my body through with ease. Ducking. Landing on solid ground before I stopped in front of a broad and ominous slab, its jagged back to the sands.

Reaching out my hand, I placed it on the stone's warm face. It beat as if possessing consciousness, the rise and fall pushing against my palm with steady ease.

Nature's door.

I braced against it, moving my feet shoulder-width apart. With my chin tucked, I concentrated all my strength upon the door. The winds stirred around my frame like a violent plague, echoing moans of a coming storm. They never caused me to carry thoughts against them. But now that I knew the beauty of love's song, their cries consumed me like a nimbus, threatening to break me apart.

The door continued to breathe until cracks formed in a steady outline that marked the edges of the boulder.

When the last line reached the sanded ground, it fell open, parting the way into darkness.

There was no time to waste, for Sumner would soon run dry if I did not act. I stepped through the doorway into the void. The door closed behind me. Not a sound could be heard. A place bereft of all things.

The ground was sturdy beneath my feet, though I could not tell if I was standing or floating. But I pushed on, my legs guiding me forwards in no direction. I kept my eyes trained ahead, hoping to see a sign of Nature's presence. But there was nothing. Not for many, many countless steps. I turned around to remind myself of the trail back. Everything was succinct. Nothing was unique.

I was lost. Perhaps forever.

Was this a trap? Had Nature discovered my plans to forbid the winds from taking Sumner's life? It was not impossible. The mysteries surrounding Nature were strange, even to the spirits that carried out her will.

The winds buried beneath the surface spooled, tightening and twisting the insides of my very being. I stopped, clutching the battered remains of my spirit, trying to ease the panic that was slowly suffocating me.

"I mustn't lose hope," I said, feeling my knees begin to buckle. "I must persist. I must discover the secret."

I forced my gaze ahead. There was a glow that had not been there before. Faint and steadfast. A sign, perhaps, of Nature herself. I pushed my feet forwards, dragging them through the abyss to carry me. Each gruelling step freed the winds from their anxious knot. Soon, they flowed freely once more, as if encouraging me to hasten my approach.

I reached out my hand, straining my fingers as I drew closer and closer to the pale light. It hung in the vacant darkness, unmoving and constant. I was so close to it now. One step. Then two. It was the third step that brought me to grasp it, and when I did, the glow enveloped me in an instant.

I was no longer in the void but standing in a cylindrical room. I could not tell what it was constructed from, but it reflected like light upon the water. Its walls were like bark, coating the ground beneath my feet and beyond. Deep lines ran across every inch, each connecting to another.

In the centre of it all was a glowing orb on a gnarled pedestal. And just behind it stood the impenetrable form of Nature.

4

Nature

SHE WAS LIMITLESS. HARBOURING everything and nothing. A beacon of both light and emptiness. The only distinguishing feature was her eyes. They shifted through the many spectrums of light. Ever changing. Everlasting.

They studied me carefully until I came to stand before the orb. It was then her wings unfolded, revealing a slender frame of moss and sand. Her arms like branches, legs the ever-kerning sea. Her sweeping tendrils, a cascade of feather, fur, and scale from every living being that called Earth their sanctuary.

Duty compelled me to bow. Lowering my forehead to my knee, I closed my eyes regarding the mother of the spirits.

"Forgive me for seeking your presence," I said.

I waited for her to respond, but none came. Raising my chin, she continued to look at me with a vacantness I could only anticipate, as if she were nothing but an illusion. I rose to my feet, keeping my hands pressed together as I prepared to present my reasons.

"You wish to know the secret to cease the winds." Nature's sultry voice echoed through the room. No voice was as powerful as that of her creations.

Her response froze the winds in my throat, forcing me to swallow. "Yes." Despite her vague attention, I was certain I did not need to draw specifics from her conclusions. For she was all things. Even me.

Her wings reached forwards, placing them on the orb between us. "Put your hand here, Aré, Keeper of the Wind."

I glanced from her swirling gaze to the muted glow of the orb. "What will happen if I do?"

"Do you not trust in Nature?" Her eyes moved to the orb. "Place your hand here. And you will discover the secret."

I shook my head. "You will not keep me from it? Or attempt to dissuade me from what I will do?"

"Understanding is not gained with words, wind keeper."

She beckoned again, and this time, I relented. As soon as my hand fell against the orb's smooth surface, it drew us into its centre. I stood side by side with Nature, whose grand appearance was now mixed into a colourful form. The nose of a fawn and the lips of an otter now lived on her face. Two folds of lion's ears twitched on either side of her head. And her hair now an elegant wave of a steed's mane.

Nature's smile omitted a bluish glow that encompassed the space we now inhabited. I looked from edge to edge, unable to conclude where we had travelled to. But when I followed the curvature of the space between us and the light, I realised we had been pulled into the orb itself.

"This is the Heart of the Earth," Nature said, seamlessly gliding in front of me. "And where your answer can be found."

Looking again, there was nothing I could see other than us. No trinkets or tombs laced with forbidden words. It was empty yet ever moving, just as the moon travelled to draw the tides. A stoic presence commanding the seas.

"I do not understand." I turned to Nature. "There is nothing here."

Nature stopped, her angled profile presenting itself to me. "That is untrue." Her pulsing gaze collided with my own. "For you are here. And so am I."

The cerulean light faded into crimson, the edges tickled by remnants of lavender and gold.

"I am Nature" – she turned to face me with her words – "the conductor of all things. But it is you who carries the songs of the seasons. Without you, the song will fade. And I conduct nothing." A single step brought her to me. Her muted hand pressing into the cool breeze of my cheek.

"The heart needs a pulse. And I direct the paths of that pulse. The pulse is you, dear Aré."

It could not be so simple. But it was internal thought that complicated many things for both mortals and spirits. Perhaps things were just as they appeared to be. My need to seek answers was nothing but a farce.

"You are saying that all I need to do is—"

"Cease the wind and it will not carry. None can do this but you. There is no spell. No ritual you must conduct. Lock them away, and it will be so."

"Lock them away," I said with a faded gasp. "Where?"

"Where wind cannot carry. Where seasons cannot breathe. Where the Earth dances with the stars."

I grasped her wrist, bringing her hand to rest across my collarbone. "Why would you tell me this? If it will render you powerless, why would you allow yourself to fall?"

She cast a comforting smile upon this unfathomed understanding. "Because I do not rule over you as you believe me to. It is you who truly breathes life into the world. I am merely an instrument of your will. Where you flow, I follow. When your winds change, I, too, change with them. The laws of Nature are not laws at all. It is the understanding that all things are connected. And if one were to falter, so would the rest of us."

Delicate fingers tightened at the base of my neck. "But remember this: consequences will follow. Not just for you, but for all you are tethered to." Nature's nose twitched as her chin lowered before me. "Are you prepared to accept them?"

The question hung between the bars of my mind. Could I truly do this? Condemn the winds for love to prosper?

Cease the balance that Nature conducted and the seasons forged as I both granted and took their lives? Was the love I had for Sumner enough to defy this grand understanding that was far simpler than I imagined it to be?

I straightened my posture, keeping a steady vigil on Nature's hand as I inhaled the Heart of the Earth. "Yes," I said with conviction.

Nature's smile faded as she stepped back from me. "You must go to the centre of all things. With an offering of greatest worth," Nature explained.

The place in which we stood dripped like heavy rain upon the leaves of the forest. It churned and mixed into the ground beneath until even Nature herself melted into an unrecognisable form. I tried to move, but my feet merged to the floor. All I could do was wait for all the colours to become one swirling grey mass beneath me.

As I stood, looking down at the mixing of the heart, I could not help but smile. Sand began to pool along the edges. Soon, the colourless above became speckled with light. The winds churned the grains across the scattered ground before me. The Earth was again present. And I stood at the centre of it.

A breathless laugh escaped my lips. I covered my mouth, too giddy in my elation of what I had discovered. Wasting little time, I leapt into the sky, spooling the winds around me as I propelled higher and higher towards the heavens.

I would love Sumner eternally. We would lie in the clouds and kiss and make love every day, for all time. No pain could live in me as long as that joy remained. And nothing would stop me from loving him with everything I was. And everything I would willingly sacrifice. To the only being strong enough to covet the winds other than I.

5

Sun

IN THE DEAD OF NIGHT, I ASCENDED TO the stars. Floating above Earth, seeing all that there was and ever will be of the world. My winds made no symphony here. Silent were the storms in the vacuum of space. As much as I enjoyed the chaos of them, it was eerily comforting to be bereft of it.

I looked beyond the horizon of Earth, past the neighbouring bodies to the root of all things. The source of life and all that were given the responsibility to maintain it. Using the now silence of a storm, I charged towards the ever-pulsing Sun. I had never had a reason to be near it before, but now that it had more than one purpose for me, it seemed as if they were waiting for me.

The aura surrounding me changed the closer I moved towards it. Passing Venus was less than tolerable. When I came to Mercury, I had to stop. It was stronger than any heatwave. Stronger still than the fires of the love shared with Sumner. I could hear the winds sizzle and snap like sparks across the surface of my skin. Though I should fear it, it did not deter me nor change my trajectory. This was something I had to do. I had to sacrifice the winds and stop the coming season of Autum.

I closed my eyes and continued. Sumner was forever in my thoughts. The blaze of his amber eyes. The sharp tips of his ears. The elegant curves of his ironed frame, as if pulled from a hearth fire before the hammer bent him to its will. He would only possess his own will from now on, without death on the horizon. Perhaps it was possible to bear his fruit? To usher in a new age of spirits that would change the course of Earth for the betterment of all.

A sense of completion opened my achromatic eyes. There I was, facing the massive Star of Earth. Without them, there would be nothing. This place would be desolate. Quiet. Forgotten. But because of them, there was a history. Stories to be told. To be created. And ones yet to be conceptualised.

The winds surrounding me cracked like lightning. They must have known my intentions as they protested before me. Begging me to reconsider what I was about to do. But my heart was too full for Sumner. There was nothing left to do but this.

Closing my eyes, I spread my arms wide, allowing the Sun to reach for me. The magma of their soul swallowed me whole, threatening to take everything there was of me.

"Aré," Sun's booming voice echoed in the chambers of my mind, "why have you left your Earthen plane to seek an audience with the steadfast flame?"

I brought my hands together, reaching deep into the wells of the chest. The winds spat and hissed as my fingers wrapped around their tail. With all my strength, I pulled them from me, reaching out into the pooling thickness of molten rock.

"I wish to make an offering," I said as the fires entered my throat. "For love to prosper, I must be parted from the wind. I will command them no more."

"And if I grant you this favour, what will I receive in return?"

"I will offer you eternal brilliance. For it is Sumner that has taken my heart. If you take the wind, you will forever be a pinnacle in the skies above Earth. Brilliant and true. None will be without your radiance."

I released the wind, watching them bend and stretch before me. Its ever-reaching hands reaching for me to carry them once more. A fragment of a tear escaped the corner of my eye, for I have never been without the wind. I had been born to bear its power since Earth's creation. And now, I was willingly tearing out a piece of myself. From whom I was born to be.

Would the Sun keep them fairly? Would they be mistreated or misused? How these questions sprang to my mind but dare not make a sound. For doubt was a terrible thing to possess. A quality of mortals and not the spirits of the Earth.

"I will keep safe these winds," the Sun said, "and in exchange, I will give you that which will burn for eternity. For if it is love you wish to possess, it is love you shall have. The truest and most coveted of love. For as long as I have left to burn."

My mouth remained agape as the Sun continued to pour his gift into my stomach. Soon, the emptiness from the winds was full of a fire so profound, what I had carried before had become nothing more than a wistful memory.

"Go now," the Sun commanded. "Our promise is fulfilled. The gift I have given you will burn with the intensity of the stars."

With a satisfying gulp, I gasped in awe at this newness I had yet to feel. The Sun expelled me from their body, catapulting me through space. I welcomed the emptiness, for I could bear no more than what was given.

I was no longer the wind keeper. I was only Aré.

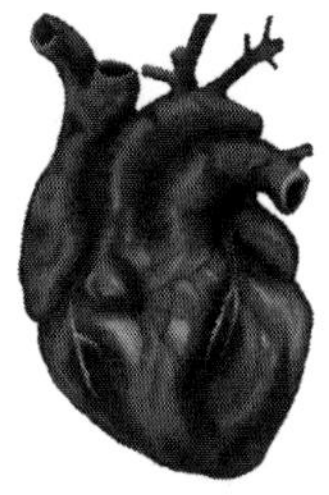

6

Eternal

SUMNER WAS SITTING ON A MOUNTAIN overlooking the cloudless day he had brought those below. I sailed towards him, my arms outstretched, ready to hold my love for all time. When his eyes flashed to my oncoming presence, he embraced me. My head sank into the comforting nook of his neck and shoulder. His arms blanketed me with matched desire and strength. He felt different from before. For now, there was nothing between us to threaten the time we had left together.

He must have noticed the change as I had, for he drew himself away, holding my arms to look me over. "Something has changed." He searched my face. His hands trailed down my stagnant locks, which rested over each shoulder as delicately as a feather in the grass.

"The winds," he uttered, his jaw tightening, "they are gone."

A subtle pressure built in my chest. I could see displeasure spreading across his face. He had not wished for me to do what I did. He had accepted his fate. To continue the cycle of Earth as it was meant to be.

I folded my lips between my teeth, taking his wrists in my hands. "I have offered them to the Sun. So that you may live."

The flickering flame of his locks rose with aversion as he tossed me aside. Sumner turned, his back seething with wildfire. "How could you do this?" he said, his voice rising from the harsh glow of the Sun's rays. "This goes against the laws of Nature."

I rushed forwards, grasping him and leaning my forehead on his shoulder. "'Tis Nature who gave me the secret. Willingly and without protest. For she saw how true our love was. Beautiful and worthy of everlasting life."

Sumner turned and looked down at me. I cowered before him. If he were to deny me, it would break me into fragments too fine to repair. "I cannot bear you to distrust me. I did what I knew to be right."

"Right for who, Aré?" I fell from him, too frightened to look into his seething eyes. "You have acted selfishly. You, a spirit of Earth, acted in your favour and no one else's."

"I have acted for us," I said, "for there is nothing more important than us. Nothing that we cannot endure together."

Sumner's body tensed. His fists planted at his sides seemed to draw their own breath, as if trying to recover from the truth of my actions. I grasped on to him, running my hands to his elbow.

"I know there will be consequences" – I began to rise to my feet – "but what if this is a way to make Earth anew? A home where Sun may always shine. Where no one is left in the cold. Where laughter and joy can flourish and prosper for age upon age. A place nurtured by us."

I took his hand, forcing his fingers to splay before placing them on my chest.

"Can you not feel what the Sun has given me? A love so powerful it can outlast the stars?"

Sumner turned away but allowed his hand to settle on my skin. The beating of my heart found the light of his touch. It bloomed in the moments he remained. The petals unfolded in his palm, which he raised to gaze upon their fiery hue. His eyes widened in wonder as a lotus reached towards him, gracing the tips of his fingers and wrapping around them as if knowing he was the reason for its existence.

"'Tis a beauty I have not yet seen," he whispered, watching the lotus wrap around his wrist, becoming one with him as it was one with me.

"None have seen it. None possess it but us." I reached to cradle his angled face in my palm. The lotus continued to encircle his arm as I moved closer to him, his hand resting back to my chest where the love had bloomed. "This is life anew."

Sumner studied my gaze, the sparks of fire from his eyes flickering across the voided depths of my own. "If this is how our love truly blooms" – his fingers gently tickled my skin at the waist, drawing me ever closer – "then, I will not condemn you for being true to your heart."

The fire settled, returning to the molten serenity of this new gift that had been given to us.

"Promise me one thing, and it must be a promise you never break," Sumner said, testing the strands of our trust yet again. "If I ask it of you, if our love becomes a burden too great for us to bear, you will take back the winds and allow me to pass so that Autum may live."

What weight words could carry. It was a promise I was unsure I could keep, even as I fell endlessly into the pools of his amber gaze. Though, the fear subsided as quickly as it came, for this to pass would be impossible. Not when the Sun could glow eternally. Not with the joy Sumner could bring to all life on Earth.

I crept closer to the curve of his lips, whispering to them and them alone. "I promise. If what you say comes to pass."

A tempting smile graced his glowing cheeks. He placed a finger on my chin as the tips of our noses touched. "Let our love bring new life to this Earth."

The lotus had completed its circle, binding us in its leafy branches. Its bloom spread wide and true above our heads as we came together. The first kiss in the new age of Sumner.

7

Calamity

DAYS TURNED INTO WEEKS INTO MONTHS into years. All uncountable as Earth ceased to turn, never changing its course. The Sun had greedily muted all hues of joy and elation from the surface, casting the land in a bitter haze of harsh yellows and browns. The oceans rose to new heights, drowning in sorrow the soil that was once teaming with life. Millions of species were dead or threatened as their homes crumbled and fell to the drought the Sun had wrought upon them. Rivers and streams lay dry like bleached bones, the lakes they once filled mere puddles of rancid water, tainted from its poisonous rays. Rain-filled clouds became nothing but a burden, never cool enough to quench Earth's unshakeable thirst. Most did not venture away from the shadows, ever clinging on to the small, darkened hope.

And Sumner, my dear, beautiful Sumner. He became as broken and withered as the Earth. No longer did he stand with poise and power. The fires of his spirit ceased along his frame. Eyes no longer blazon and true. He coiled upon whatever ground could find him, agony gripping his very core in waves of panic-filled groans that I could no longer stand. Even the night brought no comfort, for night never fell. The moon could not blaze brighter than the Sun. So he hides away, like an ever-shrinking speck in the harsh blue skies above. Always seen but forgotten.

"Aré." Sumner's dry, scratchy voice pierced my ears. "Aré!"

I turned to where he lay like a pitiful heap on the heated stone of this desolate mountain range. It pained me to look at him. Knowing it was I who had condemned him to suffer.

"Please, Aré," he begged, reaching out with a shuttering hand. The tips of his fingers falling off as easily as parched grass. "You must. You must end this insatiable suffering!"

I shook my head, the pools of my vacant eyes too frightened to break. The shame of my actions had left me empty. Emptier than when I willingly pulled the winds from my centre. It buried the love that had bloomed from their absence. The lotus stained black and drooping, bereft of beautiful life.

I could barely move. Words had become lost. I had never been so tethered. So trapped by my volition. By my greed. I, once the wind keeper, the freest of all the spirits, was nothing but a pox.

"What if Sun will not heed," I muttered with a shaken breath. "What if he turns me away as punishment for my selfishness?"

"You must try..."

Sumner continued to reach out to me. I could only watch him as pain became my eyes. The limp, dead weight of my once erratic locks sinking me deeper into despair as I watched my love clip away piece by piece. Twisting agony coiled my heart until I could no longer stand the distance. I rushed to his side, bending the knee and taking his flaking hand in my own.

"Sumner," I breathed as I laid his broken flesh against my cheek, "I am barren. Our love is as withered and frail as the Earth itself. As much as you suffer... I am afraid."

He tried to rest on his knees but fell forwards. I braced him against me, his head crashing onto my shoulders. I passed over the many seams of his back, his spine jutting from his broken skin like a rising serpent. "Oh, my Sumner, my love," I wept. "I never wanted this to be your fate."

His head rose to find my eyes. "You promised me if the burden was too great, you would grant me death."

Fear kept me tethered to his plea. Only allowing me to see and not act. How these mortals overcame such an atrocity as fear, I could not fathom. Perhaps this was something so unique to them that a spirit could only cower in the shadows of it.

What would a step forwards yield? Or back? I could not bring myself to do it. How I wished the winds were with me. I would let them carry me to wherever fear could not follow. I would leave it in the wake of their power and never allow it to draw breath again.

"Aré" – he grasped my face with bevelled hands – "I do not cast blame on you. For love was the reason, and that reason remains. But the chaos of your winds, spinning beneath your turbulent gaze, have left you. And now you are empty. And me, desperate to feel them run through me." He swallowed as rasps of blight clawed at his chest. I held him closer to me, waiting on bated breath for him to command me to do what I feared more than the Sun themself.

"Love is beautiful, but it is unworthy if it strips us of who we are. You must prove you are not so blind to this truth. You must allow Autum to bloom. Return the cycles of Earth." His voice dropped. "Your promise is the ultimate test."

A promise made from love. It had come despite my disbelief. And with a force I could never articulate. But it was the only hope I had left to hold on to that would end in peace. For the Earth. For Sumner. But for me? How could I live with the knowledge of my crimes? I have doomed all. How Sumner did not hate me beyond measure only proved that he was better than I. And I could not deny him. For my love for him was true. And to continue to allow him to remain in a constant state of misery would be an act of cruelty. Despite the fear that threatened me. I could remain afraid, but I refused to remain cruel.

I placed my tear-soaked lips to his forehead. "Stay," I said as quietly as a twilight wind. "When I return, you will see me as you did on the day you first drew breath."

His hands clutched my arms. "What are you prepared to offer now?"

"Anything." Our foreheads met, our eyes closing to keep this moment forever in our thoughts. "Anything they ask, if it brings you everlasting peace."

8

Memories

NEVER HAVE I SAILED SO HIGH AND SO fast, even without the winds to carry me. The need to release Sumner from his suffering sprang from my eyes and toiled the vines of my heart into motion. There was nothing left to distract me from seeking the solution.

I came before the Sun and reached my hand into their molten form. Even the scalding heat that enveloped me was not enough to quell the bitter sorrow that now became the very frame of my existence.

"Aré, the wind keeper," the Sun's tremendous voice bellowed through the soundless space of my mind. "Why have you come?"

I held the empty breath in my lungs as quiet tears flowed more freely down my face. Sun's coils of fire reached for them, taking each one carefully before they evaporated into their body. "These tears you shed are unbefitting a spirit of Earth." He spoke again. "They are a sign of regret."

"Yes." My voice shuttered. "Regret poisons my spirit. For my eternal love has become that of pain and suffering. Earth has been left desolate and bereft of the waters of life. And Sumner..." I swallowed a gulp of threatening fire. "His existence is agony. One that I have caused because of my selfishness."

"And now you wish to free him?"

My head hung to my chest in absolution. "I do."

I hovered in silence, the monotone hum surrounding me becoming the only song left to hear as the vicious metals stirred around me. The Sun was every and all. Retracting a bargain once one was made was not an easy task. Though, I had nothing left to give them, but myself. Was I willing to part with my very life if it put an end to the suffering love had enacted?

"What are you willing to sacrifice?"

The question snaked through the colourless waves of my greying locks and into my ears. This was the ultimate test. Where one word could either release or condemn me for all time. I could not whisper a lie. I could not let fear cower the words I must speak. I had to believe it with all my soul. That what I would give was real and not false promises.

I raised my chin to stare into the bright cacophony of bleached tones before me. "I give you all that I am."

A low rumble shifted the waves of the Sun. I remained steadfast, clenching my hands at my sides as the salted taste of tears littered the cracks of my bleached lips.

"I have no use for you as you are, for you are riddled with morality and fear," the Sun said, "but I sense the truth in your words. So, I will take something else from you in exchange for the winds you hope to recover from me." A coiled solar flare encircled me from forehead to occiput. "If what was promised is to be stripped from us, then I will strip you of what you have gained from it. All marks and memory of what has happened will be robbed from your mind. You will never again recall your actions or the consequences of them. All feelings of love, pain, and remorse will be burned to ash. Nothing will remain but who you were before Sumner's birth. Before love ensnared your heart and left you only wanting for yourself."

I closed my eyes as they continued to speak.

"If you agree to these terms, say yes. And it shall be so."

A heavy storm festered deep within the core of my existence. To forget the blight was easy, but to be ripped from Sumner? To never remember his face. His voice. The entrancing light of his eyes. The lightning that sparked from the friction of our lips when we kissed. All that would be lost forever. As if he never existed.

It was too painful to bear. But perhaps the pain was not unfounded. To be deserving of such a love should only be granted to those worthy of it. Those who would not let it consume and rob them of their morals. I, who have used love selfishly, did not deserve to hold on to the memories of how wonderful and true it had been. To remember Sumner would only lead to longing and pain unbefitting the carrier of winds. As much as I did not want it, it was what I deserved.

I conceded with a single nod. When my answer was complete, the ring of fire tightened around my crown. Cleansing waves of searing fire pulsed through my mind. It enacted screams from deep within my throat, unable to break away from the pain.

"Then, it shall be done," the Sun said. "When I have taken from you that which was promised, the winds will be restored. You will return to Earth and take back the final breath of Sumner."

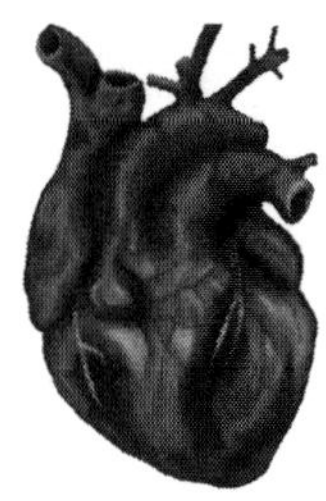

9

Autum

IT WAS STRANGE HOW I DID NOT REMEMBER this. The Earth was so dry it chipped away beneath my feet. The winds whipped the broken bodies of grass and twig as I walked. Even though they ripped into a thousand pieces, I couldn't help but sense they were elated to perish in such a way. As if my winds had not touched them throughout this eternal season of blight and famine.

Sumner was resting on the mountainside. Never had there been a season born so weak and incapable of commanding their power. This one seemed to be in agonising strife. Had he always been this way? I could sense there was something brilliant beneath the dying flames of his sight. As if he had changed from birth till now. Not all seasons matched their predecessors. Perhaps this Sumner possessed a weakness he could not overcome.

When I touched down beside him, he rose from his slumping posture. His eyes flashed with such relief. It felt new yet slightly familiar, though I could recall nothing as to why.

"You've returned." His voice was hoarse as he rose onto his knees. "And the winds with you. You've never looked so breathtaking."

"What strange words you speak. My winds are always with me. I would be nothing without them." I squinted as I looked down on him with mild regret. I had not taken the time to know him as I did the other seasons. There must have been a reason I chose to be elusive, though it was lost to me now. Despite his condition, he was a spirit of the season who took advantage of his power. The laws of Nature forbade me from taking him until it was right to do so. Never before have I seen such misconduct spread so quickly. He was surely an abomination to the cycle. A cause that Nature should have commanded me to extract sooner. But I was not meant to understand what tied her to the knowing of Earth's mighty pulse. I was not meant to act against it.

The cracks of his angled face creased with bewilderment to my words, but soon, a quiet understanding took their place.

"Sumner" – I raised my voice so that nothing would remain unclear – "you have stripped the Earth of all that would nourish it. Leaving her barren and broken. Though I do not understand why Nature had not instructed me to take your winds sooner, I am here to take them now. So that the cycle may continue. And balance be restored."

He filled his lungs with the drying scent of his last moments, closing his eyes steadily as he rose to his feet. "I accept that this will be the end of my season. I offer myself without protest. But there is one small thing I wish to ask of you."

I folded my arms, my head tilting slightly to the left. "Speak your final wish."

He opened his eyes. A still serenity stripped the aggravated tension from my winds, allowing them to flow freely between us. There was something stirring in his muted yellow orbs that made me question the frailty of them. As if he was once vibrant and full. But something had caused him to be this way, as if it had slowly stripped the vibrance from him little by little. But a loss that was worth the suffering he had endured.

Curiosity crept into my throat. I wished to ask him how he came to be this way. What had happened to him during his time since he had risen from Spryng. For no matter how hard I tried, I could not remember even that. What a stranger he was to me, and yet, how he looked standing before me pulled at the threads of my muted empathy. As if he were dear to me and not a stranger.

"I will allow you to take my winds," he said, "but I wish for you to do so... with a kiss."

My arms fell to my sides. Instinct to deny him was sudden but soon overtaken by this unspeakable longing to fulfil. I took a hesitant step forwards, bringing him closer to me in our stance. "Very well," I said with soft intonation.

How he had affected me so, I could not understand. Perhaps this was a test. His existence a cause for Nature to see how I would respond. If I was truly just a tool or if I possessed a spirit beyond the winds. A kind of mortality that one befitting my duties could easily forget I possessed.

He smiled. "Thank you, my dearest Aré." He took my hand in his. "If this is the only memory you carry of me, then I wish for it to be one you will remember."

I had no words to reply to the strangeness of his request. All I could do was go through the motions of what I had promised him. I reached for his face, allowing his hand to fall to my waist. I held his rough skin in my palms, being careful not to cause him any more pain. Regret for what I must do gripped me without purpose, hesitating to the mantra I carried out with each death of the seasons. Every inch of me tightened as the winds encircled us, carrying the particles of the decaying Earth around us in a symphony of song.

It took all my strength to drag the words from my throat, though they stuck to the edges, grating on my teeth and scratching my tongue as I moved to set them free.

"Sumner," I said, my fingers tensing on his face, "season of unending light. Your winds call for freedom. As they pass from you, know that I will carry them with great pride.

For the wind keeper holds the spirits of all seasons that have come to pass. Long bereft of life but never forgotten." I drew myself closer to him. "Your death brings new life. And your winds, an eternal gift to Earth."

A last whisper leaked from his lips before parting to accept his wish. "Our winds are our eternity."

As we kissed, a tornado grew to consume us. His winds poured from his mouth into my own. But it was not just his winds that I tasted as they passed through me to join my spirit. There was passion and longing. A love I never dared to taste. It set my winds ablaze with thunderous applause, clapping and casting the clouds above into an ominous darkness. Soon, they burst with the waters of life, relieving Earth's parched throat, soaking the soil to invigorate life once again.

Sumner dragged me lower and lower to the storm-drenched ground until I could feel him begin to scatter. I opened my eyes to watch him fall into the storm. The muted colours of his skin became one with the rain. Silent tears breathed from my eyes as the final tails of his life soaked into my very bones. The mass of debris soon began to congeal at its centre. I took a step back, watching the slow piercing form of a woman. Her oaken skin shone with a newness. An array of red, orange, and yellow tendrils encased her, until two sharp crimson eyes emerged, silencing the winds surrounding us.

The sorrow that consumed me soon fell as I shared in her presence. She was quite beautiful before the storm brewing above us. The rain kissed her skin as if she were what the rain had been longing to feel. Her fawned lips parted as she took in the moist precipitation of this new life. When she found me, she bowed graciously with a smile befitting a season of Earth.

I returned her bow. "Autum. You were born from the fallen winds of Sumner. Remember this sacrifice as you serve Earth."

"Thank you." Her voice was smooth and melodic. She rose again to meet my stormy gaze. "It would honour me greatly if you told me your name."

I paused, listening quietly to the warmth of Sumner's winds as they seemed to shift the tides of the currents within me. No season had ever changed the course of my winds. How I wish I could discover where he had found such a love, so strong and true that it could reverse the tides of Earth. His death would be one of remembrance. A kiss I would cherish for all time.

"I am Áre," I said with a smile, "the wind keeper."

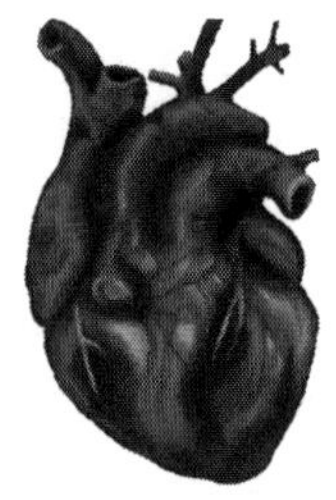

10

Time

NATURE WATCHED FROM THE SAFETY OF the heart. Centuries after the death of Sumner, Earth was at last restored. Though, land and sea would be forever changed, and many living things failed to adapt. But with change came prosperity. Soon, new life emerged. New ways of living that proved substantial for many.

Aré carried the winds with renewed vigour. The passion she obtained from the love of Sumner, she carried with the winds. Autum, Wynter, Spryng, and each new Sumner seemed hardier than the last because of it.

How one act could change the course of many was still something Nature could not fully understand. Nor was she meant to.

Nature moved her hand from the heart and stepped back. The steady hum of Earth's breath calmed her spirit. But a threat was never too far from the horizon. It only took a shift in the winds for it to fall.

Heavy footsteps echoed through the chamber. Nature waited with her doe eyes trained on a figure coming towards the heart. Skin as hard as stone lay cracked and coarse. Deep wells of cerulean leaked from each vein left ajar. His eyes were old, the only part of him that seemed to age. He wore nothing and needed nothing.

Nature lowered herself regarding the true immortal being of the universe. "My lord, Time."

Time crossed his arm over his torso and bowed to her. "Nature, it is good to see you once more on this most auspicious occasion."

"Yes, my lord." Nature rose. "The final scars of what Aré enacted have faded from Earth's skin."

"An Age of Rebirth." Time took a step towards the heart and placed his hand upon it. "Just as I intended." His weathered eyes shifted to her. "You've done well, Nature. You've always been devoted to the passing of Time. Know that your efforts do not go unappreciated."

Nature smiled. "Thank you, my lord."

Time slipped from the orb and raised his hand. "The sixth interglacial age has ended, restoring a new balance to Earth. Now we move towards the next."

With a wave of his hand, the dark reaches of the chamber swelled with light. Hundreds of lines and circles surrounded them. Each intersection marked with eternal symbols, the language of the Universe, to record every cataclysmic event that Earth and the other universes would endure.

Both Time and Nature moved towards the ebbed glow at the end of a single trail. A line cast through it, just beyond where it continued to crawl through space itself. It marked the Calamity of Sumner, the last of these events.

"Aré remembers nothing of what came to pass?" Time asked.

Nature shook her head. "No, my lord. Sun is aware of his part in your universal plan. They are not one to stray from it."

"Good." Time's finger touched the glowing pulse, tracing a faded light into the unknown, yet to be lived.

"I know it is not my place to know, my lord. But" – Nature turned to him – "when will Aré once again bring calamity to Earth?"

An assured smile cracked the rough exterior of Time. "When Wynter sets Aré's heart ablaze with the dream of eternal love."

ACKNOWLEDGEMENTS

Thank you, dear reader, for choosing this book. We really hope you loved it and found a story within that you resonated with.

We are a brand-new publishing company, testing the waters of the book world, and we want you to know you've been a part of something truly special. This is our debut publication, and our team and authors have put their all into this book.

We hope that with your support we can continue to publish amazing stories from talented writers, so if you loved this book, please leave a review and tell others about it.

Thank you to each and every writer who submitted a story and took a chance on our new publishing house. Your trust in us means everything and has allowed us to bring this book to life.

A massive thank you to Fakel Barros from Stardust Book Services, who illustrated our beautiful cover, taking our rough concept and turning it into something truly amazing. Not only did she create our cover, but she also worked on the wonderful layout and formatting of the interior, ensuring we could bring the best possible book to market.

Thank you to the people who inspire us – partners, family, friends, teachers. Your love and support is paramount.

To all those before us who blazed a path in publishing, making space for love stories and fantasy worlds, we salute you.

And once again to you, dear reader, and your tender heart. Thank you for taking this journey with us.

If you'd like to keep up to date with news about our new publications, our authors, and any general updates, you can follow us on Instagram, Threads, and Facebook or sign up to our newsletter on our website.